Three Tainted
Teas

D0099416

Three Tainted Teas

LYNN CAHOON

Kensington Publishing Corp.
www.kensingtonbooks.com

33614082861310

To the Stained-Glass Wedding Chapel in Vegas who hosted my wedding. A wedding that wasn't planned and that didn't have any of the magic or non-magic amenities, except for those that are brought by true love and good friends.

ACKNOWLEDGMENTS

Throwing a magical wedding is hard enough without adding in a killer who doesn't want the wedding to occur. So when I started writing this, I thought about the things I would want in a big first wedding. Especially if my imagination was the limit. Thanks for my readers who took a chance on a magical cozy and fell in love with Mia and the gang. My ongoing thanks to Esi Sogah for her belief in my stories, and to Jill Marsal for her support and guidance.

CHAPTER 1

"Transmogrify. To transform in a magical or surprising manner." Christina Adams set down her English language textbook from her class and reached out to pet Mr. Darcy, who was purring on her lap. "Dude, you were part of a transmogrification?"

Mia Malone looked up from the cookbook she'd been flipping through. One of the bonuses about having Christina in school was that she had access to the college's library in Twin Falls, along with the larger library system in Boise. Christina brought home several different cookbooks every week. And because Christina was in the hospitality/culinary program, they had a lot of interesting and unusual options. Currently, Mia was reading a book that claimed to have recipes that had been brought over on the *Mayflower*. But if that had been true, she didn't think the library would have it in general circulation. "Are you trying to increase your vocabulary?"

"Yeah, the professor gives us a list of words every week. Then we have to find the definition and use it in a sentence. Bonus points if we can modify it." She pulled back her currently electric-blue hair into a clip. "Don't worry, I won't rat out Mr. Darcy as being a human/cat hybrid. I'll probably use it with those brownies we made yesterday. They were so good, they were magical."

Mia crossed up her legs underneath her, going back to scanning the roast duck recipe. "I'm not worried about you outing my magical side. One, who would believe you besides someone in Magic Springs, and most of them already know. And two, Mr. Darcy isn't a human/cat hybrid. He's a cat with a human soul trapped inside. It's a technicality, but a hybrid is a result of two things mating. Mr. Darcy was just in the wrong place at the wrong time."

Mr. Darcy opened one eye and glared at Mia across the room.

"And Grans hasn't figured out a way to get him out, yet," Mia added, hoping the addition would calm the feline. She checked her watch. "I can't believe it's after eleven. What are you doing here with me on a Saturday night? Is Levi working?"

"He's got night shifts all week. Bethanie was having dinner with a friend from the coven who's getting married. Bethanie is her maid of honor." Christina set the book on the table and rubbed Mr. Darcy's ears. "But you should hear how Bethanie talks about her. I'm beginning to think she must say horrible things about me when I'm not around. I don't know why this girl would ask her to be in her wedding."

"Sometimes people don't realize that the way they

treat others will catch up to them." Mia wasn't one of Bethanie's biggest fans, but she wasn't Christina's mother either, thank the Goddess. She was just her friend and her boss. "Who is getting married? I'm surprised I haven't heard about the catering for the reception."

"The wedding planner decided the Lodge would be a better fit for catering. I don't think she even asked for a proposal from us." Christina yawned and stood, putting Mr. Darcy back down on the chair. "I'm going to bed. I'm glad Bethanie couldn't go out tonight. I don't think I could have kept my eyes open after today's event. I didn't even know they had a spring Mother's Day tea here in Magic Springs."

Mia didn't look up from the recipe. "Grans has been the chairman for years. I really need to send her a bunch of flowers, or maybe just stock her freezer again with some made-for-one meals. She's been getting us a ton of bookings lately."

"Well, she's introducing you to the right people. Your food is getting the bookings. Even Bethanie said that Amethyst's planner was stupid going with the Lodge. Mia's Morsels is becoming the go-to catering business in Magic Springs." Christina picked up her book and strolled out of the living room. "Talk to you in the morning. I'm going to call Levi and say good night."

Levi Majors was a local EMT and Christina's boy-friend. They'd had a few issues last year, but now they were solid. Mia figured they'd start talking about mar-riage once Christina finished school and decided where to look for work. Levi had stayed in town so far for the skiing, but Mia had a feeling he'd follow Christina to the Arizona desert if he had to. The boy was in love.

Mr. Darcy jumped off the chair and hurried after

Christina. Alone, Mia glanced over at the gas fireplace. Early May wasn't a time for hot summer temperature in the Idaho mountains, especially at night. Mia snapped her fingers and the fire roared to life. She cuddled back into her chair. Sitting reading next to a roaring fire was a perfect way to spend an evening. Maybe she should make some cocoa too.

Her musing was interrupted by the front doorbell ringing. She stood and glanced at the display. Bethanie stood there looking into the camera. Mia buzzed her inside and opened the apartment door. It would take Bethanie at least a minute to get up the three flights of stairs. Mia went and knocked on Christina's door.

"Come in," Christina called.

Mia opened the door but stayed out in the hallway. "Bethanie's here."

"What?" Christina stood and spoke into her phone. "Levi, I'll call you back. Bethanie just showed up."

Christina walked past Mia and went straight to the doorway to greet her friend. "What are you doing here?"

"Oh, my Goddess. Christina, you won't believe what I just found out." Bethanie plopped down on the couch, her silver, sparkling dress and black leather boots making her look like she should be at a holiday party, not a girls' night out. "Amethyst's cousin isn't going to be able to attend the wedding. She's got her med school graduation or something stupid like that the same weekend, so she needs someone's who's a size four to replace her. So guess what?"

Christina shut the door behind Bethanie and then sat back on the chair she'd just vacated. She glanced at Mia when she saw the fire, but then focused back on her friend. "Okay, what?"

"You're going to be in the wedding with me! Isn't that the best? You'll love her. She's so much fun. She was part of Kappa Si when I attended U of I before I lost my funding. The dresses she picked out are from a new designer out of New York. You're going to love it. And Tok's groomsmen are all to die for." Bethanie bounced on the couch. "This is going to be the party of the year."

Mia picked up the cookbook from her chair and nodded to Christina. "I'm heading to my room. I'll see you in the morning."

Christina nodded, but even from a distance Mia could see she wasn't happy about being a replacement bridesmaid for a woman she'd never even met. Oh, the joys of being friends with someone who just didn't get the friendship part of being friends. Bethanie always had her own agenda, even when she told you it was all about you.

Mia's phone rang as soon as she closed her bedroom door. "Hi, Grans, how are you tonight?"

"I'm good, dear, but is something wrong over there? I'm feeling some negative vibes coming from the school. Did Isaac try to call you? Or is Christina's mother visiting?"

"Neither, Grans. I think you're attaching to Christina's emotions. Her friend Bethanie is over and she's trying to talk Christina into standing in for a missing bridesmaid." Mia sat cross-legged on the bed and leaned over to grab the novel she'd been reading last night. She'd probably be able to finish it tonight.

"Well, shoot, I knew something was going on. I haven't felt Christina's emotions before. I wonder if she's starting to develop some of her innate talents."

"She's magical?" Mia stopped reading the book's back cover, focusing on her grandmother's words.

"Oh, heavens no. She just is starting to tune into her own power. She's been under her mother's thumb for so long, she didn't really develop her own sense of self until this last year. I should have thought you'd picked up on that."

"Well, yeah, but—" Mia bit her lip. Fighting with her grandmother never did anything. "Anyway, I don't think she even knows this girl that's getting married."

"I'm sure she's met Amethyst before. Mia, it's a small town. Everyone knows everybody. I'm just not sure whether Christina wants to be part of this wedding. There's a bit of a feud going on between the coven and the groom's tribe. I'm sure it will be fine, but you know how things are when there's alcohol involved. Tempers flare."

"Wait, how did you know what wedding we were talking about? Oh, never mind. Anyway, you said the groom's tribe. Is he a witch too? Or is she marrying a mortal?" This was getting more interesting by the minute. Maybe she'd have to see if Bethanie could get her and Trent invited to the wedding. Mortal and witch weddings were always fun to watch because most of the time either the bride or the groom wasn't honest with the other until after the vows were cast. Then the bond makes the witch's true self apparent to the mortal spouse. It made for some interesting arguments during the reception.

"No, dear. Tok's tribe is from the northern Idaho woods. He's a shape-shifting wolf."

Grans's pronouncement wouldn't have surprised Mia more if she'd said an alien from outer space. "Shapeshifters aren't real. Besides, the only modern sighting of a werewolf was in Wisconsin. We're a long way from there."

"They're cousin packs. Although the main tribe—or is

it a pack? Anyway, the main branch of the family came originally from Europe. But when the black plague ran through the Continent, they packed up and moved to North America for health reasons, as well as freedom from persecution. It's not much different from the witches' story who came to America with the pilgrims, looking for a less judgmental land. Instead, they got England across the pond." Grans yawned. "Anyway, if you're all right, I'm heading off. I've got my potions to stir before heading to bed."

"Okay. I'll come by and see you tomorrow." Mia hung up the phone and thought about what Grans had told her about Magic Springs. And about her own magic. If she as a magical creature existed, what other nonhuman people were on planet earth? Were they all low risk and easy to get along with like she was? Or were there darker forces at play that she could only dream about?

Either way, it wasn't something she was going to solve tonight. She might as well work on the problem of feeding the homeless or world peace. She might have better luck solving those issues.

She picked up her book and curled up on the bed, falling into the story right where she'd left off last night.

An hour later she heard the door open and shut, then the sound repeated a few minutes later. Christina must have walked her friend down to the first-floor exit and she was back now. A small knock came on her door.

"Come in." Mia set the book down. Christina would probably want to talk about this. She braced herself for what she was going to hear. "What's going on?"

CHAPTER 2

Mia wasn't surprised when she'd got a call the next morning to step in as wedding planner for Amethyst and Tok's nuptials. She *was* surprised, however, that the wedding was the next weekend. She tripled her normal price for these events and kicked herself when Amethyst's mother agreed without a hesitation. She should have quadrupled the charge. "May I ask what happened to your last planner?"

"Of course. She and I had a different vision for the wedding. My daughter is only going to be married once, according to her, so I need to make this as perfect as possible." Cassandra Uzzi paused. "The fact you're Mary Alice's granddaughter made it easier to explain the special circumstances to you. Chelsea was just so human. She never listened."

"Well, I hope I can pick up from where she stopped

without a problem." Mia glanced at her calendar. "Can I stop by today and we can walk through the plans? Did she leave what she'd started?"

"The book is here. But I've got lunch plans and by the time I get back, I'll need to get ready for an evening event. Just come by anytime and pick up the book. If you have questions, Selena, my assistant, will be here. She's up on all the things that need to be changed."

Great, she'd underbid the event and she had a client who was too busy to talk but not too busy to fire her if she didn't live up to her expectations. "Please leave a deposit check with Selena, then." Mia quoted an amount that was more than her usual deposit, but she didn't know how long she'd actually be on the project. Might as well pay herself first.

She stood and took out a new notebook and started writing down everything she knew about Amethyst and Tok's wedding. Where, when, who—When Christina dragged herself into the kitchen and poured a cup of coffee, she grinned. "Good morning, sunshine, I'm glad you're awake. I need your help."

"Coffee first, work later." She sat down at the table and sipped the coffee. "I'd tell you my megillah, but it's a long-drawn-out story."

"One of your vocabulary words?" Mia didn't even try to hide her smile. Living with Christina was always entertaining.

"Yep. And I think I nailed the usage, don't you? It's cute, right?" Christina's eyes closed as she sipped the coffee. "Your coffee here is better than the coffee shop where we go to study. Maybe you should just open coffee bars all over the area."

"I'd get bored with just serving coffee. But it's a good

thought for an expansion." Mia made a note on her calendar to look at her business plan. "Speaking of expanding. I have good news. We have an event next weekend."

Christina's eyes flew open. "Perfect, then I can tell Bethanie I can't play bridesmaid with her. This is amazing news. What are we catering?"

"We're not really catering the event. And it's Amethyst and Tok's wedding, so I guess, yes, you *can* be there." Mia refilled her coffee cup.

"Aw, man. Seriously?" She leaned back in her chair, her eyes closed. "I guess I need to rethink my friendship with Bethanie. She seems to get me into a lot of uncomfortable situations."

"Maybe it's just stretching your comfort zone. I'm sure if Amethyst could find another friend to step in, she would have." Mia studied the list. "I can't go much farther on this until I know what the first wedding planner has completed. Do you want to drive over to Amethyst's house with me later?"

"I guess so. Maybe I can meet this chick and at least know who I'm standing up for next weekend." She glanced over toward the cabinet. "Do we have any of those muffins left from Tuesday's orders? I think I need to gain a few pounds so I can't fit into that dress."

"I'm not sure your plan is going to work. You seem to burn off everything you eat." Mia stood and got two chocolate chip muffins out of the plastic bag she'd put in the cupboard yesterday. "Do you want yours warm?"

"No, I'm fine just the way they are." Christina held up her hands. "Levi says Trent's out of town at some grocery convention. I'm surprised he didn't ask you to come along."

Mia didn't meet Christina's gaze as she tossed her a muffin. "He'll be back on Monday."

"I knew it. He did ask you, but you said no." Christina curled up her leg underneath her. "Why? Don't tell me you're not in love with the dude. Cuz I know you are."

"Love's a strong word." Mia sat at the table and peeled the paper wrapper from the muffin. She broke off a piece and ate it before continuing. "I don't know. It would have been a free trip to Vegas. You could have handled the orders. And I wouldn't have been here to say yes to this wedding planning, which may turn out to be a total disaster."

"So why did you say no?" Christina's voice was softer, kinder now.

Mia shrugged. "I just didn't feel it. I mean, it would have been a fun trip, but are we ready for a week just the two of us?"

"He would have been in meetings a lot of the days. You could have gone restaurant hunting and eaten some amazing food. My professor talks about how Vegas has turned into a place where every chef wants to open a restaurant. It used to be New York City, I guess."

Mia sighed. She'd overthought the trip so long by the time she'd decided to go it had been too late to buy a second ticket. "I probably made a mistake on that one."

"Well, you'll just have to be extra nice to him when he comes back so he knows you missed him." Christina's phone rang. "That's Levi. He must just be getting off. What time do you want to go to Amethyst's?"

"Let's say ten?" Mia thought that would give her enough time to read the planning book and still get phone calls made if she needed to. And she needed to order

some books on wedding planning, just to refresh herself
on the process.

Christina nodded as she answered the phone. "How
was your shift?"

Mia watched as her housemate moved out of the kitchen and into the hallway toward her bedroom. Mr.
Darcy meowed from the floor where he was currently sitting, watching Mia.

"Yes, my emotions are a little up and down this week.
I think I need to either go for a run or do some spell casting later to see if I can work off some of this excess energy." She reached down to stroke Mr. Darcy on the back
and he took off to the front door.

She stood to go let him out, but his resident spirit
witch, Dorian, must have decided to help a cat out and the
door creaked open. Mr. Darcy slipped through the crack
and then the door closed with a thud. At least he was closing the doors he opened with magic. Mia wished she
could use magic for the little things around the house.
Like cleaning or mopping. But just her luck, the magic
would get the best of her and she'd be living a version of
The Sorcerer's Apprentice. But it might be fun while it
lasted.

Gloria, her kitchen witch doll and familiar, giggled.

Mia finished her muffin, then threw away the paper.
She'd put off getting ready for the day and, instead, went
into her newly acquired library to see if there were any
books on wedding planning. They'd be old and out of
date, but she might be able to salvage something.

Mia grabbed the key to the library. She kept the area
locked more for its safety than worry that someone would
wander inside. St. Catherine's Academy had been closed

for years, but who knew who had been hanging out in the abandoned school before Mia bought the place. And besides, the real reason was something Mia didn't want to think about. She was pretty sure the spirits that hung around the school were just manipulating her one more time. Just because it was so much fun. Not. Her grandmother was researching the history of the school and any reported spirit activity. When they found something else out they could deal with it. Right now wasn't the time.

She unlocked the door and stepped quietly into the room. The hallway had pictures of former classes and school attendees from the school's beginnings. Mia wondered if she'd looked that pained during the class pictures she'd been part of every year in public school. When she turned the corner this time she wasn't surprised by the large grizzly bear that greeted her. She'd talked to the Lodge administration about taking it for the lobby, but so far they hadn't made up their minds. She should reach out to the Magic Springs historical society too. Maybe they'd have a use for a six-foot, stuffed bear on wheels.

She eased through the stacked furniture and perused the shelves. She'd pulled out all the cookbooks from the library and they were now sitting on the window seat in her kitchen. Much to Mr. Darcy's displeasure. If the library had been set up according to the Dewey Decimal System, wedding planning books should be near where she'd found the cookbooks. The library had an old-fashioned card catalog, but there were so many desks and other pieces of furniture stacked next to it, it would take her a week to get there and another week to move the furniture back away from the bookshelves. The first thing she was going to do when she got back to her office was put a date on the calendar for a yard sale, then have Trent and Levi lug all these desks out of here. Well, except for a couple for decoration.

She found the shelves where the hole of missing cookbooks was and started scanning the shelves to the left of that. Of course she didn't find anything. Then she went right. By the time she was done she had five fairly new texts about wedding planning for the young bride. The material might be ancient, but the process should have stayed about the same, right?

She was almost out of the room when she heard a noise behind her. She turned around and a book lay on the floor. Right where she'd just been. "Okay, then, what do you want me to see?"

She went back and picked up the book. It was an old book about the beginnings of what was now Blaine County, the area that included Magic Springs. She frowned and looked around the room. "What is this supposed to tell me about wedding planning?"

There was no answer. Not even a giggle from her tricky familiar, Gloria.

She tucked the book in with the others and shrugged. "If you're not talkative, I guess I'll be going."

She left the room and locked the door, heading back to the apartment to start reading through the wedding books, a plan forming in her head as she did.

Christina came out to the kitchen a few minutes before ten. "I'm as ready as I'm going to be."

Mia looked up from the book she'd been reading and held back a gasp. "Why are you dressed up? We're just going there to pick up a book."

"These people are considered coven royalty. The dad has been on the coven board for more years than most people have been alive. They have pull in Magic Springs. I want to make a good impression."

Mia stood and pushed a lock of Christina's blue hair out of her eyes. "You just be you. That's all you have to be to make an excellent impression."

When Mia pulled her ancient van into the driveway of the Uzzis, she wondered if she'd made a mistake not taking Christina's lead and changing. The house was architecturally beautiful and had to be ten thousand square feet. Even Christina's family home would look tiny in front of this one. And the Adams's had money.

Christina turned and looked at Mia. "You see? I told you. My mom would be so happy I'm here and 'making friends.'" She did the air quotes.

"Well, we're just here as the help, or at least I am. You're in the freaking wedding party. I guess that makes you someone special, at least in their eyes. If I get a chance, I'll snap a picture of you that you can send to your mom. When she asks about where it was taken, and she will, you can say, 'Oh, that's my new friend's parents' house.' That should get you next semester's tuition paid without a hassle."

"Mia, you are scheming and awful and I adore you. Your best shot is with me on the steps. Let's get the picture before we ring the bell." Christina fluffed her electric-blue hair. "I can always count on you for ways to deal with my mom."

Mia felt just a little bad as she stood near the van and watched Christina position herself on the stairs. She snapped several pictures for Christina's use and then tucked the phone into her pocket. Time to go meet the neighbors, so to speak.

Mia knocked on the door, which was opened almost

immediately by a man dressed in a butler's suit. She nodded and stepped forward. "Hi, I'm Mia Malone. Mrs. Uzzi left me a book for the wedding? I'm the new wedding planner."

"Yes, come in. I'll get Selena, Mrs. Uzzi's personal assistant. She has the information. Please follow me. Can I get you refreshments? Coffee?"

Mia glanced around the large foyer. "Coffee would be fine. This is such a lovely house, and so large."

"The family enjoys their time here in Magic Springs. This is one of their larger homes." He paused at the doorway to a sunny living room. "Please make yourself comfortable. Selena will be right with you. Your coffee service will be delivered shortly."

After he left them alone Mia sat on one of the white couches. She perched on the edge. "Wow, you were right. Stand by the fireplace and I'll get another shot before anyone comes in."

Christina grinned. "I'm so glad you're my friend."

Mia had just tucked her phone away again when a tall woman in a red pantsuit came into the room.

"Miss Malone, I'm so happy to meet you. I'm Selena Andrus." She held out a hand, and Mia noticed she had a diamond ring on her left hand and a large diamond on a chain that sparkled as she walked. "The family is so happy you agreed to help them out of the bind that woman left them in."

"I'm happy to help." Mia shook her hand and nodded to Christina. "This is my assistant, Christina Adams. I hear she's also going to be part of the wedding party."

"Yes, Miss Amethyst told me that you agreed to help her out. I can't believe Willow didn't calendar her time better." Selena nodded toward the chairs. "Please sit down. Our coffee will be here momentarily."

As soon as she mentioned it, a woman walked in with a tray. She set it down and poured a cup. She held it out to Mia. "Cream and sugar?"

"Black's fine." Mia took the cup. After everyone else had been served and they were alone again, Mia set the cup on the table. "So tell me about the wedding plans so far. Do you know what needs to be completed?"

"There are some contracts Chelsea still has. You'll need to get in touch with her. From what I saw, it's a matter of mostly keeping the parts moving. The actual wedding will be at the Lodge in the ballroom. Neither family is part of an organized religion, but we have an ordained minister who is coming from back East." Selena stole a glance toward Christina, then refocused on Mia so quickly that she thought she'd imagined it. "He's part of an older sect that the families have agreed will work nicely. He'll be flying into Hailey next week. His travel plans are in the book. Someone will need to pick him up and take him to the Lodge."

"Okay, I'll make a note of that." Mia had taken out a notebook and was furiously writing down things that Selena had mentioned. "Chelsea—is she local or do I need to catch her before she leaves town?"

"She's out of Boise but has been staying at the Lodge. I hear she'll be leaving tomorrow, but you should be able to catch her today."

A sound came from the doorway, and a large man with a huge smile walked into the room. "I hear we have a celebrity in the house. Mia Malone, I was at the mayor's breakfast you catered last fall. The food was amazing.

I'm so glad you've agreed to step in to solve our little problem. Once I found out what my wife was paying you, I demanded she double it. So I believe you'll find this check enough to cover your new deposit."

"Mr. Uzzi, that's too generous." Mia took the envelope. The price she'd quoted had been jacked up already. Now the father had doubled it? She'd be able to replace the furnace at the school with this one job alone.

"Call me Drunder. We're the ones imposing on your generosity." He put a hand on the back of Selena's chair and the woman stiffened. Mia wondered if anyone else had seen it. "I just wish we could repay you for the inconvenience. I know, you should come to the party tonight. The new in-laws have arrived in town and this will give you a chance to meet everyone in a casual environment. Selena, call the Lodge and tell them there will be two more for dinner. Unless the two of you want to bring a date?"

Mia met Christina's gaze. She shook her head. "I think we're both stag for this event. We'd love to come if it's not an imposition."

"Of course not. We'll see you at the Lodge at seven. Christina, it will give you some time to chat with Amethyst. She's so happy you are able to step in for Willow. She was brokenhearted when her cousin called and canceled."

Mia saw the flicker of anger on Selena's face. So there was more to the story. Maybe they'd find out what that was tonight.

CHAPTER 3

"Let's hope this doesn't turn into a bacchanal." Christina reached over and adjusted the red cocktail dress she'd loaned Mia. "I'm going to have my homework done fast this week if this keeps up."

"I'm hoping for a quiet dinner party where we get to meet our new clients and your new friend." Mia pulled the dress up so it didn't show quite as much cleavage as it had with Christina's adjustments. "Thanks for the loan of the dress."

"I've got tons. One of the joys of growing up in a home that worships events over people. That should be one of the professor's words. I don't know what it might be, but if there isn't one, we should make one up." She nodded toward the Lodge's entrance. "You need to understand these people. They act like they're normal, but don't be alone with them. The rich are different. They take what they want. And the way you look, someone's going to think you're tonight's dessert."

"Thanks, but I can take care of myself." She gave Christina a hug. "Besides, you're young and pretty. You would probably be their first choice."

Christina shook her head. "I grew up playing these games. I know when to disappear. Just stay near me and I'll get you out of anything that starts looking like trouble."

"I appreciate the assist." Mia took a deep breath and headed to the Lodge door. Being successful at this wedding planning would bring in a lot of new business. Especially here in Magic Springs. Most of the wedding planners she'd met lived in Boise and traveled up to do the events here. If she was local, she might just snag more business. She'd tucked business cards into her purse, just in case.

The Lodge lobby was always breathtaking. The room was three stories high, with a balcony that looked down from the second and third floor. The staircase looked like it was out of *Gone with the Wind* or some movie prop. The last time she'd been here, they'd been decorated for Christmas. Now all the glitter was gone, but the room still looked like the ski lodge they'd started out to be. The concierge could get you tickets for the ice shows with famous past Olympic skaters or reservations at the local restaurants, or have you all set up for a day of downhill or cross-country skiing or snowshoeing. Or, for the romantics, the Lodge also contracted with a company that did horse-drawn carriage rides. It was the destination hotel for Magic Springs.

Mia thought about the book about the history of the area that the school had encouraged her to read. Maybe there was something about the Lodge she needed to know.

She took a flyer on the carriage rides from the desk, wondering if Chelsea had already set one up for the couple's getaway vehicle. At least until they got out of town, where a limo could be waiting to take them the rest of the way to the airport.

"You look a million miles away," Christina said, bringing Mia back to the duty at hand. Playing nice with the families.

"Sorry, I was wondering if I had time to check in with Chelsea now to grab those contracts." Mia glanced at the clock in the lobby. No such luck, but she had a thought. "Let me leave a message for her at the desk and give her my number. I'm sure she'll be as anxious to get those contracts off her hands as I am to get them."

Christina shrugged. "Maybe. From what Bethanie said, the woman was really hard to work with. She wanted to change Amethyst's colors just so it would look better in the ballroom. I love blue and silver. In fact, Bethanie showed me a picture of the bridesmaid dresses, and they're lovely."

"Some people just want things their way. In this business it's all about what the bride and groom want. And if you can please the families too, you're lucky. You can't be putting your own spin on things. It's their day." Mia wrote out the note and gave it to the front desk clerk. "There. Now I feel a little better about hopefully getting those contracts before she leaves."

"She'll probably just leave them for you at the desk." They walked to the back of the lobby, where the ballrooms were located. Christina nodded toward a group standing at one side of the large room. "There's the bride's family."

Mia pointed to the other side of the room, where there was another group of people. "And there's the groom's family."

Christina paused in the middle of the doorway. "And the bride and groom are standing in the middle. I guess we should start there."

"Good instincts. It looks like we've got some bridge building to do." Mia followed Christina to introduce herself to Amethyst and Tok.

After initial introductions were made Amethyst showed them the engagement ring. "Tok has excellent taste. I didn't even tell him what style I wanted and he picked this out all on his own."

Tok McMann pulled her close to his side. "Actually, sweetheart, I had some help. Bethanie took me to the jeweler in town. But I do know what my precious loves."

Mia thought about the finder's fee Bethanie probably got for bringing Tok into the store, but she figured it wasn't something the couple needed to know. "The ring is beautiful. And your wedding's going to be beautiful here in the ballroom as well."

"That's why you're here." Amethyst looked nervously between the two families. "I'm less worried about the way the wedding is going to look and more about bringing these two groups together. Our families have a history of not being exactly close."

"Amethyst's being kind, as usual. Our fathers hate each other. There's some bad business in their pasts. I would compare this to the Hatfields' and McCoys' feud." He squeezed his fiancée's hand. "But we're going to get through this. We're in love and nothing that happened years ago is going to stop this wedding."

"That's so romantic. Like *Romeo and Juliet*." Christina bubbled, then thought about what she'd said. "Well, without the deaths."

Tok laughed, and the sound filled the room. Mia liked the guy. She could see why Amethyst had fallen for him. "Yes, let's avoid any deaths around the wedding. She might want to kill me after we get married and she finds out what a slob I am, but for right now, she's blind to my faults."

Amethyst laid her head on his shoulder. "I'm not blind to your faults, dear, I just overlook the things that annoy me. I'm sure I have things that will annoy you as well."

"Besides your family, you're perfect in my eyes." He pulled her closer.

He didn't see the flash of anger that Mia caught in the bride's eyes, but it was gone as soon as it came. Yes, this wedding was going to be interesting. "I'd love to meet with the two of you tomorrow to go over what has already been set up and any changes you need to make. The wedding's fast approaching, so if we need to make changes, we need to do it now."

"I can meet you at one tomorrow." Amethyst stepped away from Tok and opened the calendar on her phone. "What about you, Tok?"

He didn't take out his phone. "I don't have anything planned except to be where you want me to be until our wedding day. And I guess all the days of our life afterward. Although I do have to go back to work after we get back from the honeymoon."

"Well, except for your bachelor party on Friday night," Amethyst said as she keyed the appointment into her phone.

Tok chuckled. "Well, Hulk has gone to the trouble of hiring entertainment, so I guess I should go to that. Where are we meeting tomorrow?"

"I could come to your house," Mia offered.

"Let's do it at your place if you don't mind. I've been dying to get into that old schoolhouse. I've heard rumors all my life about the hauntings and goings-on." Amethyst squeezed Tok's arm as she looked around the room. "Besides, that way it's neutral ground."

Mia wondered about how neutral it actually could be with these two families, but she agreed, meeting at the school was probably better. "That's perfect. I'll see the two of you at one tomorrow."

"I know I haven't said this, but Christina, thank you so much for standing in for Willow. We could have dropped a bridesmaid, but I really wanted it to be even for the pictures and the visuals. The weird thing is you look a lot like her. She's the exact same size, same colored hair, but your face is a little different. And she has green eyes. Anyway, having things even is best with this group." She glanced between the two families. "I think it sends a message that we're equal partners in this marriage."

"Dinner is served in the Elk Room," James, the head chef for the Lodge, announced from a spot at the door. "Please come this way. It's next door on the right."

As people moved toward the exit, Mia paused by the door. Christina stopped too, but Mia waved her off. "Go ahead and save me a seat. I want to chat with James for a minute."

"Cool." Christina caught up with Bethanie, who had

been talking with one of the men from the McMann side of the room.

Mia waited for everyone to be gone before she greeted James. "So, this is an interesting assignment. What can you tell me?"

"Besides the fact that you'll be dealing with two groups of the most selfish and paranoid people I've ever met? Neither family likes giving an inch to the other family and they all think that wedding planning is a blood sport. Honestly, I'm so glad you took the job. You might not be later, but the other wedding planner, Chelsea, was a nightmare to work with. She kept changing things but not telling me, then yelling that I didn't listen. A week and a half and this will be done. I'd cancel now if I thought the Lodge would back me. Management likes the revenue from weddings and we're charging them for every change now."

"Yeah, that's what I thought I got myself in to." She walked with James to the next room. "At least we're both being compensated well for this project."

"Speak for yourself. I'm on salary. But you can bet in October I'm using this wedding as an example of why I deserve a raise." He held the door open for her. "Have fun in the lion's den. At least the food is amazing tonight."

"Says the man who cooked it." Mia squeezed his arm. "I'll check in with you on Monday to make sure we're still on the same page. That gives me the weekend to pull everything together."

"Good luck. The bachelor party starts here tomorrow night, but then they're all heading out into the woods. They're supposed to be back around midnight to close up the party here." James pointed out toward a window that

showed the drifts of snow covering everything. "I like nature, but drinking around a bonfire for hours? They're
crazy."

"Bachelor parties are not on my to-do list, thank the
Goddess." She paused before she left James in the hallway. "Grans says the McMann family is a little different."

"If what she means by different is that they are rich?
Yep. I like living in Magic Springs. You never know who
you're going to meet. I did a catering job for a major
movie star last week." He glanced over her shoulder and
into the dining room. "I haven't lived in Magic Springs
long, but I'm thinking the bride and groom might have bit
off more than they could chew here. Both of the families
have traditions and needs that not even Santa could provide."

Mia thanked him for his time and his assessment. Then
she strolled into the room, looking for Christina. Instead,
she found a tall, handsome man at her side.

"I'm Tok's brother, Gary. They all call me Hulk. It's a
childhood nickname. Not one I would have chosen, but,
like family, you can't choose what people call you." He
grinned and pointed to a table on the other side of the room.
"We're over there. Your assistant is sitting with the Uzzi
family. They wanted to get to know their new bridesmaid. I
take it she's human?"

"Yes, she's human. Of course, so am I. My kitchen
witch status doesn't change my species." She waved at
Christina to let her know she saw her and then followed
Gary to their table.

"Are you sure about that?" He held out the chair for
her. "Our shifter talents give us a heightened set of
senses, including smell. I can smell a witch from about a

hundred miles. And lovely as you are, you smell like a witch. Your friend, she doesn't have it in her blood."

"I never thought of it like that." Mia sat at the table and nodded to the two other couples. They were all shifters from what she could tell. "Thank you for explaining that. I'll have to give it more consideration."

Gary introduced her to the other couples and then the first course was served. A woman to her left, whose name was Lita and who was Tok's sister, if Mia remembered correctly, leaned closer. "So you're the new wedding planner. Are you crazy or what?"

"Excuse me?" Mia's forkful of salad paused in mid-movement.

Lita laughed, and Mia smiled as the same feeling she got from Tok eased from the woman. "I didn't mean to insult you, but wow, this wedding has to be a pain to manage."

"I haven't gotten into the details yet." Mia wondered if she really had made a mistake. Hopefully, this first job wouldn't be her last in the wedding arena. But it might end up that way. "I run a catering company and cooking school out of the old St. Catherine's Academy here in Magic Springs. I'm looking to expand my business offerings. You know how it is in a small town."

"Of course." Gary shot Lita a look that apparently was meant to keep her from saying anything else he deemed stupid. "We're very glad to have someone new in the driver's seat. I don't think humans can understand creatures as well as another creature. Even if we are from different species."

Mia didn't want to explain again how she saw herself not as a witch but as a human. And definitely not as a creature. She wondered if this attitude was part of the ar-

gument between the two families. "I'm happy to be part
of making sure this wedding is perfect for Tok and
Amethyst."

"Just wait until next weekend. Then we'll talk." Lita
laughed again and refilled her wineglass. "I like your
spunk. We should be friends."

After dinner the group moved to the bar for drinks.
Mia tried to exit the party, but Gary took her over to
where his parents were seated.

His father stood and shook Mia's hand. "Brody Mc-
Mann and my wife, Marilyn. Please sit down. We have
some issues with the current guest list we'd like you to
bring up to the Uzzis."

Mia glanced across the bar, where Mr. and Mrs. Uzzi
sat. "Maybe we should just bring them over to talk about
this."

"Oh, no. That's not the way these things are done."
Marilyn exchanged a look with her husband. "That's why
we need a wedding planner. When Drunder fired Chelsea
yesterday we were ready to make Tok call off the wedding. Of course, with you on board now, you can be our
spokesperson."

"I'll do my best." Mia thought about the large check
sitting on her desk, waiting to be put in the bank. She
could just return it, then get a plane ticket to Las Vegas
and spend a nice few days with Trent. Maybe she'd stay
there until after the wedding was over. "So what do we
need to get changed?"

Marilyn pulled out a piece of folded paper. "These are
all family members from Wisconsin that we need to have
put back on the guest list. The other planner let the Uzzis

pull them, but if we don't invite them, it will be a slap in their face. We can't insult family that way."

Mia glanced over the list. It looked like about thirty people. "I'll bring this up tomorrow with the couple. We're meeting to talk about their wedding plans."

Marilyn's eyes lit up. "Maybe I should tag along, just so we can review what our family needs out of the event."

"Actually, I need to chat with the bride and groom first," Mia lied. She already saw where this was going. It wasn't like she hadn't been warned. Several times. She hadn't heard that Drunder had been the one to fire Chelsea, though. She held up the paper before tucking it into her purse. "Maybe we can get together early next week sometime. This is really helpful, though."

The bar band started paying a soft, slow ballad. "I think this is our song." Gary took her hand and pulled her to her feet. "Sorry, folks, but I did see her first."

"Oh, but I . . ." Mia didn't get another word out before she found herself being led out to the dance floor. Trent was going to have a field day with this. Although they weren't officially exclusive, they actually were; they just hadn't said it to each other.

On the dance floor, Gary twirled her around and lightly put his hand on her waist and grabbed her hand. "And you're welcome. I told the folks I'd bring you over to chat with them, but I figured that was enough manipulation for the newbie for tonight. I hope your boyfriend isn't going to come punch me in the nose for this."

"He's out of town on business." Mia watched the McMann family watching them. From the pleased looks, they must have assumed Mia was entranced by Gary and would be putty in their hands.

"Oh, well, there is a boyfriend, then." He chuckled.

"My loss. I was beginning to think that I might just come back to Magic Springs after the wedding and charm you into falling in love with me. I'm always a day late and a dollar short."

Mia couldn't stop the laugh that came out. "Sorry to burst your bubble. I'll let you know if it doesn't work out, but for right now, I'm pretty happy."

"That's horrible news." He leaned closer. "So after this dance, where do you want me to leave you?"

"I need to check in with my assistant and then I'm getting out of here. I've got a lot of work to do." She nodded over to where Christina was sitting with Amethyst and Bethanie. "That table will work fine."

"Then let's dance over there so it doesn't look like you planned your escape." He twirled her again. "I do really like dancing with you."

Mia didn't know how to respond. She finally decided on a generic, "I'm enjoying your company too."

He laughed as the music ended and kissed her on the cheek. "Now, was that so hard?"

Mia found herself standing in front of the table she'd pointed out earlier. Gary was walking away toward the open bar. She turned to Christina. "I'm done. Are you leaving with me now or do you want to stay longer?"

"Oh, you can't leave yet. I told my mother I'd bring you over to her table. She has some things she needs to chat about." Amethyst stood and took her arm. "Do you want a drink? Maybe a glass of wine or a beer?"

"I'd love a sparkling water. It's getting a little hot in here." Mia followed her to the other side of the room where the Uzzis sat around a table. Selena sat next to the woman who Mia guessed was Cassandra Uzzi.

"After that dance with Hulk I don't blame you for being all hot. He's a hunk, just like his brother." Amethyst bumped Mia with her shoulder. "I'll be right back."

"Well, I see you met the in-laws." Cassandra made a point to stare across the room toward the McMann table. "What are their demands now? I saw she gave you something."

"It's a list of guests. I thought I'd check it against the current list in the book, and if it's a substantial increase, I'll talk to Amethyst and Tok about their wishes." Mia just wanted to chat with Christina and get out of there. Sparkling water or not.

Before Cassandra could respond, a woman entered the bar and walked to the McMann table.

"Well, I guess they'll let anyone in this bar." Drunder Uzzi stood, glaring at the newcomer. "I'll go handle this."

Amethyst put a cold bottle of water in Mia's hands. "Uh-oh. I can't believe she actually had the nerve to show up here. My dad's going to kill her."

"Who is that?" Mia sipped the water, feeling gratitude for the cool bubbles that were quenching her thirst.

Without looking at Mia, Amethyst nodded toward the escalating scene. "That is the woman you're replacing, Chelsea Bachman. My father caught her stealing from the wedding account."

CHAPTER 4

Mia had arrived home a little after ten. Her new clients had her freaking out. The scene between Drunder Uzzi and Chelsea had turned into a screaming match. The Lodge sent in security guards to remove Chelsea from the party. Christina had decided to stay as Bethanie promised to drive her home. If that fell through, one of the Lodge's van drivers would give her a ride home. Mia wasn't worried, at least not about Christina.

Mia had noticed her new friend, Gary, had followed the former wedding planner out of the bar. Mia would have tried to chat with her, but after that scene she didn't think it was the best time. The Lodge had another bar that was open to the public on the other side of the first floor. They'd probably ended up there, although, in Mia's eyes, anger and alcohol really didn't mesh well.

Now it was the next morning and Mia was just waiting

for a reasonable time to go chat with Chelsea. If she waited too long, she might miss her and have to drive to Boise to pick up the contracts if Chelsea didn't play nice and leave them at the front desk. But if she went too early, well, Mia assumed the woman had been drunk before and after the fight last night from her condition during the heated discussion.

A text chimed on her phone. It was from Trent. She read it. **Going on a trip to see Hoover Dam. It was either that or learn to play blackjack. I want to keep my fortune intact, so I chose the excursion.**

She laughed and texted back. **Probably a wise move. I've got a new wedding planning contract. It might just kill me. Free for dinner Monday?**

Of course. Got to run, the bus is leaving. Take care of yourself, a quick response came back.

She tucked her phone and the wedding book into her tote along with a list of questions she had for Chelsea. It was time to go wake the sleeping lion.

Mia strolled into the Lodge lobby a few minutes later. She'd found a parking spot easily and now headed to the front desk, just as a group of men strolled toward the exit.

Tok called to her, "Hey, pretty lady. What's going on in wedding world today?"

"I'm here to talk to Chelsea. Don't tell me you're already on your way out." She thought they'd planned to meet at the school at one.

"We're doing some hunting this morning. Then the party starts at five. The bonfire is a tradition for all young men who are taking on a mate. Of course, we've modernized the tradition a bit. No sacrificing virgins or killing a goat during this event."

Mia stared at him.

Tok started to laugh. "Oh, no, you totally believed me. I'm kidding, Mia. The bonfire is traditional, but we don't kill people, or animals even, unless we're hunting."

She took in a deep breath. "Of course you're kidding. I didn't get enough sleep last night."

"Seriously, you're all right? I swear, you're as white as a dove." He reached for her arm, but she shook her head.

"Like I said, I didn't get a lot of sleep last night. I'm fine." She nodded to the coffee cart the Lodge had set up in the lobby. "First order of business is a cup of coffee."

"Let me get that for you. I feel bad I scared you." He didn't wait for her protest, just ran over and poured a large coffee. He turned back to her. "Cream and sugar?"

"Black's fine."

A hand settled on her shoulder and she turned to see Gary, aka Hulk, standing next to her. "You have Tok wrapped around your little finger. Where did you go last night? I looked for you after our dance."

Funny, I saw you chasing after Chelsea, Mia said on the inside. Instead, she smiled and took the coffee from Tok. "I went home early. I've got a lot of work on Tok and Amethyst's wedding to get done before next weekend."

"The Jeeps are waiting for us." Tok slapped his brother on the back. "I'd let you stay and chat up Mia, but rumor is she's involved."

"Rumors fly fast here in Magic Springs." Mia smiled. "This time they're right. I am seeing someone."

"My loss." Gary nodded and joined Tok as they strolled across the lobby to the front door.

Mia sipped the coffee, then went to the front desk. "Can you ring Chelsea Bachman's room?"

"Of course." The front desk dialed a room, then frowned. "No answer. And she has a wake-up call at six that she hasn't picked up yet either."

"You might want to send someone up to knock on her door. If she's flying out, she'll miss her plane."

The front desk clerk glanced around. "Sorry, I don't have anyone. Look, I know who you are, Miss Malone. I'm friends with Levi and Christina. You need to talk to her and I need to make sure she's awake for checkout, so can you just go up and knock on her door? I gave her your note last night and she said she'd be glad to get this crap . . ."

Mia waited for the rest and the girl turned pink.

"Sorry, I mean she said she wanted to give you the stuff." She nodded to the elevator. "Third floor, room 315."

"Thanks. I'll try to be quick so she can make her flight." Mia headed to the elevator. When the doors opened Mr. and Mrs. McMann stepped out. "Good morning."

"Well, hello, Mia. I'm looking forward to chatting with you more. Can we sit down over coffee?" Marilyn paused at the door while Mia held out an arm to keep it from closing.

"I've got an appointment first, then I'll come down to the dining room. If you're still there, I'd love to spend a few minutes talking about what Tok wants for the wedding."

The woman's face tightened for a minute, but then she smiled. "That sounds lovely. We McManns have a few customs we need to make sure occur. I'm sure you've dealt with this kind of thing before."

Mia didn't want to say that she had *no* experience in

wedding planning, so she smiled and stepped into the elevator, punching the button for the third floor. "I'll chat with you later."

When she stepped off the elevator the smell of orchids filled her senses. There were three pots sitting on the table in front of a mirror in the floor's lobby. Two wingback chairs were sitting on each side of the table. As she left the elevator, she wondered about the décor. She never saw anyone sitting in these waiting areas. Except for kids who were with their parents and couldn't stand for the three seconds it took for the elevator to arrive. Why waste decorating budget on this area?

She moved down the hallway and saw signs directing her toward the left for rooms 300–345. The Lodge was huge. She passed by a few maid carts, their owners in rooms working on cleaning up for the next guest. It wasn't a job she'd ever wanted to have. She'd heard horror stories from the maids who worked at the Owyhee. Food service might be hard, but housekeeping had to be the worst job ever. Except for maybe front desk clerk, which would be boring. Honestly, Mia was glad she was out of the hotel business altogether.

She found Chelsea's room and knocked on the door. No answer. She knocked again and this time called out. The door moved with her more forceful knock and she realized it was open. The safety lock had been set to keep the door from shutting. A trick she used to get her luggage into a room. Maybe Chelsea had already packed up and she'd missed her leaving on the other elevator.

She pushed open the door and stepped into the room. The smell hit her first. Blood, and a lot of it. She grabbed a washcloth from the bathroom by the door and covered her nose.

Then she walked into the bedroom and saw a woman on the bed. Dead.

She got out of the room, using the washcloth to open the door, then went and sat in one of those unused elevator chairs as she called Mark Baldwin, the local detective. When he picked up she couldn't speak for a minute.

"Mia? Is that you? Is something wrong? Not your grandmother?" He asked her question after question.

Finally, she responded. "You need to come to the Lodge. Room 315. There's been a murder."

She'd waited in the chair until he and his deputies came out of the elevator, then she pointed to the hallway. "To your left. I'll be downstairs in the bar. I need a drink."

"Mia, what happened? Were you attacked?" Baldwin nodded to the others. "Go on, I'll catch up with you."

"I'm fine. Shaky but fine. I came here for a meeting with Chelsea this morning. Chelsea Bachman. She was the wedding planner for the Uzzi-McMann wedding. I took over the job after she was fired." Mia rubbed her face. "She still had a bunch of the contracts and stuff, so I was meeting her so she could transfer them over to me this morning before she went back home."

"You were meeting in her room?"

Mia shrugged. "She didn't answer the phone and the front desk said she hadn't picked up her wake-up call either. I was being nice, trying to wake her up before she missed her flight. Especially because she was so drunk last night."

"You saw her last night?" His walkie-talkie buzzed. He pushed a button. "Hold on, I'll be right there."

She pushed the elevator button. "I'll be downstairs."

"If you're thinking about going to the bar, go easy on

the alcohol. I saw your van out in the parking lot. I don't want to have to take you home."

The elevator doors opened and Mia stepped in. She felt hollow and numb. She'd never seen anything like that. It was just too much.

A vision of a traditional wolfman flipped through her mind. Had she been killed by a creature? Or was this a run-of-the-mill killer who wanted it to look like the in-laws? Both good questions, and ones that Baldwin would never ask because he didn't believe that witches lived in his little town. How would he accept shape-shifting wolves?

She turned away from the coffee shop where the Mc-Manns were enjoying their breakfast and instead went into the almost-empty bar. She sat on a stool and opened her tote to grab her phone. The washcloth was in the tote as well. She set it on the bar, not wanting to steal from the hotel.

James walked through the back of the bar and stopped next to her. "You look like crap. What can I get you?"

"Coffee. Maybe a shot of Kahlúa in it? And some whipped cream?" Mia tapped her fingernails on the bar, focusing on her phone. Who should she call to report she just saw the worst thing she'd ever seen?

She finally pushed the phone away. She wouldn't call anyone. She'd talk to Baldwin before she left. Tell him she needed the contracts or anything about the wedding, then go home and work. Work would help her get that scene out of her mind.

"So what has Baldwin here?" James put the drink in front of her, then leaned on the bar, watching.

Mia took a sip before answering. "Chelsea's dead."

James blinked, then took a bottle of Jack from behind the counter. He took a shot, put the bottle and the glass away, then focused on her again. "What did you just say?"

"Chelsea, the wedding planner. She's dead. And I swear to the Goddess, it looks like some wild animal got to her. Her room's a mess." Mia sipped her drink. "I was supposed to meet up with her before she left for Boise, but last night, well, she got kicked out of the wedding party, but you knew that, right?"

"Yeah, I got pulled in from security because I was technically running the dinner-and-drinks event after Chelsea got fired." He poured a glass of water to sip while they talked. "I can't believe anyone would kill her. Especially one of the McManns."

"You think a McMann killed her?" Mia's head jerked up and she met James's gaze.

He shrugged, sipping the water. "You're the one who said she looked like a wild animal got to her. That's not usually what humans do."

"Unless they were really mad, or maybe trying to frame a McMann." Mia paused, thinking about last night. "The guy they call Hulk, Gary? He followed her out of the room and to the bar. Maybe he spent the night with her and it went bad. He's out hunting with the rest of the groom's party."

"You seem to have a handle on all the players," James remarked.

Mia shook her head. "I knew this job was going to be a problem when the money came too easy. I should have said I was too busy. Or gone with Trent to Vegas on Monday. That way I wouldn't have been here to say yes."

"You're always the one to step in and save the day for people. It's kind of in your nature." He took another sip of water and drained the glass. "Chelsea wasn't much of a human being, but she didn't deserve to die. I hope you find out who did this, and soon. The wedding's going to be enough of a powder keg with the issues the two families bring to the altar. We don't need people pointing fingers at one another about a murder too."

"Well, Mia won't need to be solving this case quickly because she's the caterer and, in this case, the new wedding planner. She's not in law enforcement." Baldwin sat next to her and James straightened. "Can you get me a Coke?"

"Of course, sir." James poured the soda and then looked at Mia. "Just call out if you need anything else. I'll be in the back. The drinks are on the house."

Mia watched James leave the back of the bar and then turned toward Baldwin. "It's awful, isn't it?"

"It's not pretty, that's for sure." He took a sip of the soda, then pulled out his notebook. "How in the world are you always one of the first people on a murder scene?"

"Unlucky, I guess." Mia sipped her coffee, which was starting to make her feel a little more stable. "Look, all I wanted was a quick chat with the woman to get the contracts for the wedding that I'm missing and to see where she was at in planning the wedding when she got fired."

"And you thought she was actually going to be helpful? Man, you are naïve." Baldwin made some notes in his book.

"Helpful or not, the contracts were the Uzzis' property, so she'd have to turn them over to me or she'd risk her reputation. She knew that. She wouldn't have done anything to ruin the next job opportunity. The catering/event planning world is pretty small, especially in Magic Springs."

"That's true enough. So, tell me about this morning." He opened his notebook. "No, tell me everything that's happened since you took this job. There might be something there. Maybe she was killed so you could get the job. Is your friend Christina around?"

"Don't even start. I had the job before she was killed. They called me right after Mr. Uzzi fired her." She met Baldwin's gaze and realized he was kidding her. "So not funny. She gets hives when you're around."

"Well, she's just so fun to tease." He clicked his pen. "Okay, so when did they call you about taking over?"

CHAPTER 5

By the time Baldwin released her, Christina stood in the doorway to the lobby, waiting for her. Mia grabbed her stuff and headed toward her. Baldwin had promised to release the contracts as soon as possible. Which meant she probably needed to do some digging and figure out what exactly she didn't know about the wedding to see if the vendors whose contracts weren't in the book would provide her a copy. "You didn't have to come. I can drive myself."

"You're upset. I can drive you home. It's not a burden. Besides, your grandmother called and told me to walk down here and get you. She can be pretty persistent. I didn't know what happened until Levi called me when he got off shift." Christina held out her hand and Mia gave her the keys. "I'm sorry you had to see that."

"It was awful, but I'm not the one who died, so please

don't treat me with kid gloves. Grans called you, huh? She must still have that spell on that ties into my emotional status. Either that or the rumor mill works faster in Magic Springs than I thought." Mia tucked her tote under her arm and hurried toward the door. She wanted out of the Lodge. She had a meeting with the bride and groom this afternoon. She didn't need the images from Chelsea's room still in her head.

"Does Baldwin have any idea who killed her?" Christina started the van and eased it out of the crowded parking lot.

"Not that I know. Let's change the subject. How was your night? You stayed out with Bethanie a while." Mia wanted to talk about anything but the murder.

"You know Bethanie. She's always saying how much fun we'll have, then she flakes. You would think I'd learn. She took off with one of the McMann boys and left me stuck there waiting for a ride home. Finally, James saw me sitting in the lobby and offered to drop me off. He's a good guy." Christina glanced at Mia as she pulled the van into traffic. "Don't be upset. I knew the chance I was taking hanging out with Bethanie, but I wanted to give her one more chance to be a real friend. She failed. Again."

"You need to know who you can trust." Mia closed her eyes and leaned her head back. The coffee had kicked in, but the small bit of alcohol in the drink had done nothing to relax her or dull the anxiousness she felt. "I'm going to take a long bath, then dig into what I can figure out on the wedding. Maybe Tok and Amethyst can fill in the blanks."

"I think Tok just says whatever you want, so I don't think he'll be much help. His mom is very nice, but she's intense. She was asking about you and how you fit into the town. I think she was fishing to see if you're in the coven, but I figured if you wanted to reveal your other side, that was your business." Christina grinned as she pulled the van into the driveway and stopped in the parking lot. "I did get to tell her what a number my brother did on you and what a saint you are for not holding it against me. Now she thinks you're amazing."

Mia opened the door and climbed out of the van. Heading to the door, she kept pace with Christina, who unlocked the door when they got there. "I am amazing. Right now, I'm amazingly anxious."

A sound came from upstairs and Christina's eyes widened as Mr. Darcy came running down the stairs, shooting out the cat door to the outside. "Stay here. I'll go see what's going on. If I don't come back, call Baldwin."

"This is ridiculous, I'll go up with you." Mia kind of hoped someone had broken in and was upstairs. Maybe hitting someone would make her feel better.

"Don't be stupid." Christina pressed the keys into Mia's hand. "Just do what I say. If I scream, go outside, get in the van, and leave."

Before Mia could stop her, Christina ran up the stairs, taking them two at a time. When she got to the third floor and disappeared into the open door of the apartment, Mia clutched her phone and the keys tighter. She heard something, but it wasn't a scream. Was that laughter?

Christina appeared at the top of the stairs. "Come on up, you have a visitor. I should have known."

Mia ran up the stairs, following Christina back into the apartment. She smelled the spaghetti sauce first. When she entered the kitchen she saw her grandmother cooking lunch on the stove. "How did you get here? Your car isn't in the parking lot."

"It's at Al's Repair Shop. I went out to start it to drive here and it just died. He's going to get her fixed up and back to me as soon as possible, but I thought Muffy and I would come stay with you so you don't have to come to the house to get me when I need to go somewhere." Her grandmother leaned over and gave her a kiss on the cheek. "Of course Mr. Darcy and Dorian aren't very happy to see Muffy at all. He went running out of here just now."

"Yeah, we saw that." Mia sank into a chair and Christina offered her a soda. "If you're okay here, I'm going to go soak in the tub for a while. Then I've got a meeting with my new clients."

"Of course I'm okay being here. I was here alone until you got here, right?" She tasted the sauce and added some herbs. "Go relax. You're wound tighter than a clock."

Mia rubbed the back of her neck, which did feel like a band of iron. She stood and set the tote on the chair. "I'll be back in a few. If I'm not out of there by the time lunch is ready, bang on the door because I've probably fallen asleep."

But as she sat in the steaming, deep tub, instead of feeling tired, the bath was pushing off the weariness. She breathed in the lavender she kept on hand to calm herself and closed her eyes. This time Chelsea's face didn't show in her mind. Instead, Trent was there, laughing about a trip they'd taken up the mountain to look for snow in September. The river was gently flowing next to the place where they'd pulled over for a quick picnic lunch. The day had been perfect.

A gentle knock sounded at the door. Christina called, "Are you asleep?"

"No. What do you want?"

"Time to eat!"

She'd just gotten in the bath. Lunch couldn't be ready. But it was. Mia wondered if she'd actually fallen asleep. When she dressed and walked into the kitchen, her grandmother was watching her.

"That's better."

Mia slid into a chair. "Seriously, you need to stop spelling me without telling me. I take it you changed up my bath salts?"

"Just a little potion I've been working on." Her grandmother put a plate of spaghetti drenched in sauce with a couple of slices of garlic bread in front of Mia. "Soda or coffee?"

"Coffee, please, and thanks for the carbs. I needed a pick-me-up after that bath." Mia twirled her fork in the pasta.

"Carbs tend to counteract the side effects of the potion. Without a heavy lunch, you'd need to sleep for a few days." Grans set a cup of coffee in front of her. Christina sat next to her, focusing on her pasta. "Tell me, did you have a dream during your bath? Was it a positive memory?"

"Yes and yes. I take it that was part of the potion?" Mia picked up the cup and took a sip. "Is this why I haven't seen you around for a while?"

To Mia's surprise, her grandmother blushed.

"Wait, what's that about?" Mia glanced over at the kitchen window seat, where Mr. Darcy was sleeping next to Muffy. She lowered her voice and whispered, "Are you seeing someone?"

Grans peeked over toward Mr. Darcy, then whispered back, "Let's table that subject."

Mia was floored. First she'd been shocked that Grans

had been dating Dorian when she came up for the food bank redesign last fall. And after Dorian was killed she assumed that would be that. Now Grans was dating someone else? As far as Mia knew, Grans hadn't had a man in her life except Dorian since her husband had died over fifty years ago.

"Close your mouth, dear, it's not attractive." Grans pointed to her plate. "And don't you have an appointment in thirty minutes?"

"I'll eat. I'm just adjusting." Mia focused on her lunch, and the three women around the table were quiet as they ate.

"When's Trent getting in tomorrow? Are you going to go pick him up at the airport?" Christina finally found something to talk about.

"Levi is picking him up, but he said he'd stop by around three to say hi." Mia yawned. "I'm still beat. Do you want to help me with the chat with Amethyst and Tok? It might help me get all the pieces I need to put this together."

"Sure, I'd love to. I got a few books on wedding planning from my school library yesterday. One of them has a checklist we can use. That way, we can figure out if Chelsea missed anything."

Mia's phone buzzed with a text. She glanced at it and grinned. "Things are looking up. Baldwin had one of his staff send us the front page of all the contracts that were in Chelsea's room. We won't have the full thing until they release them, but at least we don't have to guess who's bringing the flowers."

"Send the file to me and I'll go down and print them off before the meeting." Christina stood and took her empty plate to the sink. "I'll take the book with the list down and make a couple of copies of that too. I'll leave the other books in the living room on the coffee table."

"Thanks," Mia called after her. When she heard the front door of the apartment shut she twirled more spaghetti on her fork. "I don't know what I'm going to do without her."

"Why do you think she'll ever leave? You've given her a place to stay, a job, and, really, a family. At least one that listens when she talks. The only thing that's going to pull her out of here is that boy, Levi." Her grandmother finished her lunch and picked up her plate. "The things we do for love."

"Ain't that the truth." Mia focused on finishing eating so she wouldn't be asleep during the meeting. Hopefully the carbs would counteract this feeling. Otherwise she'd have to curl up into a ball after the meeting and sleep off the remnants of Grans's potion. She hated being a guinea pig.

She finished eating, ran into the bedroom to grab a cardigan and some flats, then ran a brush through her hair. It would have to do. She hurried downstairs and met Christina in the lobby area, setting up a table where they could chat. She had already set the wedding book there, as well as notepads and pens. The checklists were on top of the wedding book, as well as the contracts.

Christina pointed to the book. "I haven't had time to match up the contracts with the section of the book where they belong. Do you want to do that and then we can run down the checklist?"

They still had fifteen minutes before the couple was due at the house. More, if they got lost on their way to Mia's. She opened the book and picked up the first page. "Florists are Magic Springs Floral."

"Check," Christina called out as she made a physical check on the page. "Next?"

By the time they'd gotten through the scans it was almost one. Mia straightened her notes. "Why don't you go grab a bucket and fill it with sodas and ice? Then bring out glasses and cookies and set it all up over there."

"Perfect." Christina paused before leaving. "Do you want more coffee?"

"Please." She drank the dregs from her cup and handed it to her. "You're the best."

"Glad you think so." Christina winked and headed into the kitchen.

That left Mia alone to flip through the book and wait for the happy couple. Something was off about the whole wedding thing. And why was Mia in the middle of it? Had she been hired on someone's recommendation? Or was there more of a method to this randomness?

A knock on the door and then a voice called out that broke Mia out of her musing. "Hello? Is anyone there?"

Mia stood, waving Amethyst and Tok inside the lobby. "Come on in, we're set up over here."

"I haven't been in the building since Senior Sneak Day." Amethyst glanced around the room. "You've done wonders with it. I always hoped someone would buy this place and restore it. It must hold so many memories for people."

"You broke into an abandoned house for Senior Sneak Day?" Tok grinned down at his bride. "Boy, do you know how to party?"

"We visited here first, then we drove into Twin and went to Shoshone Falls. The water was running fast and the falls were beautiful that year. Some years it's just a trickle. Then we went to Sara Johnson's cousin's house and got drunk." Amethyst smiled up at him. "What did you do on your Sneak Day?"

"We didn't have a Senior Sneak Day. I was home-schooled by the tribe. There were five kids in our 'high school' class. We learned, took tests, then helped the kids coming up with what we'd learned. We should home-school our future kids."

"You probably should look at my report card before you put me in charge of that project." Amethyst laughed and pointed toward the table Mia had set up in the lobby. "Anyway, we're here to talk about the wedding, not our school experiences. Mia, you were raised in Boise, right?"

"Guilty as charged. I went to a private Catholic school for elementary through high school, even though my family didn't attend church. I guess they thought private school was better than the public schools, but I had plenty of friends who went to public school and loved it." Mia nodded toward the cookies and sodas Christina had just brought out. "Grab some refreshments and we'll get started."

Mia sat down and sipped her coffee. She turned to Christina, who was standing nearby. "Thanks for setting this up for us."

"Not a problem." Christina greeted Amethyst as she joined them at the table with a soda and cookies. "Nice to see you again."

"I hope you had fun last night. I'm sorry Bethanie took off on you. I heard that the hotel staff had to drive you home." Amethyst looked genuinely concerned. "Next time that happens and I'm around, let me know. One of Tok's brothers could have driven you."

"Or not. They were three sheets to the wind before the

dinner started." Tok grinned at Amethyst. "But we could have found someone. Bethanie is a flake."

"Honey!" Amethyst looked horrified at the word.

"I know, she's one of your oldest friends, honey, but she's a total loser. You've had your own issues with her stranding you." He put his arm around his future bride, softening his words as he spoke.

Amethyst leaned her head on his shoulder, meeting Mia's gaze. "I'm afraid he's right. It's hard to admit that she's as flawed as she is at times. I blame her family."

Mia's opinion of the couple rose by 10 percent.

"This just proved that I need my own car. I've been talking about getting one, and with me going to Twin for classes it's time. I'm always just bumming rides from people. I'm thinking I'll get one in smalt." Christina grinned at the trio.

"And where is Smalt?" Mia finally took the bait. This had to be one of Christina's vocabulary words.

"Smalt is not a there, it's a what. It's a color. Blue, in fact." Christina pointed to the book. "But we're not here to talk about that. Let's make sure this wedding is amazing."

Mia loved the way Christina transitioned the conversation. She was great at the client management of event planning. "You're right. Guys, I was able to review the plan and compare it to the contracts Chelsea had already obtained, and it looks like there are three areas we need to review today."

The meeting went on for a couple of hours, but by the time Tok and Amethyst left, Mia had a good understanding of what still needed to be done and who she needed to check in with to make sure everything was going well.

Christina walked them out of the school to the parking

lot, then came back inside, locking the door after she'd returned. "That went well."

"That went amazing." Mia pulled out the notebook she'd been taking notes on and pulled off the sheets she'd been writing on and laid them flat on the table. "Let's figure out everyone we need to call and what needs to be done each day before next Saturday. Then we can divide the list between us."

"Sounds good." Christina started making her own list as they talked. When they were finally finished she set down her pen and stared in the direction of the door.

"Okay, what's wrong?" Mia could tell when something was bothering her assistant.

Christina pressed her lips together as she turned back to meet Mia's gaze. "I don't know if it matters, but don't you find it odd that neither one of them said anything about Chelsea? Or asked how you were after you found her. It's like she doesn't exist anymore in their lives. It's kind of cold."

Mia had noticed the same thing but had pushed it out of her head. Now, questions rolled through her brain. Questions about the families she was working with. Families who were becoming one with this act of joining. And why no one was talking about Chelsea.

CHAPTER 6

Trent arrived at the school the next day with a bag in his hands. Mia buzzed him inside and then opened the door to the apartment to greet him. Christina and Grans had left about thirty minutes before to do some shopping and to stop by Grans's house to pick up some things. Mia figured it was just a way to let Mia and Trent have a little bit of time alone. She'd take it even if she saw through their ruse.

"Hey, beautiful." He pulled out a bouquet of flowers from behind his back and handed it to her. Then he kissed her.

She broke the kiss and tried to peek into his bag. "What's this?"

"Dinner. Christina called earlier and told me that she was taking your grandmother to dinner at the Lodge. So I thought I'd cook for you." He put his free arm around her and they walked into the kitchen. "Rumor is you not only found another job while I was gone, you also found a murder victim. I can't leave you alone for more than a few hours without you getting in trouble, can I?"

"I didn't go out to get involved in a mystery, I just wanted the job and the referrals I'll get from this one wedding." She stopped and held the fridge door open. "I can offer you a glass of wine or a soda. I didn't go to the store this week."

"Oh, you missed me that much?" Trent started unpacking the bag. "It's fine. I brought a six-pack of this new Sun Valley IPA. You can tell me if it's worth the hype."

"Why would me not going to the store mean I missed you?" She got a glass. Trent liked to drink his beer out of a bottle.

"Because you couldn't bear to go to my place of employment and know I wouldn't be there. You really should get over that. You'll starve if we ever break up." Trent handed her an open bottle.

"I know how to drive to the next town over to get groceries. Or even order delivery. If I was ever that upset." She'd just poured the beer when the doorbell went off on the front door. Mia stepped over to the desk and turned on the video. Gary McMann stood there with a bouquet of flowers. "That's strange."

"Is there something I should know?" Trent stood behind her and sipped his beer.

Mia shook her head. "Nothing I know about. Let me go see what he wants. He's the groom's brother, so maybe it's something to do with the wedding. I think the mother wants to run the show on this party."

"If you say so. But the flowers tell another story." Trent stepped back so she could go around him.

She unlocked the apartment door so it wouldn't lock her out and headed downstairs to see what Gary needed. She opened the door. "Hey, Gary, how can I help you?"

"I just came by to thank you for the dance on Thursday." He handed her the flowers. "I was wondering if I could take you to dinner."

"Sorry, I've got my own personal chef upstairs. Besides, I told you I had a boyfriend." Mia glanced around the driveway. A huge blue truck jacked up with oversize tires sat in front of her house. "Oh, my Goddess. I don't see how you can even drive that."

"Get in and I'll take you for a spin. It's fun. Especially in mud." He grinned, and the sparkle of his smile reminded Mia of the wolf in the Red Riding Hood story.

"I don't think so. Besides, like I said, my boyfriend's upstairs cooking me dinner." She stepped back and moved to shut the door.

"Seriously, Mia, this hard-to-get attitude is going to get you nowhere with me," he called out as she closed the door.

She stuck her head out of the small crack. "Good, then it's working. Go away."

"That's not nice. I brought you . . ."

She didn't hear the rest of the discussion because she'd already shut the door. Apparently, Gary didn't handle rejection well. She ran up the stairs and into the apartment. Trent stood between the kitchen and the living room in the doorway.

"So I'm officially your boyfriend now? A real couple?" He watched her walk in, his gaze dropping to the flowers in her hand.

Mia turned toward the hallway and opened the first door. She tossed the flowers on her grandmother's bed. She walked back into the kitchen. "Hopefully she'll get home in time to put those in water."

"You didn't answer me." Trent followed her and sat down at the table when she did.

"And you shouldn't listen in on people's conversations. It's rude." Mia sipped her beer. "Maybe I just said that to get rid of him."

"Maybe. But I thought it was wiser to stay up here so I didn't punch the jerk in the face." He sipped his beer. "Tell me about the dance."

"One dance, and it was at the meet-the-in-laws after party. Man, those people are serious about controlling the wedding details. The groom's mother was going all mother-of-the-groom-zilla on me, which I didn't realize was even a thing. Gary saved me by taking me out to the dance floor. Then he dropped me off with Christina. That's the story." She sipped her beer.

"He's a shifter, isn't he?"

Mia frowned. "You could tell that from the camera feed?"

Trent shook his head. "No, his scent is on you from when he greeted you. He must have touched your hand when he gave you the flowers. On most women, that would have been enough to convince you to have his babies."

Mia laughed and took another sip of her beer. She realized Trent wasn't laughing. "Oh, my Goddess. You're serious."

"Totally. There's a lot of mythology around them, but mostly it's animal call-of-the-wild stuff." He focused on Mia. "Don't be alone with him. He won't give up easily."

"Chelsea left the party with him. Well, he followed her out. She's human. Would she have fallen at the touch of his hand?" A knot was forming in her stomach. Had the killer just made a house call?

"Like I said, don't be alone with him." He finished his beer, then stood up. "Want to help chop veggies?"

Mia decided not to focus on Gary's interruption. She wasn't going to let him mess with the first night she'd had with Trent for over a week. "I will if you tell me about the Vegas trip. What did you see besides that creepy dam?"

"Hoover Dam is an engineering masterpiece. And it's creepy as heck, especially if you look down at the canyon." Trent pulled out peppers and onions from the bag and gave them to Mia. As they worked together to cook dinner, he told her about his week in Vegas.

Mia didn't know a lot about healthy relationships, but this felt right. Good, even. She let herself be pulled away by the joy of the evening. She'd think about murder and killers tomorrow. It was good to have Trent back and she needed him to know how much she'd deeply missed him.

When Christina and Grans returned later that night, Mia and Trent were curled up on the couch watching a superhero movie. They'd watched it before, but it was a fun distraction and they could talk around the action plot.

"There are leftovers in the fridge," Trent called out, not moving from his spot on the couch with Mia curled up next to him. "Chicken fajitas with homemade tortillas."

"Is it pukka?" Christina asked, her eyes blinking innocently.

"It's my version of Mexican. Probably Tex-Mex if you're trying to label it." Trent glanced between Mia and

Christina. "I've never heard of pukka. Is that a chef term?"

"It's a vocabulary word. Christina is trying out her use-a-word-in-a-sentence skills with us." Mia glanced at Christina, but Grans spoke first.

"You should tell that professor of yours that you shouldn't use a ten-dollar word when a ten-cent one will do." Grans snapped her fingers and Muffy sat up from the pillow by the gas fireplace where he'd been sleeping. "I'm turning in. It's been a long day."

Christina waited for Grans's door to shut. "She's been grumpy since dinner. I think she saw someone she knew at the restaurant. And I think he was with another woman."

"I knew she was seeing someone," Mia blurted out, sitting up from where she'd been lying. "Did you get a good look at him?"

"No. It was right when we were leaving. I'm not even sure he saw her. But she definitely saw him. I only could see his back. He wore a pukka Brooks Brothers coat. It was nice."

"Original? That's what pukka means?" Trent had sat up as well and was watching the women talk.

"Bingo. I think I'll use that sentence as my example. Thanks, Trent. I'm too full to eat anything else. I guess I'll see you in the morning." She reached down and picked up Mr. Darcy. "And there you are, sleeping under the wing chair. Time to crash."

This time Mia was the one to wait for a door closing. "I didn't see Mr. Darcy there. Dorian must be crushed."

"I don't understand. About what?" Trent pulled her back down to sit next to him with his arm around her.

"He heard us talk about Grans dating again."

Trent pulled her closer. "It was bound to happen. And he's actually dead, so he can't do anything about her dating except wish her the best. I was just out of town for a week."

"Hey, now, nothing happened with me and Hulk."

He giggled. "You have to be kidding. That's his name?"

"That's what the guys call him. He introduced himself as Gary." Mia reached up and kissed Trent. "You know there was nothing to that dance, right?"

He kissed her back. "I know that, but does the Hulk?"

Mia shrugged and snuggled back up to finish watching the movie. The sooner this wedding was over, the better. Everything was getting complicated. And she hadn't even finished putting the pieces together that the last planner had put into place. Sometimes the job wasn't worth the money even when the money was good. This was turning out to be one of those times.

She turned down the sound. "Tell me what you know about Tok and Gary's tribe. Do they live around here?"

"Mostly in the mountains. There are several compounds down Lupine Road off the highway near Galena Summit. According to local lore, they've lived out there for decades, maybe longer. They don't send their kids to school. They don't pay taxes, but for some reason the feds and the state people leave them alone. And they're amazing hunters. I've been out with my dad when I've seen one of their trucks piled high with deer. Apparently, they don't believe in hunting regulations either because it wasn't deer season when we saw them. Dad always said to give the McManns a wide berth. What they want, they take." Trent took her hand in his as he talked.

Mia could feel Trent's energy turn cold as he talked

about the groom's family. "I got that from my talk with the mother. Tok is sweet. He's letting Amethyst do anything she wants for the wedding. He doesn't seem like he just takes what he wants."

Trent sat up and turned to face her. "Mia, don't underestimate him. He's playing nice about the wedding because Amethyst is what he wants. Having a witch in the family is a huge boon for his people. It wasn't that many years ago that they came down from the mountains and kidnapped women. The mother? She was a human who went missing from Sun Valley as a young girl. She's been sucked up into their lifestyle now."

"If she'd been kidnapped, why would she stay? Even now, wouldn't she want to go home?"

Trent rubbed his face. "The rumor is she doesn't have a family to return to now. Her house was burned down the night she was taken with her parents inside."

"That's awful." Mia sat up. "Maybe I should bow out of this. I could return the deposit and the book. I don't know if I can work with people like that."

Trent took her hand. "Honey, we all have demons in our background if you look hard enough. The Uzzis aren't squeaky-clean either. All I'm saying is don't get close, and please, don't be alone with this Gary."

"Maybe I should hire you to be my bodyguard for the week." She rubbed his arm, but he grabbed her wrist and kissed it.

"Mia, you're a genius. I'll work for you this week while you get this done. That way I can watch you and Christina during the festivities. Maybe we'll need Levi to pull some shifts too." He turned up the movie volume. "I love it when a plan comes together."

Mia took the remote from him and paused the movie. "Hold up there, Sparky. I'm not sure I want you to take time away from the store just to play watch dog."

"It's the smart thing to do. I still have time. I took two weeks when I thought you might come to Vegas with me. At worst, you get someone to do the heavy lifting. And we get to spend time together." He smiled and leaned back on the couch. "Or are you telling me you want to spend more time with that Gary guy?"

"You're an idiot." She threw a couch pillow at him. "If I wanted to spend time with Gary, I would have kicked you out this afternoon. You're right. I need the money. It's a great boon to the replace-the-furnace fund. And it lets me give Christina hours this week besides just the deliveries. She's good at this event stuff."

"Guys?" Christina stood in the entrance from the hallway. "Levi's on the line and he wants to know if he should take next week off from the firehouse. What's he talking about? Can someone tell me what's going on?"

Trent stood and took the phone from her. As he walked into the kitchen, he said into the phone, "I take it you heard most of that?"

Mia patted the couch. "Come sit by me. I need to tell you a story about our new clients."

CHAPTER 7

Monday morning, Mia and Christina were in the kitchen, cooking for the next day's deliveries. Keeping his promise to stay close this week, Trent had arrived earlier that morning with a box of pastries from the store's bakery. Currently he was wandering through the school looking for more secret passages. They still hadn't been able to keep the passage in the chemistry lab closed. No matter what Trent did, the locks fell off or broke within a day of him installing them. So she kept the door to the lab locked. She made a note to chat with her grandmother to see if she'd made any progress finding one of the witches who had been involved in the school's original building process. She needed to know how the wards were spelled in order to close the passageway.

Mia had just finished putting in a cake for desserts when she realized how quiet Christina had been all morning. Mia grabbed a dish towel and stepped over to where she was chopping vegetables. "Hey, sorry I've been quiet this morning. There's a lot going on. Are you okay?"

"I'm fine. Just processing. I know Magic Springs is different. Heck, I know you and Trent and Levi are witches. That information didn't faze me at all. Your grandmother scares me at times, but I think that's more of her personality than her special powers. But now you tell me there are real shifters in Idaho? And that I hung out with them a few nights ago? Those guys, they just seem normal. Maybe a little over-the-top, live-in-the-woods, mountain-man types, but not different to shifter level. I thought that was fiction." Christina set down her knife and took a sip from her water bottle. "I'm beginning to think I don't know anything about this world."

"And you're thinking you'd rather close up the Pandora's box you opened when you moved in with me." Mia laughed at the look Christina had. A mixture of guilt and shock. "Don't worry, I didn't read your mind, I just know how non-magicals think. My mom raised me in the normal world. She'd rather I'd turned my back on this world like she did. Instead, I dived in headfirst, thinking I knew everything. Like you, I'm finding out I have a lot more to learn."

"So you didn't know either?" Christina climbed on a stool and watched Mia.

"Did I know that shifters or werewolves were real? No." Mia grabbed a soda from the fridge. She needed some sugar to keep going today. Then she sat on the stool next to Christina. "I always knew about magic and witches. It seemed normal, more like a job. And Grans always focused on the good we do for the world. Like her new potion to help people with trauma in their past. She wants to use her skills to help others. I think that's a calling. Like deciding to be a doctor or a politician. But I didn't know creatures like shifters existed. Maybe that's not PC to call them creatures. Maybe they're just human with a special something in the mix."

"The entire McMann family seems nice." Christina sipped her water, obviously thinking. "I just keep coming back to whether shifters are real and I've met one or more, so I know that's a fact. Then, the question hits me that what else is real out there that I don't know about? Well, I know ghosts are real too. I'd forgotten about Dorothy."

"So now you know three types of people who aren't 'normal' in your eyes. You've also met people who were raised in different socioeconomic households and from different parts of the country. You were telling me about the ultrarich the other night and that they are different from us. Are you frightened of them just because they're different?" Mia sipped her soda. She had her own doubts about the shifters and their motives, but all in all, people were people.

Grans burst into the kitchen holding the bouquet in front of her by two fingers. "Where did you get these flowers?"

Mia laughed and patted Christina on the arm. "We'll talk more later. Good morning, Grans. How did you sleep?"

"Mia, answer my question. Where did you get the flowers?" Grans held them away from her like they were on fire.

"I thought you might like them. Trent wasn't going to let me put them up in the living room because Gary

McMann brought them over. Why, don't you like yellow roses? They're so pretty." Mia stood and pulled down bowls so she could start making the stuffed meat loaf they were delivering this week.

"They have a listening spell on them." Grans put them in a metal trash can and poured olive oil on them. Then she snapped her fingers, and the flowers burst into flame. "I can't believe you didn't feel it. I barely slept last night. The spell kept nagging at me and when I awoke this morning I realized it was the flowers."

"You're kidding." Mia watched as the flames burned down, thankful her fire inhibitors hadn't gone off. It would have ruined the food they'd already prepared. "Why would Gary want to listen in on my conversations?"

Mia's phone rang and she glanced over at the caller ID. It was blocked.

Grans pointed to the phone. "Answer the call. It's him."

"How do you know?" She held up her hand. "Don't bother." She punched a button and put the call on Speaker. "Gary, how are you this morning?"

"Good morning, beautiful. So, you found the spell. Not that I suspected you in the woman's death, but you did find the body. Tell me what you know." Gary's tone was crisp.

"I know you were trying to listen in on my conversations. Couldn't you have just asked me what you wanted to know?" Mia sipped her soda and waited.

Gary laughed. "I tried, remember? You were busy with your boyfriend. Look, someone's trying to make this look like someone from our tribe killed Chelsea. I've seen the coroner's preliminary report. It screams attack from a wild animal on the third floor of the Lodge. Which we all know isn't possible."

"I saw you follow her out of the party. What was that about?"

The sigh was audible even over speaker. "I was the one who invited her to the party. But that was before she got fired. I felt bad that she got kicked out. I didn't know she was going to get in a fight with Drunder. I went to see if she was all right. By the time I got back to the party, alone, you were gone."

"So you had your mom put a spell on the flowers to see if I thought you were the killer?"

He paused. "You're always surprising me. I didn't think Mom's skills were common knowledge. But anyway, yes. My family didn't do this. No one in the tribe would have done this. We're not killers."

Mia wanted to ask why his mom was still stuck with the tribe since she'd been kidnapped, but she decided to let that go. A son should never be burdened with the sins of his father. "It's really not my job to find killers. You need to be talking to Mark Baldwin."

"I've already chatted with the good detective. Not only is he totally blind to the idea of otherworldly people, but he also doesn't know his town is run by a coven. What's up with that?"

"Mark's a good man. He just tends to believe in what he can see." Mia paused, thinking about the murder. "Answer me one question: Why would anyone want to frame you or a member of your tribe for Chelsea's murder?"

"That's easy. They want to stop the marriage between Tok and Amethyst. Our families have been at odds for years. If this marriage happens, we'll have to stop the fighting. Some in our extended family feel like that's a betrayal of the tribe. My immediate family, on the other hand, think it's time we moved into the modern world and stopped acting like spoiled children. The world is getting smaller, we need all the allies we can get." Gary paused. "Look, I've got to run. Family meeting. I just wanted to apologize for the listening spell. It was wrong of us. I'll be more open in the future."

After he hung up Mia met Grans's gaze. "So, what do you think? Is he being honest with us?"

"Now that he got caught? Maybe. I still think you need to steer clear of the McManns as much as possible." Grans glanced around the kitchen. "What can I help with now that I'm here?"

Mia glanced at the schedule. Gary's call had put them behind a bit. "Can you start the spring vegetable soup? I want to make sure it gets enough time to develop a deep flavor profile."

"I'd love to. I need something to keep my mind busy today."

Christina and Mia shared a glance, but from a shake of Christina's head, Mia decided not to bring up the events of last night. Maybe she'd be able to get her grandmother to open up later, when they weren't busy.

She'd started working on the stuffed meat loaf when her phone rang. This time it was the Lodge kitchen. She recognized the number. "Hey, James, what's going on?"

"You have a tasting in about ten minutes. Your bride and groom are already here. Are you coming?"

Mia swore under her breath. "Seriously? I thought that was Wednesday."

"It was, then it got moved up in case the families needed to change any of the selections. I take it you're cooking for your weekly deliveries."

Grans made go-ahead motions with her hands and Christina nodded.

Mia swore. "I was. Let me get cleaned up and I'll be there in no more than fifteen. Thanks for the call, James."

"No problem. You know I want you to be successful with this event so we can get these people out of my hotel. So anything you need."

"Unless you know how to clone someone, I think we're good." She hung up and brought down the schedule. "I can make the meat loaf when I get back. It's going to be a long day, but we can still do it."

Trent stood in the doorway and pulled out his keys. "Let me drop you off, then I'll come back and make the meat loaf. You have a recipe, right?"

"Yes, but . . ."

"No buts. Get your apron off and wash your hands before you get into my truck. I don't want to get it dirty." He held open the door. "And without having to find somewhere to park, you won't be late. Just call me when you're done and I'll be waiting outside the front door."

Mia pulled off the apron and pointed to the notebook on the counter. "Recipe is in there. We have seventy-five orders for tomorrow. You'll need to make it in batches."

"They'll be done before you finish playing nice with the wedding party." He leaned close as she walked by on her way to the office to grab stuff. "Just mind what I said about being alone with this Gary guy."

"Yes, sir." Mia gave him a quick kiss on the cheek, then went to retrieve the wedding book, her notebook,

and the folder where she'd put all the rest of the paperwork. She needed to sit down today and do a day-by-day
plan for this week so this double-booking didn't happen
again. Not all the vendors would be as nice as James to
give her a call.

When she got into the truck she slipped on her seat
belt. "Any luck with the secret passages?"

"No, from what I see, we only have the one. Unless the
others are cleverly hidden. Has your grandmother found
any of the men who were part of the build yet?" He
started the engine and pulled the truck out of the driveway.

"Not yet. She's been distracted lately. I'll ask her as
soon as I get back. And I hate to ask, but when is Levi
coming? I think we are going to need both of you this
week. I hate the thought that Christina and Grans being
alone at the house, even for this short time." She chewed
on her bottom lip. She'd made sure the front door was
locked, so all they had to do was stay in the kitchen.

"He should be there by now. I called him earlier when
I overheard your chat with Gary."

The Lodge was the next turnoff on the road, but they
were stopped at the one stoplight in town. Mia thought
about confronting Trent about eavesdropping, but she
wanted to get his thoughts and she would have answered
the call if she'd known he was in the room anyway.
"What did you think of his story?"

"Could be true. Or he could be trying to deflect blame
onto someone else. We need to have a powwow tonight
after dinner to talk this out. I think we all have pieces of
the puzzle we need to share." The light turned green and
he put his foot on the gas. When they arrived at the Lodge

he parked in front of the doors to the lobby. "You be careful in there. If I don't hear from you in two hours, I'm coming in Rambo style."

"I love that imagery." She leaned in and kissed him. "Thanks for helping out."

"Meat loaf is my game." He watched her leave and didn't move the truck until Mia was inside the lobby.

She saw the truck pull out as she left the lobby to make her way toward the dining room. James met her at the door and handed her a travel-size cup of coffee. "Thought you might need this. Both sets of parents decided to join in today's tasting because we're doing both the rehearsal dinner and the reception dinner. I pity you. If you need rescuing, just raise a hand in the air and I'll come out and pull you out of the pool."

"You're not giving me much hope that this might be a pleasant encounter." She took the coffee and sipped it.

He laughed as he reached out for the door handle. "They're already fighting over invites. I think the bride is ready to burst into tears and the groom wants to run away. Have fun."

He pushed her toward the table and Amethyst looked up. "Oh, good, you're here. I think we need to come to some closure on the total number of guests before we can do the tasting."

"Okay, that might be true." Mia sat down at the table and turned to the page where the guest lists were tucked into a plastic sleeve. "Honestly, I thought Chelsea might have already finished this part of the plan, so I didn't dig into it. Let's see what we have right now."

"I don't see how we can be slighted. . . ." Marilyn McMann started, but her husband put his hand on hers.

"Dear, the girl just said she hadn't looked it up. Let her

give us some numbers. She's being paid to sort these things out for us." He nodded to Mia, who took a breath as she pulled out the last noted page.

"Okay, so the room seats five hundred. That's our maximum because we've already committed to the hotel. We can't go over that." Mia wrote "500" on the top of each list. Then she divided it in half. "That means you each can invite two hundred fifty people. Or one hundred twenty-five couples. It's a no-children wedding, right?"

"Many of our friends have children." Cassandra Uzzi shook her head. "We don't have to count them, correct?"

"Sorry, no, any child counts as a person, even babies, in the five hundred fire code regulation. We wouldn't want to exceed that due to safety protocols." Mia pulled out her phone. "Okay, so if a couple has two kids average, that drops your invites to sixty-two or sixty-three families. I think it might be easier on our decision-making to let your guests know that they'll have to get a babysitter for each night."

"There is no way we can cut our list down to sixty-two couples," Marilyn said.

Mia broke in before she could go on. "Okay, then, I think we've made a decision to have it be a no-children event, right? Amethyst, Tok? Are you two good with that?"

"That's perfect. I hate hearing kids yelling at weddings. It makes the event seem less formal and less sacred." Tok squeezed Amethyst's hand. "What do you think?"

"I totally agree. So our next step is to take back the lists and make sure we're at one hundred twenty-five couples apiece, right, Mia?" Amethyst gave her a thankful smile as she took the guest lists from the book. "I know we already sent save the date and real invites to at least four hundred people, so this is just the extras that we seem to be adding in daily. We'll handle this and get you a final list tomorrow. Next step?"

"Well, that would be the food. Now that we have a final number of five hundred, we can look at the meals to see if they fit into the budget. Traditionally, the McManns as the groom's family would pay for the rehearsal dinner. Which leaves the reception food up to the Uzzis."

"Then why are we meeting here together?" Drunder grumbled.

My question exactly was what Mia didn't say. Instead, she smiled at the four gathered around the table. She passed out a list of menu options to each person. "Hopefully we can agree on two different meals so your guests won't be eating the same meal each night. James is going to bring out a few of the more popular dishes for us to taste, unless there's something on this menu that you don't want served. But if there's something specific you want, we can focus on that."

"We need to have beef on both nights." Brody McMann pointed to the listing. "Our guests expect that."

"It's something we can discuss. Typically, one family chooses the meal for their respective nights, with input from the other family. Like the marriage we're gathering to celebrate, these meals are the first joining of the families. Food is the best way to bring people together." She pointed to the first entrée. "Who wants to taste the prime rib?"

Everyone's hands raised.

"Good first start." She nodded to James, who was standing near the kitchen door, waiting for their decision. "Okay, what about the halibut?"

They went through the list of options quickly without much discord. Mia stood as the first plate arrived and excused herself. "I'll go chat with James to let him know what we want to taste."

When she got into the kitchen, she blew out a long breath. "That was rough."

"Are you kidding? You're great at this. You really need to add wedding planning to your list of services. You took that table from wanting to kill one another to actually agreeing on things." James squeezed her shoulder. "You're amazing."

"The day isn't over yet. We still have to get agreement on both menus." She glanced out the small window and watched as the four seemed to be talking and enjoying the food. She handed him the menu list. "Bring out the next round. Let's see if we can get this done before someone says something stupid."

CHAPTER 8

To Mia's surprise, the tasting ended right inside the hour and they had final menus for five hundred people. She'd pushed the limit by not counting the wedding party, but James and the fire department would just have to deal with a few more people. Besides, there were always people who said they were coming and didn't. She sagged against the bench outside the main entrance to the hotel while she waited for Trent to arrive. Next on the list? She had to cook for the rest of the day. By the time she was done she was going to fall into bed. Except she couldn't.

The one thing that today's almost-missed meeting had taught her was that she needed to set up a schedule for the next week. And everything needed to go on the schedule. Thank goodness she had Levi and Trent to help out. She didn't think she needed a bodyguard as much as Trent thought she did, but she did know she needed help getting the work done. If they thought they were "protecting" her and Christina, well, that was okay too.

"It's a beautiful morning. Taking in the sunshine?" Gary McMann stood near the bench, watching her.

"Actually, just waiting for my ride." Mia glanced around. There were several people in the parking lot as well as two valets standing near the stand. She wasn't alone with Gary. Trent couldn't yell at her when he arrived.

"I heard you were the music that soothed the savage beast in the tasting meeting today. Tok said you even calmed down Mom." He took out a bag of beef jerky and put a piece in his mouth. He held out the bag. "Do you want one?"

"No, thanks."

"I'm trying to quit smoking, so this is my replacement. I'm not sure I'm going to be able to get through this week without at least one pack." He tucked the jerky away into his jacket. "So, who do you think killed Chelsea?"

The quick change of subject surprised Mia. "Actually, I'm not sure. She'd just fought with Mr. Uzzi, who'd fired her. She was hanging around a bunch of shifters who might be a little overanxious due to a relative's wedding. Or she might have had a horrible ex-lover who didn't like the fact she was getting on with her life. I've been too busy with this wedding to really think about who might have wanted the woman dead."

"I see you're still open to someone besides the shifters as suspect number one." He squatted down and surveyed the area. "I feel like it has something to do with Tok and Amethyst. When they announced their engagement neither family was happy with the situation. And if you take out the wedding planner, maybe the wedding wouldn't happen."

"Not true. They'd just hire another wedding planner." Mia saw Trent's truck turn in off the road. She stood and took a step toward the driveway. "Like this one that has to get back to working her other job."

"Mia, you need to be careful. If preventing the wedding is the motive, they might not stop at just killing the first wedding planner." He walked toward the entrance.

Gary's words shocked her and she turned to face him. But he was already gone, the door to the hotel swinging shut. His words brought on a chill as she refocused on Trent's truck in front of her. She opened the door and arranged her tote on the floor. Buckling in, she waited a beat before she could trust her voice. Finally, she took a breath and said, "Thanks for picking me up."

"Tell me what's wrong." Trent drove the truck out of the overhang and toward the road. "You're white as a ghost."

She leaned back and closed her eyes. "The tasting was horrible. Both sets of parents were there and it was like herding wild cats. When one would calm down the other set would freak out. I hate working with angry people. I feed people. It makes them happy. I like happy people. This is a wedding. It's supposed to be about being happy. But no, everyone wants to kill the wedding planner."

"What? Did someone say that?" Trent shot a look at her.

She shook her head. "Not exactly. The tasting is done and the choices are made. And they all started to act like normal people afterward. It just took a lot of energy to get there. Then Gary . . ."

Trent interrupted. "I told you to stay away from that guy."

"No, you told me not to be alone with him. Which I wasn't. I can't just stay away from one of the wedding party members. Anyway, let me talk." She'd never felt so tired. This wasn't the fun experience she'd hoped for.

"Sorry. Go on. I'll control my alpha male response."

His words made her smile, which apparently had been his plan because she saw his knuckles relax on the steering wheel. "Thanks. Anyway, Gary found me out on the bench after the tasting. And he brought up the fact that maybe Chelsea's death was due to her role as the wedding planner. He said neither side was happy when the engagement was announced. Then he warned me that the killer might just want to take out the replacement planner as well."

"Well, isn't he a bringer of great news." Trent turned the corner and drove up the drive to the parking lot by the house. "Although, to be honest, I can't say I wasn't thinking the same thing."

"So you agree with him on one point at least. You both think I'm in danger. Great." She opened her door and swung the tote over her shoulder.

Trent caught up with her before she reached the front door. "I'm not letting anything happen to you. Don't worry about it."

She looked up into his brown eyes and touched his cheek. "Honey, I'm not worried about someone killing me. I'm not going to give anyone the chance. I'm upset that someone would go to this length to stop the wedding of two people who are so desperately in love, they can't see any differences in themselves or their families. What if they can't get to me so they go after Amethyst? What if

Christina gets in the way? I've never felt so scared in my life."

"We'll solve this. We'll find out who killed Chelsea. Not just for her sake, but to make sure everyone else is safe. We might be just pawns in the food service industry, but we have a few tricks up our sleeves. And we have the crew to brainstorm with. Nothing is going to happen to Christina. Not on Levi's watch. And nothing's going to happen to you." He glanced toward town. "Baldwin's going to have to take care of the rest of them."

Mia glanced at her watch. "I can't waste any more time on this. I've got to get tomorrow's deliveries done. Where are we on the list?"

Trent listed off what they'd gotten done while she was gone. Mia had to admit she was impressed, but there was still so much more cooking to finish. She made a beeline to the kitchen and started barking orders as she washed her hands and put on a clean apron.

Levi laughed as she listed off what was still in line to be done.

"And why are you laughing?" She narrowed her eyes at him.

"Because Trent just lost five bucks to Christina. He said the first thing you'd do when you walked into the kitchen was comment on all the stuff we'd finished, and Christina said you'd focus on the work to be done." Levi pointed to his brother. "Pay up, dude."

"Am I that predictable?" Mia glanced around the room and saw all the cakes had been finished and both ovens were filled with meat loaves with the next batch ready to take their place.

"When you're stressed, yep." Christina came around and patted Mia's shoulder. "Don't worry about it. We love you anyway. I'm going to start the frosting for the cakes."

Mia gave assignments to Levi and Trent and then started on her own project. From the way things were looking, they should be packed up and ready no later than six. Maybe she'd get takeout from the Lodge for the crew this evening, which would give her time to review the wedding book and write out a plan for the next few days. Having a plan would stop this stress she felt. She hoped.

Sitting around the dinner table that night, Levi was telling a story about the new coven member who'd moved into a mini mansion near the ski lodge. Apparently, the man was from Southern California and had been part of the movie business in his prime.

"Maybe Cindy knows him." Mia glanced at her grandmother, who was focusing on her chicken enchiladas. Cindy was an actress and Dorian's daughter. She'd spent a lot of time with them a few months before, after using her magic to curse her talent agent. "Grans?"

"I don't know everyone who Cindy knows, dear." But Grans didn't meet her gaze. Instead, she changed the subject. "I talked to Charles Silas Miller this week and he's going to be at the Uzzi-McMann wedding and reception. He's willing to talk to you about your questions on the building of the school."

"That's great." Trent met Mia's gaze. "Can I attend the reception and meet with the two of you? If I had specifics on how the protection spell was placed on the secret entrance, I might be able to get it off and close that problem entirely."

"You have to be there anyway. You and Levi are helping Christina and me. At least, that's your cover story. Unofficially, you're our bodyguards. And you're on the payroll until this wedding is over or canceled. Whichever comes first." Mia glanced at the chocolate cake that sat on the counter. "I've got to go work on the schedule. Can someone cut me a slice of cake when you do desserts and bring it down with a carafe of coffee? I have a feeling I'm going to be working for a while."

"I'll bring down the cake. Do you want ice cream as well?" Trent cut into his pork chop, not watching her face.

"Sounds perfect." Mia excused herself from the table and set the plate in the sink. Then she grabbed the wedding book and a light jacket from her room. She kept the heat low in the building except for in the apartment to try to keep the energy costs down. She'd hate to think what she'd pay a month if they heated the entire school.

Mr. Darcy followed her out of the apartment and down the stairs. He had his own secret entrances, but so far he hadn't shown her where they were. Of course, with Dorian's magic, the cat could just leave by the front door if he wanted to.

She unlocked her office and set her coffee down on the desk. Then she turned on her computer and, as she walked around the desk to sit down, saw she had a fax. She picked up the paper and froze.

"'Cancel the wedding or else.'" She read it aloud a couple of times. What did the killer want her to do? She couldn't cancel a wedding—that was up to the bride and groom. She set it on the desk, then snapped a picture of it. She sent the picture to Baldwin's phone and added, **CAME BY FAX.** And listed her fax number.

He texted right back. I **SUPPOSE YOUR FAX NUMBER IS ON YOUR BUSINESS CARDS.**

She answered, **YES AND ON THE WEBSITE.**

She waited for the response. When it came it was one word.

FIGURES.

And that was that. She set her phone down on top of the fax and took out the wedding planner. It was time to work. If Baldwin decided to shut the wedding down, she'd follow his orders. But until then, she had work to do.

Trent came into the office with a tray about an hour later. Mia had gotten through the book and made a list of everything she still didn't know, as well as the wedding week schedule. It was all typed up in a nice Word document and she'd just printed off three copies. One for her, one for Christina, and one for the bride and groom. She'd made an appointment to see James in the morning to go through the I-don't-know list with him.

She looked up and grinned at the man with the tray. "Yay, I'm done for the night. And—" she held up the papers she'd stapled together—"I have a plan and a schedule."

"I've never seen anyone so happy about making a work schedule." He moved the papers to set down the tray as Mia grabbed the carafe to pour herself one last cup of coffee. He held up the fax. "What's this?"

Mia sat down and moved her plate and fork closer. "It looks like Gary's theory just got another upvote."

"Mia, this is a threat. It's serious. You should tell Baldwin." He stood, holding the fax toward her.

"That's a great idea." She pointed to the visitor's chair. "Sit down and eat before your ice cream melts. This is amazing."

He stood there, watching her eat. Finally, he sat and picked up his plate. "You could have led with that."

"What, that the cake's amazing?" She put up her feet on her desk and stretched her legs as she ate.

"That you'd already contacted Baldwin."

"Someday you're not going to treat me like I'm an idiot." Mia pushed her phone toward him, unlocking the screen. "That's the response I got."

He read the texts, then set the phone down and went back to his dessert. "Can you even track a fax?"

"Probably. He has my number. All he has to do is reach out to the phone company. I'm sure it will be some random mailbox place, or worse, the Lodge's business center. No one is ever in there. You could slip in and send a fax without anyone noticing."

"There's a computer system that lets you send faxes through your computer. So he wouldn't even have had to touch a fax machine," Trent added.

"The joy of modern technology. Maybe that would allow some computer cop to track it better. We can only hope." She sipped her coffee. "What's happening upstairs?"

"Mr. Darcy came back. We were in the living room, talking about tomorrow's plan, and the door just opens. He walks in and the door closes after him. You really need to talk to Dorian. What if a nonmagical person was here when he did it?" Trent finished his dessert and put the plate on the tray. Then he poured himself a cup of coffee.

"He doesn't seem to do it when humans are here. I had a guy here checking the gym lights last week and Mr. Darcy went to the back door and cried to be let out. Then he winked at me when I opened the door." Mia smiled. "I'm not sure if I think it's cute or I'm concerned."

"I'd be the former. Anyway, they want to talk to you about deliveries tomorrow if you're ready to go upstairs." He sipped his coffee. "I'm sorry this is happening."

"That's what I get for thinking I'm going to make easy money with wedding planning. The Goddess must be laughing right now."

"Man plans, God laughs." He leaned over and kissed her. "I can't say I'm happy you're even considering staying with the wedding planning gigs. Especially after this."

"I think it has two possibilities. Either they know Gary told me that I might be on the killer's list, so they're pushing the point." She stood and locked the door as they moved out of the office.

"Or?"

She tucked the keys into her jacket pocket and took Trent's arm. "The killer is trying to stop the wedding. Which leads me to ask the question, why?"

CHAPTER 9

Christina and Levi were tasked with Tuesday's delivery duty, which gave Mia and Trent a little time before they needed to leave for the Lodge. Grans sat at the kitchen table with them as they finished one last cup of coffee.

Mia glanced down at Mr. Darcy. "Grans, you need to have a talk with Dorian about using magic to get what he wants. It can't be good for Mr. Darcy."

"Your cat is fine. Dorian's soul is attracting all the residuals of using magic. Especially what he does for his own use. Although I think the rule of three isn't affecting him because Mr. Darcy's cat body is fooling the Goddess. Or whoever pushes out the Karma bounce." Grans frowned and went to Mia's desk. "Although I think there are some studies on the effect of spirits and magic. Maybe it might hold a clue to a banishment spell that wouldn't affect Mr. Darcy's soul."

"Mr. Darcy has a soul?" Mia reached down to rub his head, but the cat nipped at her.

"Of course he does. I swear, when this is over we're continuing our magic lessons. You need a basic refresher." Grans glanced at Trent. "Unless you want to take her under your wing as instructor. She might listen more to you."

Trent held up his hands. "I'm just a normal human. I don't have the power to be a teacher."

"Give me a break. You might be able to fool the town with this whole transfer of power to Levi, but I see what you're doing. I'm just surprised your mother doesn't know." Grans stirred her coffee.

When Trent didn't respond she laughed and pointed at him. "Ha, she does know. How in the world did she create a spell to divide the power?"

"I don't know what you're talking about." Trent sipped his coffee and didn't meet Grans's gaze.

"Oh, yes, you do. I'm visiting Abigail and having a little talk with her. She's more powerful in her spellbinding than she lets on."

Trent fidgeted in his chair. "I wish you wouldn't. She doesn't know about Levi and me."

Mia pointed her finger at him. "I knew it. You reached out to Levi when we were stranded. So much for just brotherly intuition. You two are sharing the inheritance. I didn't think that was possible."

"Believe me, I didn't either. I meant to transfer it and we did the ceremony, but I guess it didn't take all the way. Levi still has his power and I have as much or more than

I had before." He glanced back and forth between the women. "The coven can't know this. It's against the laws."

"I'm not telling the coven squat." Grans held a hand over Trent's arm. "You are burning with power. How do you hide it from other witches?"

"I just cover it with an invisible blanket. Unless I want to use it. Then I can access what I need. I don't know how it works, only that it does." Trent's phone buzzed. "Great, that's Levi."

"Answer it." Mia nodded. "We can discuss this later."

He picked up the call and started to leave the kitchen but paused instead. "No, I'm fine. No one forced it out of me. They know. And you might as well tell Christina. I know you two are in a no-lies time. I guess it's time to honor that."

Trent ended the call and set his phone on the table. "Any more muffins?"

"Does that mean you're taking on Mia as a student?" Grans studied him as he moved toward the cabinet to get a muffin.

"No way. I like being out of the magic business. Even though I'm not out, everyone thinks I am. If they knew, I'd be poked and prodded. And if I started training Mia, they'd figure it out. You know they keep an eye out on that sort of stuff. Just in case the new witches get a little froggy." He glanced over at Mia, who had just been listening to the discussion. "What, no comment from you?"

She shook her head. "The more I know about you and this magic thing, the more I'm surprised. Anyway, we don't have time to discover the mysteries of the universe. We have a wedding to finish planning."

"What's on our schedule today?" He unwrapped the muffin and leaned over to read her list.

"First up, let's go visit James at the Lodge and make sure everything is in order for the rooms and catering. I'm so glad he's doing the catering for this. I'm not sure I would be able to get that done as well as herd all these cats." Mia ran her finger down the list. "Then I want to go visit the bakery and check in on the cake, and the florist. Then you can buy me lunch."

"That sounds awesome." He met Grans's gaze. "Are you sure you don't want to go with her instead of me? I hear you have a strong right cross."

"I only hit someone once and he deserved it." Grans pulled out her notebook. "Besides, I'm working on a protection spell in case someone tries to zap Mia. It should be full force by the time you get to the Lodge. I'll have to reconnect with you daily, though, to make sure it's still active."

"Whatever you need to do." Mia tucked her notebook into her tote. "Christina is doing a bride's bash at the Lodge tonight. Kind of like a bachelorette party, but they're having it in Amethyst's suite."

"Then maybe the four of us need to have dinner and drinks at the Lodge tonight. That way we're close by just in case." Trent stood, tucking his phone in his jeans. "I'm ready when you are."

"Grans, do you want to do dinner at the Lodge?" Mia paused, wondering if her last trip with Christina would make her say no.

"Who am I to turn down a free dinner from a handsome man?" She waved Mia away from the table. "Go do your job. I'll be working here so come get me when you're ready for dinner. And don't expect me to stay out late waiting for Christina. You'll need to drive me back at a reasonable hour."

"Sounds good." Mia and Trent went downstairs and out the door. The spring morning was warm but not hot. Which was why Mia typically grabbed a light jacket. "You're good with her."

"Your grandmother is fun to be around. I lost both sets of grandparents when I was just a boy. I like having someone with some history to talk to about things. Especially things around Magic Springs. Although I never expected her to figure out that I was cloaking my magic. I've been doing this for years and you two are the only ones to even question that I didn't lose all my power." He started the truck.

They didn't talk on the way to the Lodge, both lost in their own thoughts. Trent pulled up to the main entrance. "You go on in. I'll park and be right there. Are you meeting in the dining room?"

"That or the kitchen." She climbed out of the truck. "I'll see you in a few."

As she walked into the lobby, the McMann brothers walked out of the elevator. Tok saw her and hurried over. "Please don't tell me we have a meeting today. I was just about to take off for a run."

"No meetings with me. I've got to check in on the Lodge arrangements, and then the cake and flowers. You go have fun. I'm here to do the work." She turned toward the dining room.

Gary caught up with her. "Hey, I hope I didn't scare you the other day. I thought about what I said and realized it might have been misconstrued."

"You mean after I talked to you that I might have thought I was the next one on the killer's list to stop the wedding? No, I got the point. So tell me, why would someone want to ruin Tok and Amethyst's chance at a happily ever after?" Mia knew she should just leave it alone, but she was tired of the games.

"You think there's only one person out there for you? A soul mate?" Gary laughed harshly. "And next you'll be telling me you believe in unicorns. Look, Amethyst is fine, but Tok should be marrying someone of his own kind. It's not right for him to, well, marry outside his tribe."

"Unlike your mother?" Mia took in the shocked look. "Yeah, remember, I know your mother is a witch. And there's another story there too, but let's put that aside. Your parents seem to get along just fine. Why isn't love enough for your brother?"

"I know he loves her, but seriously, *is* love enough?" Gary stuck his hands in the pockets of his jeans. "The wedding has already cost one person their life. Why risk it?"

Mia felt him before she saw Trent and way before he put a hand on her back in support. He leaned toward her. "Is this man bothering you, Mia?"

Mia didn't take her gaze from Gary. "No, he was just going on a run with his brother."

Gary nodded but didn't say anything else. When he was out of the building Trent turned to her.

"Seriously, are you all right? I could feel the tension all the way to the parking lot." He fell in step with her as they walked to the dining room.

"I'm fine. He was just explaining to me why Amethyst isn't good enough for his brother." She rolled her shoulders. "Five days and this will be over. If I don't kill someone myself and force Baldwin to take me into custody."

"Okay, then, Trouble. I'm getting coffee and then I'll be in the corner, reading the paper. Let me know if James overcharges or anything like that. I'd like to get in a fight with someone. The last encounter this morning was less than satisfying. Although I do have a policy never to fight a shifter. They cheat." He kissed her on the cheek and then went to the coffee bar.

Mia made her way into the dining room and stopped by the hostess stand. "Is James available?"

"Just a second." She touched her ear or, more accurately, an earphone in her ear, and spoke to James. "You have a visitor."

She nodded as he talked, then turned back to Mia. "He'll be right out. I'm supposed to seat you and bring you coffee."

"Bless James for thinking of me." She followed the hostess to a table.

The only other occupied table held an older couple. Mia noticed the man kept looking over at her, and finally, after several comments with what must've been his wife, he set his napkin on the table and walked over to the table where she sat. "Miss Malone?"

"Yes, that's me. I'm sorry, do I know you?"

"My name is Charles Silas Miller." His eyes bounced with humor, and Mia thought she might just be able to be friends with this guy. "I hear you and your grandmother have been looking for me. You can call me Silas. I've never cared for that first name anyway."

"You worked on the wards for St. Catherine's. I bought the building, and I was wondering if we could talk a bit about the entrances. Especially the one in the chemistry lab." She leaned forward, excited to hear what Mr. Miller was going to say.

James arrived at the table. He looked between Mia and Silas. "I'm sorry, am I interrupting something? I'm afraid I only have this slot to get the wedding finalized."

"Just hold on a second and I'll be with you." She stood and stepped closer to Silas. "I guess I'll have to chat with you on Saturday."

"I'm sorry, I'm not staying for the wedding. I've been called back to my coven. Political issues, you understand. Maybe we can talk the next time I'm in town." Silas nodded and started to step away.

"Wait. Please come talk with Trent Majors. He's my boyfriend and has been trying to help me fix the problem." She wondered how much of Trent's secret she could reveal. Finally, she found a way to step around it. "He comes from a magical family here in town and is well versed in the ins and outs of protection spells."

"I know the Majors family well. Abigail is a very unusual witch." He nodded as he saw Trent watching them. "Yes, I'm sure I'll be able to explain the process of removing the wards to him. If that's what you want. You know if you remove the wards, you might be opening the school up to other influences. It's a very old building. There might be a lot of things lurking around the property."

"Please explain all this to Trent and then I'll make the decision when I'm not so rushed." She squeezed the older man's arm. "Thank you so much. I was worried we'd never cross paths."

"Oh, my dear. When you reach my age, you realize that you always cross paths with those you're destined to meet. I'm so glad I was able to connect with you. You're very special, young lady." He kissed her cheek, then moved away from her and toward the table where Trent now stood, waiting for Mr. Miller.

When she got back to James, he nodded toward the

older man. "I haven't heard that guy say more than two words in the two weeks he's been here at the Lodge. He just points to what he wants from the kitchen. But with you, he's a Chatty Cathy."

Mia smiled as she sat down to talk catering. "What can I say? I've got a way with people."

When she'd finished confirming the Lodge commitments Silas was gone from Trent's table. Trent saw her packing her stuff into her tote and he finished his coffee and stood. When she reached him, she said, "Next stop, the bakery. I tried to talk to someone yesterday, but they don't answer their phone."

"I'll get you there in less than ten minutes. Were you comfortable with what James has planned?" He pulled on his jacket and took his keys from his pocket.

"It will do. I wouldn't have made some of the choices, but I'll assume that Amethyst did unless Chelsea was just going rogue with this wedding." She leaned closer. "Did you have a good chat with Silas?"

"I did, but I think it's better we talk about that at the house. I felt someone trying to overhear my conversation with Mr. Miller. I'd hate to give them the information now, when I've tried to hide it for so long." He opened the truck door for her and smiled. "I can tell you that it's good news."

"Thank the Goddess." Mia checked her makeup in the mirror, then applied more lipstick. "I wonder what kind of cake Amethyst ordered. There wasn't a picture of the wedding cake or the groom's cake in the book."

"What is a groom's cake?" Trent started the truck and they headed into town.

"It's an old Victorian tradition. The wedding cake was

too feminine for the groom to eat, so he had his own cake. Now it's served at the rehearsal dinner." She patted the book on her lap. "Apparently, Tok wants a dragon cake."

"That's totally cool." Trent turned toward her. "Will it spit fire?"

"I don't think so, unless we give it a bit of magic." She shook her head. What happened to grown men when you mentioned a dragon? "I hope it's purple. I've always wanted a purple dragon."

When they reached the bakery it wasn't crowded, so Mia stood in line while Trent grabbed a table and took a call. The young woman running the register boxed up muffins, pastries, and coffee. It was a different person who had been here the first time Mia had visited Sunshine Bakery. This woman kept the line moving, so it wasn't long before it was Mia's turn.

"What can I get for you?" The woman smiled, holding a set of tongs in her gloved hand.

"Two large coffees, black, and two apple turnovers. And I need to talk to Nellie about a wedding cake that's being delivered on Saturday." Mia pulled her wallet out of her purse. They'd have dessert first, then lunch.

"Delivered from here? That's impossible." The woman set the two cups of coffee on the counter and slipped lids on them. "Nellie's gone this week on a cruise to Alaska. I'm pretty sure there are no orders pending for cakes."

Mia handed her a credit card. "Can you check? I've got a bride and a groom who are going to be really upset if they don't have a wedding cake and a groom's cake.

The clerk quickly put two turnovers into a bag and pulled off her plastic glove. She waved off the credit card. "My treat. I don't think you're going to like what I

find out for you. I'm sure there are no cakes pending. I'm
not a decorator, so all we have are the basic bakery items
that our baker does each morning. Let me check."

Mia felt her stomach twisting. This wasn't good. Not
at all. She stepped over to the table where Trent was still
talking on the phone and dropped off the cups and bag.
When the woman came out of the back with a notebook,
she hurried back to the cash register. "What did you
find?"

"Well, there was an order for a cake and a groom's
cake for Saturday, but it was canceled last Monday. It was
the only order for the week, so Nellie decided to take her
vacation. She got the last ticket for this cruise according
to the travel agent." She turned the notebook around so
Mia could see the fat canceled stamp and a signature.
"Do you know a Chelsea Bachman?"

"Yes, I do. She was the wedding planner for this wedding before she was fired last week." Mia swore under
her breath. "And you don't have a decorator available?"

"Sorry, no. Nellie does all the custom work." She
turned the page over and ripped out the next page. "But
we do have pictures of what the bride and groom ordered
and I can give you a copy of the order form. Maybe you
can find someone around the area to bake the cakes."

Mia took the information and thanked her. Then she
went and sat next to Trent, who had just finished his call.
"I'm so done with this. That witch canceled the cake
order."

"Which witch would that be?" Trent opened the bag
and handed her a turnover.

"The only one who really isn't one. Chelsea. After
Drunder fired her, she canceled the cake. And who knows

what else." Mia tucked the papers on the cake into her tote. "I need to call all the vendors to see what kind of damage she did. Hopefully, it's just the cakes."

Mia had a bad feeling she'd be dealing with at least one other cancellation. She just hoped it wasn't too late to fix the mess that Chelsea had caused.

CHAPTER 10

There were five of them for dinner at the Lodge that night. Mia and Trent had just arrived after visiting several other vendors. Several had been "canceled," but Mia was able to revert the cancellations because the businesses didn't want to anger the Uzzi or the McMann family. Now, she just had to figure out what she was going to do about the cakes. She was scrolling through her contacts when James stopped at the table.

"Hey, it's not that I don't appreciate the business, but you guys were just here this morning. Anything going on with the wedding that I should know about?" James pulled a chair up near Mia and sat on it backward.

"My predecessor canceled as many of the vendors as she could get a hold of, so now I'm going through the list to make sure everyone knows that there's going to be a wedding here on Saturday. I'm surprised she didn't try to cancel the venue with you." She set down her phone.

"I was out of town the first of the week. I wanted to get some sun for the weekend, so I took off Friday and didn't get back until Tuesday. I think I had a message from her, but by then I'd heard that she'd been canned." He glanced around the crowded dining room to make sure everything was going as planned. "I guess I just have amazing timing."

"I guess." She sipped her wine. "You don't know a cake decorator around here who would be available for a couple of days, do you? I can bake the cakes, but I'm not much of a decorator."

"Man, the cakes? That's cruel." He nodded to a waiter who was trying to get his attention. "Let me think about it. There has to be someone here or in Boise who could pinch hit for the weekend."

"I've got pictures and descriptions of what they chose. And like I said, I'll bake it. I just need someone to assemble it and make it pretty."

James stood. "I'll see what I can find out."

As he walked away, Christina set down her fork. "Maybe one of my professors decorates or knows someone."

"That's a good idea. Could you send out a couple of SOSs before you go to your party tonight?" Mia hoped that with several people looking, they'd find someone.

"I don't have to go to this party. I can just come home and work with you," Christina said hopefully. "I'm beginning to understand why Amethyst's cousin stepped away. They are all so intense about the wedding and the dress and the hair. They're even bringing in someone to do our makeup on both Friday and Saturday. Amethyst's mother bought me a dress to wear for Friday's rehearsal. I showed her several of the dresses I already own, but she said I needed something new."

"That's nice of her." Grans patted Christina's hand. "Cassandra's just helping where she can. I suppose she feels really out of control, what with Marilyn in town."

"Do those two have a history?" Trent zeroed in on what Grans had almost said.

Grans glanced around the dining room. "You could say that. Marilyn and Cassandra went to school together. They were best friends, at least until Marilyn left with Brody. Then Cassandra broke all ties with Marilyn. It broke Marilyn's heart."

"I thought Marilyn was kidnapped and her parents' home burned down." Mia glanced at Trent.

"Don't look at me. That's what I was told by my mom." Trent held up his hands.

"That story went around for years. Marilyn's parents' home did burn down, and her parents were killed in the fire, but that was years after she'd run away with Brody. I think they were heartbroken that she left the coven. I'm not saying it was their fault the house burned, mind you." Grans finished her soup. "A lot of times, Magic Springs stories tend to grow more fantastical with time. I guess it's all the magic floating around."

The conversation paused for a minute while the waitress delivered their meals. After she'd refilled the drinks she left to take care of her other tables. Levi leaned in. "Mom has done some cake decorating before. Not professional or anything, but she's pretty good."

"I'll keep her in mind." Mia dug into her pasta. She was starving. They hadn't stopped for lunch after meeting with the florists and finding out their order had been canceled as well. Mia had to get in control of this wedding, one way or another. It was maddening. Yesterday she'd been late to a planning meeting. So she'd fixed that issue by getting all the appointments and meetings in one place. Today, she found out some of the contracts she'd found in Chelsea's room had been canceled by the woman herself. What would tomorrow bring?

"Don't bring tomorrow's troubles into today." Her grandmother pointed a fork at her. "This is really good trout."

"Stop reading my mind." Mia focused on her meal.

"If you didn't broadcast so loudly, I wouldn't have to listen to your thoughts." Grans laughed as she took a sip of wine. "Besides, I know you too well. Even if I couldn't read your thoughts, I would have known what you were thinking."

"We still need to talk about me skipping the party today," Christina reminded them.

Mia shook her head. "Nope. You need to go and play with them for a while. Levi and Trent will be here in the bar, waiting for you to finish."

"And where will you be?" Trent asked.

Mia took a sip of wine. One glass was all she could afford to consume tonight. She needed to be sharp when she started working. "I'll be home baking cakes."

"Not alone. Levi can wait for Christina. I'll come back with you and Mary Alice." Trent cut his steak and checked the doneness. "You two are not going to be alone in the school. Sorry."

Mia started to say something, then stopped. "I guess you're right."

No one at the table said anything for a few minutes.

Mia glanced around at the other four. "What's the problem?"

"I've just never seen you give up as fast as you just did. You must be worried." Christina met Levi's gaze, and he nodded as well.

"Let's just say I don't want my first job as a wedding planner to be my last."

Grans went upstairs to feed Mr. Darcy and Muffy. Trent had made a plan for what would happen next. She would bring the dog down to run around the backyard while she sat on the bench. That way Trent could keep an eye out on both Grans and Mia.

Mia pulled out the mixing bowls and got her ingredients ready to make some cake bases. She glanced over at Trent, who was scanning the backyard while he waited for Grans to come downstairs with the little dog. "You're freaking me out a little with all this protection stuff."

"Let's just say I have a bad feeling about all this. At first I thought the killer was that Gary guy. He'd been with Chelsea; things got a little rough and he went crazy. So he was trying to make it look like someone was trying to stop the wedding. But right now? I actually think someone is trying to stop the wedding."

Mia nodded. "I guess you heard the timeline at the florists too."

"The woman who they talked to about canceling couldn't have been Chelsea because she was already dead by then." He nodded. "I caught that."

"So who is trying to stop the wedding? I keep coming back to that question. Is the fact these two are getting married that much of an affront to either the witching or the shifter worlds? Marilyn seems more worried that the people she wants at the wedding are there. If she wanted to stop it, would she still be inviting people to come into town?"

"Silas is leaving town. He says he thinks it will be safer somewhere else," Trent reminded her.

"Yeah, but the only person who has died so far has been a human. And she got in a fight with the father-in-law. Has anyone looked at Drunder's alibi?" Mia started putting ingredients into the large mixing bowl.

"That's a question for Baldwin. Have you even talked to him lately? Usually you're throwing him clues and suspects during a murder investigation. He's probably missing you." Trent went to open the door and Grans came into the kitchen with Muffy in her arms. "I appreciate you humoring me by shortening Muffy's walk."

"You're just being careful." Grans glanced over toward Mia. "Something more of us in this room could learn."

"Do you want me to go outside with you?" He walked through the kitchen with Grans, ignoring the pointed barb at Mia.

"We'll be fine. I put on a small protection spell this morning, so I should be aware if anything gets close." She put Muffy down just outside the door and walked out toward the bench.

"I certainly hope that small protection spell works against bullets too because if we are being targeted, I don't think it will be a magic spell that attacks us." Mia snuck a glance out the window to watch her grandmother. "She's a pain in the butt, but I love her."

"She's just worried about you." He leaned against the cabinet, where he could keep an eye out the window and on the other kitchen door. "It's kind of cute."

"When you're not on the other side of her worrying. Sometimes she can be a bit smothering. Anyway, enough of my family issues. What did Silas say except he was hightailing it out of Magic Springs? Anything we can use to fix the spell on the house?" She turned on the mixer and leaned on the cupboard, watching the beater mix the wet ingredients.

"I'm not sure. He's afraid if we do try to break the spell on the secret entrance, the rest of the wards will fall as well. He thinks part of the reason the building is holding up so well after all these years is the wards. He's afraid you'll have a pile of crumbled bricks if you mess with them." He smiled as he watched Muffy as he started barking at a squirrel in the tree. "Little man, you're asking for trouble."

"Well, shoot. I don't want to ruin the entire building." Mia turned off the mixer and put in the dry ingredients. "Can you ask your mom what she thinks?"

"I can, but Mom doesn't know much about building spells. I guess it's kind of a dying art. Only a few of the witches in Magic Springs took on the craft. And Silas, well, he is the last of the trained practitioners." He leaned to the left so he could see Muffy, who now had gone toward the trail near the back of the property. "That dog is going to get his nose bit by a mad squirrel. He's got his feet up on the tree truck and is barking up into the branches."

"The squirrel is way too fast for him. He's probably already in another tree." Mia turned on the mixer again. "It just seems like that would be a craft that people would pay good money to keep around. If houses were protected with a spell, they'd last longer and maybe their thresholds would be stronger and keep out the bad players from the world."

"I'm not disagreeing with you." Trent stood and frowned. "Sorry, I need to go get Muffy. He's off on the trail, and now your grandmother is heading after him."

"Stop her. She doesn't need to be chasing after that dog. I guess I'm going to have to put up a fence. I didn't want to break the landscape image with the trail system in the back, but if Muffy's going to be around a lot, I need to protect the little guy." She turned off the mixer and leaned down to pull out sheet pans. "Shoot. I forgot to turn on the oven."

Trent stepped outside the door and called to Grans. "Sit down and enjoy the evening. I'll get him."

Mia could hear her grandmother's response, something about not being foolish, but then she heard loud footsteps and a small scream.

She dropped the pans and headed to the door. Grans was still halfway to the edge of the property, but Trent was gone. Mia stepped out the door and waved to her. "Come inside. Let Trent deal with this."

For once her grandmother didn't argue, which made Mia all the more frightened. When Grans got to the door, Mia pointed to the kitchen behind her.

"Do you see him?" Grans asked?

Mia shook her head. She wasn't sure if Grans was talking about Trent or Muffy, but neither man nor dog was in sight. It was like they'd disappeared down the trail. She stepped inside and pulled the door shut, clicking the locks in place. "Do me a favor, stand here and let Trent in when he comes back. I'm going to go check the other doors and make sure the locks are set."

Grans grabbed her arm. "Mia, be careful."

Mia kissed her grandmother on the top of the head. "Always."

She hurried into the living room and checked the lock on the front door. Then she glanced out the side window. Nothing. The fear in her gut wouldn't give up, so she ran up the stairs to the second floor and checked the locks on the chemistry lab. Locked. Solid. If someone was in the room and tried to get into the building, they'd have to break through several dead bolts and a bolt lock.

Of course, Mia wasn't stupid. She knew that someone with the right type of magical power could probably blow the door off the hinges. But that was a different worry. She hurried back down the stairs and back to the kitchen, where she found Grans, Muffy, and Trent. Grans sat at the small table with Muffy on her lap and Trent was starting a pot of coffee.

"It's a little late for coffee, isn't it?" Mia glanced out the door as she walked past to where her grandmother sat. She didn't see anything out in the backyard.

"I want to stay up until Christina and Levi get back. I'm a little concerned." Trent didn't turn around until he'd finished setting up the coffee maker. He glanced over at Muffy. "The junkyard-wanna-be-mean dog over there had a piece of jeans in his mouth that seem to have some blood on it."

"He bit someone?" Mia reached down to stroke the small dog's fur and he was shaking.

Grans squeezed him tighter. "Muffy has never bitten anyone. He'd only do it if he was provoked."

"Or if he was convinced he needed to protect you," Trent added to Grans's statement. "The dog isn't dumb. He was in the middle of the trail, barking but standing his ground. He scared the guy off just past your property line. Then, when he saw me, he gave them one last bark and came trotting back to greet me."

"I'm seriously putting up a fence to block off that trail. I should have thought about that access point before I bought this place." Mia checked the oven, then picked up the pans from the floor. She put those in the sink and grabbed two others from the cabinet. "Well, I need to get some cake layers made anyway. I guess you can stay up with me."

"I think Muffy and I are going upstairs and reading for a bit before we turn in. It's been a stressful day." She looked between Trent and Mia. "If that's all right."

"I checked the locks; they were fine." Mia looked at Trent. "She should be fine in the apartment, right?"

"I'll walk you up myself and check out the place before I leave. I'm sure we're all just being a little paranoid after Muffy's big adventure." He opened the kitchen door that led to the living room and propped it open. "I'll be back in a few. Do you need anything from upstairs?"

Mia shook her head. She'd love a glass of wine or a beer to brush off these nerves, but she'd already had one tonight and she had to make at least two more cake batches. Especially if she was going to be the one to decorate. She needed practice cakes.

He followed Grans out of the kitchen, then leaned back into the doorway, catching Mia's gaze. "Just don't open the door to any strangers—or anyone you know, for that matter—until I get back."

"I wish I would have thought of that." She brushed

him away with both hands. "Go and get her set up. Bring down a set of apartment keys so she doesn't have to leave the door unlocked."

He grinned. "I wish I would have thought of that."

"Now you know how it feels. Get going." She focused on setting up the first three pans and getting them settled into her oversize ovens. As she was doing that, she wondered when the fun part of wedding planning was supposed to happen. All she'd been doing for the last few days was putting out fires. There were so many things she was going to do differently next time.

If there was a next time.

CHAPTER 11

L evi called just after eleven. "We're in my car and on the way back. Just wait until you hear what Christina found out."

After his brother hung up on them without telling them the information, Trent refilled the coffee pot. "I think when this is all over, Levi and I are having a talk about never hanging up on me."

"He just wanted to add some suspense to our night. Besides, he didn't know we already had one issue to-night. He's been sitting at a bar not drinking for the last four hours. He was probably bored out of his head." Mia pulled out the last cake from the oven and set it on the is-land to cool. "We can probably move this party into the living room. Are you hungry? Want some popcorn or an-other type of snack?"

"I'm fine. You'll have to ask Levi when he gets in. The

boy still eats more than a family of four." He set up a coffee tray and put cups on it. He moved the carafe over to the cupboard where the coffee brewed.

"You should live with Christina. She's always snacking. Then she eats meals too. I wish I had her metabolism." Mia reached up with one arm, then the other. She laughed at Trent's quizzical look. "Just stretching. Remind me not to take on another magical wedding for, oh, I don't know, a hundred years?"

When Levi and Christina got there, as Mia had predicted, they decided they needed snack food to accompany their story. Not surprised, Mia made popcorn while Christina put a tray of appetizers in the oven to warm up. That was one of the joys of catering; they always made just a little extra for nights like this.

"How was the party?" Mia asked as she finished putting toppings on the three bowls of popcorn.

"Fun. She had people come in to do mani-pedis, including the chairs with the foot massagers. They'll be there day of the wedding too. It must be nice to be rich."

Mia didn't say anything, but her thoughts must have shown, so Christina continued. "You know what I mean. I'm not rich, my parents are. And the way our relationship is going, Isaac's going to be the only one mentioned in the will." She held out her newly painted nails. "They're amazing, right?"

Mia had to admit the manicurist had done a nice job. And each nail had a wedding motif on it. The cake, wedding bells, a bride, a groom, and finally, a tiny church sparkled on both hands. "It's really cute."

"She's actually really nice. Not like Bethanie. Of course, Bethanie tried to get her to talk bad about Chelsea, but Amethyst was really sweet and sad about her death. Then

Bethanie ragged on her about her cousin dumping her."
Christina glanced into the oven through the window, turning on the light to check the doneness of the appetizers.
She turned off the light. "Five more minutes. Anyway,
Amethyst said she grew up with this cousin. That they
were thick as thieves for years. And now she won't even
call her back. I felt bad for her."

"Did she say why they don't get along now?" Mia took
a handful of the popcorn and taste tested it. That was her
story anyway.

"Something about her marrying Tok. I guess Amethyst
just assumed she'd be in the wedding party. When she
called her to tell her the news, she got a lukewarm con-
grats and some mumbled she'd have to check the date.
Then a few weeks later, she sent her an email saying she
had a conflict. Amethyst thinks it's some old rivalry with
the families. But that's stupid. Didn't that go out with
Romeo and Juliet? Shouldn't you be able to love who you
love without worrying about what your family thinks?"
Christina put an arm around Levi, who had just returned
to the kitchen.

"Are you talking about us? I haven't even met your
parents. Why wouldn't they love me?" Levi grinned at
her. "But you have to add in the Hatfield and McCoy leg-
end. That's more relatable than the Shakespeare story.
And probably true."

"Shakespeare didn't just make up the story. You know
there was some poor girl out there who killed herself because she thought her boyfriend was dead. He just took
that real story and made it into our favorite star-crossed
lovers tale." Christina countered as the buzzer went off.
"The appetizers are done. Are we staying down here to
eat?"

Mia shook her head. "Let's head upstairs to the apartment and put on a movie. I need to get out of this kitchen for a while."

"Sounds like a plan. You two go ahead and we'll carry up the food." Trent handed her and Christina each a carafe of coffee. "I mixed these to half decaf, half regular so we have a chance at sleeping tonight."

"I've got a bottle of rum crème upstairs that we can add with some whipped cream to ease out the caffeine as well." Mia smiled. "We'll check locks as we go upstairs. I'm probably being paranoid, but it doesn't mean I'm wrong."

"After today's issue with Muffy, I'm not going to question your hunches. Did you ever call Baldwin?" He watched as she went over to check the back door and close the blinds she'd installed on the window so no one could see inside.

"I texted him. He's coming over tomorrow morning to get the piece of fabric Muffy collected. I don't think they'll be able to DNA test all the wedding guests, though, if this is a wedding-related issue." She rolled her shoulders and waited for the others to finish loading up a platter for the appetizers and grabbing popcorn bowls. "I just want Saturday to get here and this to be over. Sunday's going to be a sleep-in morning and then a go-to-the-Lodge-to-eat-a-huge-brunch. And you're all invited to my we-got-through-this party."

"I'm down for that." Levi was the last to leave the kitchen.

Mia turned off the lights after he cleared the door. Then she locked the door between the kitchen and the lobby area. She nodded to Christina. "Go up with the guys. I'm checking the gym doors and making sure they're locked too. I'll do a sweep of the gym as well."

"Not alone. Either Christina goes with you, or I do." Trent juggled the bowls of popcorn in his arms.

"Mia, I can go with you." Christina took a bowl from Trent. "You guys go on upstairs. We'll be up soon. But listen for any screams. One of us should be able to get a doozy out before anyone attacks us in the gym."

"You're making me feel so comfortable about leaving you down here." Trent glanced between the two women, apparently questioning his decision.

"Look, the school has been locked up since we came in and we did a lock sweep after the Muffy incident. We'll be fine. The worse we might encounter is a wandering ghost. And hopefully, if we do, maybe they will have a clue about what's going on around here this week." She turned toward the gym. "Come on, Christina, let's get this done before we have to reheat the food again. Or worse, they choose an action movie for us to watch. Isn't it our turn to choose the movie?"

"Yes, it is. And I've been wanting to see that new Regency that came out a few months ago. It just landed on the streaming service." Christina winked at her as they entered the gym.

Mia flipped on the large overhead lights and the empty space lit up. Risers still lined the walls, but they were pushed back into their storage position. "You check the bathrooms and I'll go make sure the door is locked. Then we'll hit the front door on the way upstairs. You were kidding about the Regency, weren't you?"

"Of course. I've already watched it." Christina grinned. "But they don't know that."

Mia headed over to the large doors. These doors opened wide into the backyard patio, which used to be a playground, so not only were they locked but Trent had chained them closed as well. When the fire marshal came to visit once a year, Mia conveniently removed the chains so he wouldn't question the safety of the idea, but she and the other residents of the building knew that in an emergency, the key was hidden in the women's bathroom supply area.

She jiggled the locked doors. And the chains were still in one piece. But she felt a power on the other side. Someone had tried to access the locks by magic. Had this happened at the same time as the Muffy incident? Or had that been a smoke screen? Either way, the witch who'd tried to get in hadn't gotten past the school's wards, which were installed by Silas Miller. And they apparently hadn't known about them. Which made Mia wonder if most of the coven would have known about Silas's work. It could have been a lost practice and the younger generation didn't realize the older buildings in Magic Springs all had a magical barrier to keep out anyone who was trying to enter by using magic.

"What's wrong?"

Christina's question made Mia jump and she realized she was still here, studying the doors. "I think someone tried to get in."

"It looks normal. Or are you picking up something else? Something I can't see?" Christina studied the doors again. "Nope. Nothing from the cheap seats here."

Mia laughed. "I'll have Trent take a look tomorrow. He got some tips from Silas."

"Bethanie says her great-uncle is crazy. He's going back to California before the wedding because something feels off." They made their way out of the gym and Christina waited as Mia locked the doors that went from the gym to the lobby area.

Mia headed straight to the front door to check locks. Then she armed the security system. "I think his 'feeling' is spot on. The last wedding planner was killed and the only reason I can see for her death is to stop the wedding. Someone canceled wedding vendors after Chelsea's death, so we know it wasn't her doing all of it. I think the killer would have been smarter to leave her alive. Chelsea could have done some damage to the wedding before people realized she wasn't talking for the bride and groom anymore."

"You need to do this professionally. I bet you could solve all sorts of cold cases all over the world. Maybe even find out who killed that president who was shot. Isn't that still in question?" Christina followed her upstairs to the apartment.

Her suggestion gave Mia the chills. She didn't want to investigate murder. She wanted to cook for and feed people. Make people happy with celebrations and weddings. But somehow she was beginning to think the world was just throwing murder mysteries her way to see what she'd do. One day she was just going to ignore it. Maybe then it would stop happening. Mia opened the apartment door. "I already have a job I love. And a business to develop. I'll leave sleuthing to the professionals."

As they came in the door, the men turned from the menu on the television to greet them. Trent half stood, but Mia shook her head. Somehow, he'd felt the unease about the gym door. "Everything's all locked up tight. What movie are we watching?"

Trent held up his arm and she curled up on the couch

with him. "I'm thinking a new superhero movie. One where everything is dark and you think they're going to lose until the last part of the movie. Then they win and everyone's happy, well, except the bad guy."

"Sounds perfect." Mia pushed her worries out of her head and focused on where she was, right now.

"So a pandowdy is a deep-dish spiced apple pie. Finally, a vocabulary word I can expect to use in my future life in the food service industry." Christina wrote down the word and the definition in her notebook the next morning as they gathered around the kitchen table. "I really like this journal method he has for the class. You do the reading, then you write down your impressions and feelings about what you read. And he said I can add a place for my word-of-the-day listing. I'm going to bake a pandowdy for next weekend's brunch."

Mia sipped her coffee and reviewed her schedule. The wedding party was getting final fittings for their dresses and tuxes at one. And if she didn't get a cake decorator today, she was going to have to spend at least one session with the practice cakes she'd baked last night to see if she could make a dragon. The wedding cake would be easier to fake than this stupid dragon cake Tok wanted.

She was doodling in her notebook a design for a dragon when Grans came into the kitchen.

"Good morning, children. I take it someone already took Muffy out?" Grans poured her coffee, then reached over to where Muffy and Mr. Darcy slept on the window seat.

"I did. He was a good boy." Christina met Mia's gaze. "The gym doors looked normal to me."

"Why wouldn't they be normal?" Grans asked as Trent came into the room.

He nodded a greeting toward her, then sat next to Mia after filling a cup. "I checked them out and you're right. Someone had been trying to get inside. It's not a very sophisticated spell, but the residuals are there. Could our killer have magic?"

Everyone at the table paused. Finally, Christina shook her head. "I don't think it's a coincidence. Maybe someone thought you'd be alone because I was at Amethyst's party."

"Maybe." Mia shook her head. "The point is, the school protected us. Like it's supposed to. I don't think we want to mess with the wards, even if it means the secret passage will have to stay open. We'll just need to check it more often."

Christina jumped up. "We didn't check the chemistry lab door last night. I'll go do that. I might not be able to feel magic, but I can see if the lock was busted."

Levi came into the kitchen. "I'll go with her."

"Okay, so that's covered." Mia glanced at her schedule. "Christina, you need to be at the Lodge by noon so you can get your fittings done."

"What are you doing today?" Grans asked.

Mia looked down at the drawing that looked more like a dog than a dragon. Maybe being purple would help the identification. "I'm going to teach myself to decorate cakes."

"I don't think . . ." Trent began, but then the doorbell rang.

Mia looked up at the display television in the corner of the room. "Hold that thought. Looks like I need to talk to

Baldwin first. Trent, Grans, he'll probably want to talk to you as well, so I'll bring him upstairs."

"Sounds good." Grans stood and went to the fridge, where she pulled out cookie dough. "I'll bake him some cookies to take back to the station while we talk."

Her gesture was genius, Mia thought as she headed downstairs to let in Magic Springs's police chief. Feeding him and his crew kept the school and Mia in their good graces, even when she called a patrol car out to the property to investigate things way too often.

He was fanning himself with his hat by the time she got downstairs. "Mark, come in. I didn't realize it was that hot outside."

"I'm afraid standing in the sun heats me up way too quickly these days. Sarah keeps trying to get me to go down to Boise for some tests, but who has time? Besides, it's only really hot here one week a year, two at most. I can suffer through those days. So you had another intruder? I talked to Trey at the security company on the way over and he said he didn't see any activity."

"I don't think they got through, but we wanted to report it, just in case." Mia nodded to the stairs. "Why don't you come upstairs for a nice glass of iced tea and a treat?"

"Sounds good." He narrowed his eyes. "You're not trying to get on my good side before you tell me what stupid thing you've done lately, are you?"

"No, I haven't done any stupid things lately that I can think of." She opened the apartment door. "I think the dumbest thing I've done recently is take on this wedding planner job. I swear, I'm going to think twice about accepting new clients."

"In Magic Springs you need to vet your clients carefully. I've been doing some research on the McMann family. They have some unresolved skeletons in their closet, that's for sure." He leaned closer. "They've been suspects in several disappearances up in Whitehall, the closest town to their compound. The sheriff there has a contact inside the family who has been giving him information."

CHAPTER 12

As they entered the apartment, he stopped for a minute and took a deep breath. "Someone's baking chocolate chip cookies. Your grandmother used to make them all the time when she babysat me." He hurried into the kitchen.

"That's because you always said they were your favorite." Grans stood there with a spatula, looking into the oven. "Give it a few more minutes and this first batch will be done. Sit down. Do you want milk or coffee to go with the cookies?"

He grinned. "Coffee, please."

"Mark was just telling me that the McManns have a sordid history in their hometown." Mia poured the coffee and set it on the table. "Maybe one of them is responsible for Chelsea's murder?"

"It sure looked that way to begin with." Mark sipped

his coffee. "The only problem is the cuts were too precise. We're thinking someone with medical training must be the culprit. But of course, it could be someone who just thought they were a surgeon. It's all so jumbled right now. I hate this part of the investigation. I want the answer to be easy and fast."

"Like a neon sign hanging over the killer's head pointing to him?"

Baldwin laughed and his shoulders relaxed. Mia could feel the comfort spell Grans was baking with the cookies. If Baldwin didn't relax after this stop, nothing would ease his anxiety.

He pointed to Mia. "Exactly like that. You really should be an investigator."

"People keep telling me that." She shook her head. "I like cooking and event planning. You can keep the dead bodies and thefts. Anyway, about the person who tried to break in." She went on to tell him the facts as she knew them.

Then Trent told him what he'd seen as Grans got out the first batch of cookies and put two on a plate for him. By the time it was her turn to talk, she had a box halfway filled with cookies, waiting for the last batch in the oven to finish cooking.

Mia nodded to a chair. "Sit down and talk to Baldwin. I'll finish up the box."

By the time they were done and Baldwin was on his way home with the box of cookies, Mia felt drained. "We didn't get much done today."

"The day's not over. And I have a surprise for you." Trent glanced at the security camera feed. "We have another guest."

Mia glanced up at the monitor. "Is that your mother?"

"Yes, it is. You can thank me later. Although I think she's going to want to use your kitchen." He stood and hurried to the apartment door. "I'll go let her in and bring her upstairs so you two can talk."

Mia met Grans's gaze. "Do you know what's going on?"

"I haven't got a clue. Tell Abigail I'm sorry I missed her, but I'm going to go lie down. I'm a little wiped out." She stood and squeezed Mia's shoulder as she walked by. "If you need me, I'll be the one snoring in my bedroom."

Mia refreshed her coffee and took the final batch of cookies from the oven. Grans put in the batch after filling Baldwin's box just because. Now, Mia figured it was just because she must have known someone else was coming over to the house. Sometimes Grans's predictions were a little off and sometimes, like now, so random that they became prophetic. Mia had feelings at times when she thought something was going to happen, but she didn't have a good track record with them. Mostly about fifty-fifty. Gran was more like ninety-ten, with the ninety being the times she was right. It had been a game between her and her grandmother. One that Grans always won.

"Mia, so nice to see you." Abigail Majors swept her into a hug. "I'm so glad we are going to be able to spend some time together. I'm always telling my son to bring you over on date night, but he always has an excuse."

"Sorry, Mom, but it's mostly Mia's fault. She's scared of spending time with the parents." He winked at her. "Anyway, do you want some coffee? Maybe Mia could show you what she's working on that she needs your help with."

"Wait, who said I needed help? With what?" Mia tried to go through the options. Maybe Abigail was a secret wedding planner.

"Coffee would be lovely. And Mia, you don't have to be embarrassed. Cake decorating is an art that takes years to perfect. I ran the bakery at the store before Sunshine came in. I've done my share of wedding cakes. Trent tells me the groom's cake is something special too. I have to say, my fingers have been tingling since he called me." Abigail sat at the table and reached for the wedding planner book. "Do you mind if I glance through this? It will give me a sense of the couple. It's always a good idea to know who you're baking for, don't you think?"

"Of course. There's a picture of both cakes Sunshine was doing for them before the cakes were canceled. Do you think it's possible to get it done before Saturday? Maybe we should serve the groom's cake at the reception too, rather than the rehearsal dinner. It would give you more time." Mia moved her chair over and opened the book to the page where the cakes were. "Amethyst and Tok are a lovely couple. I'm worried I won't be able to pull off the type of wedding they deserve."

Abigail glanced up from the book. "You realize that most of the coven and probably most of Tok's pack are hoping you can't pull off *any* type of wedding. These cancellations aren't just about a fired wedding planner. There's real animosity between the two families."

"It can't be that bad." Mia rolled her shoulders. "Besides, what's the saying about the sins of the father shouldn't affect the child?"

"I think the saying actually is more like the father's sins do affect his offspring." Trent set coffee on the table.

"Mom, if you think this is too dangerous, just say so. We'll figure out the cake without you."

"Are you kidding? That poor couple will be cutting a birthday cake you bought from a Twin Falls supermarket if I leave it to you." She sipped her coffee. "No offense, Mia. No, if you're determined to help them with the wedding, I'll make the cakes. Trent said I might be able to use your kitchen?"

"Yes. Of course." Mia tried to keep the grin from her face, but she knew it was a losing battle. "You don't know what a relief this is. I was going to try to practice this evening, but I never would have been able to pull off a cake that looked even close to what they asked for."

"I'm going to need some things. Sunshine should have the supports I need. Tell that girl who's at the counter that Nellie said I could have them. She'll believe anything. We can reimburse her for the costs later. And it will save me a trip into Boise for supplies. We just don't have the time." Abigail pulled out a notebook from her purse and started making a list. She handed it to her son when she was done. "Trent, be a dear and run over to the store after you stop at the bakery and get me a few things."

"I can do that." He looked at his cup, which was about half empty. "Can I finish my coffee first?"

"Yes. I'm not a slave driver." She patted his arm. "Besides, I want to look through this book a little more. I love weddings."

"Doesn't every woman?" Trent downed his coffee. "I'm out of here. I should be back in thirty minutes, tops. Do you need anything while I'm out, Mia?"

"No, I think I'm good. I have to get a list of things together to decorate the smaller ballroom tomorrow to get it ready for the rehearsal dinner. Then Friday morning I'll be in the main ballroom all day with the florist and the decorator to set up the wedding venue." She glanced up and saw Abigail and Trent watching her. "Sorry, it's something I do. When I get stressed I start listing out all the things I need to do. In order. The process gives me a plan that allows my stress level to even out."

"Mia also stress cooks." He grinned at his mom. "She has a lot of the same coping mechanisms you do."

"I do not stress cook." Abigail lightly slapped Trent's arm. "I've just found that I think better when my hands are busy doing something else. It's a common solution."

"Yeah, you could be sitting at a bar, drinking." Trent stood and kissed his mother on the top of the head. "Can I bring back sandwiches for lunch at least?"

"That sounds perfect." Mia glanced over toward Abigail. "Do you want to see the kitchen? Or do you need more time with the wedding information?"

"I'd love to see your kitchen." Abigail stood and grabbed her tote.

Mia grabbed the book and her keys. "We can make a pot of coffee downstairs, and I think I have cookies from this week's meal delivery. I can work in the office and finish confirming all the vendors while you play in the kitchen."

"You might never get me to leave." Abigail followed her downstairs and paused in the lobby. "The place looks so small now. When I attended, the school seemed so large. I was always getting lost my first year, even though they kept the elementary kids in classrooms down here."

"I took out some walls when I started renovating to open up this lobby area. Then I combined two classrooms to make a lecture/classroom over there, next to the kitchen. I'm thinking about changing a few of the classrooms to where there are cooking stations so I can do hands-on classes. But I'm not sure about the rest of the rooms on the second floor. Like you said, you can get lost here." Mia pointed out the new classroom and where she'd made changes to expand the lobby.

"You've done amazing things. I'm not sure if you want people in the building all the time, but you could remodel the second floor into offices. Maybe some that are food or event friendly? Or even for those life coaches, so they'd have a safe place to meet with clients. Although, because you live on site, you might not want people around all the time." Abigail sat on one of the couches. "My husband wants to turn our home into a hunting lodge. Why on earth would I want a bunch of men in my house every weekend for three or four months? He just doesn't get my need for privacy."

Mia sat next to her as she glanced around the lobby area. It was a fine line. How much of the school was home and what was business? But really, all of it felt like home. "I don't know, renting out office space might be profitable, but then again, there would be people in the house, I mean, the school. I think it would have to be the right people and the right businesses. Maybe I could rent a room for an author's writing space."

"As long as they didn't write late at night and keep you up." Abigail rubbed the throw pillow. "And there's the witch part of our lives. It's not easy to hide that from people when they have free access to your private space."

"I'm not really . . ." Mia stopped. She was about to say she wasn't a witch. "I mean, we're different from most of the coven. I know Grans does a lot of spells and potions, but I'm more focused on getting this business going."

"Mia, you need to realize it doesn't matter what label

you put on your magic or what limitations you accept as your own. You are a witch. I can feel your power even now, just sitting and talking with you." Abigail held up a hand when Mia started to deny. "Look, I know you've been looking into your family's background, the history of the school, and of Magic Springs. All I'm saying is, you need to keep an open mind while you research."

Mr. Darcy jumped on Mia's lap and rubbed his head against her hand. Researching was kind of a strong word for what she'd been doing. Mostly, she'd forgotten about all the issues while she tried to focus on the business. But she needed to get back to reading Dorian's diary because Grans thought he had a theory about the school and Mia's heritage. "You're right. I do need to work on that, with an open mind. Just as soon as this wedding is over. Are you ready to see the kitchen?"

Abigail wandered through the kitchen, her arms outstretched as she took in all the appliances, bowls, and baking items. She stopped at the cakes Mia had baked the day before. Opening a drawer, she pulled out a small knife and took a small sliver from the edge, tasting the cake. "This is good. We can use this for the groom's cake. And, I think you have just enough baked for me to get started on that when Trent gets back. Tomorrow morning I'll bake the layers for the wedding cake, and in the afternoon we'll make creams and finish up the dragon. Then Friday we'll assemble the wedding cake. This is going to be so much fun."

Mia smiled, then nodded to the outside door. "That's locked tight, but if Trent comes in that way with the supplies, he has a code to the security system. If you want to go out that way, let me know and I'll disarm the alarm. I'll be working in the office just outside the kitchen door.

And thank you so much for stepping in. Amethyst and Tok are going to be so thrilled."

"Thank you for opening your kitchen to me. I won't abuse your trust." Abigail started humming as she went to set up her workstation.

Mia thought about the discussion on the future uses of the school. She had imagined renting out the second floor into offices, but that was before she moved into the school and it had become her home. She hadn't felt this way about anyplace she'd lived for years, even before she bought the house with Isaac. The Victorian had been lovely and she'd enjoyed redecorating it, but even as she had, she thought she was decorating it for someone else. They'd always planned on holding the property until it appreciated enough to make a killing, and then selling it and buying another one. Not a home. The school felt like a home, and not one she could see selling just because it was worth more than what she'd bought it for.

She opened the wedding planner book and went to the first vendor. Opening a notebook to a fresh page, she wrote down the business name, the contact name, and the phone number. Then she listed a few questions she had about the wedding, if any. Finally, she picked up the phone and dialed the first number.

By the time Trent was back with the supplies and the sandwiches, Mia had a headache and a bad feeling. She'd found two more services that someone had tried to cancel, but it had been too late. He poked his head into her office when she was talking to the limo company that was taking Tok and Amethyst from the hotel to the airport.

"I told the caller I'd be there Saturday night at six as scheduled. If no one was there, I'd leave for the airport anyway. I have a fare coming in on the seven p.m. flight from LA. However, there are no refunds within thirty days of the event," the man said again. It had to be the third time she'd heard the same response from Mia's count.

"We don't want a refund and the bride and groom will be outside exactly at six. I'll have the concierge meet you to load up their luggage before they come out of the reception." Mia waved Trent into the room. "But can you remember who tried to cancel it? I think someone's playing a joke on the groom."

"Not a very funny joke, if you ask me. But no, I didn't ask for a name. She told me that she was handling the Uzzi-McMann wedding and needed to cancel." He chuckled. "I'm glad it's not canceled. I love weddings."

After thanking him again, Mia hung up and leaned back in her chair, closing her eyes. "There have been more attempted cancellations. But they messed up on the tuxedo shop. The guys have already been there to pick up their tuxes. So when this mystery woman called last night, the woman just laughed and told her the men had their suits and they needed to be returned by Monday morning to avoid additional charges."

"Someone's still trying to mess with the wedding, but they don't have the schedule anymore." Trent leaned against the doorframe.

"Yeah. I think the first few calls were Chelsea, trying to get even with Drunder for firing her, but this woman is obviously still alive and unaware of the wedding schedule." Mia stood and stretched. "So, lunch is served?"

"We're eating out on the picnic table. Mom has iced tea poured in glasses and real plates from your kitchen for the sandwiches and salads I brought back. And she found cookies in the pantry. I hope they weren't already spoken for." He walked beside her as they made their way out to the kitchen.

"It sounds perfect. Just the break I need from all this chaos." She pulled out her phone and frowned as she looked at the caller ID. "It's the Lodge. I'd better pick up."

"Hello?"

"Mia, it's Amethyst. I just called to tell you the wedding may be off." She sniffed loudly, and Mia realized she was trying hard not to cry.

"Oh, no. What happened? Did you and Tok get in a fight? Stress around the wedding is common and nothing to worry about. I'm sure he'll come back and apologize." Mia put the call on Speaker so Trent and his mother could hear the discussion.

"Oh, no. Tok's right here with me. It's my father. Mia, he's been arrested. They think he killed Chelsea."

CHAPTER 13

After she'd finished talking to a very upset and emotional Amethyst, Mia's phone rang again. "Hello?"

"Mia, dear, I know Amethyst just called you, but please, keep going with the wedding planning. We are going to get these two married if it kills me and Drunder. I'm sure this whole arrest thing is nothing more than a smoke screen. There are people who don't want my daughter marrying a McMann. And those people will stop at nothing. But as the Goddess is my witness, we are having a wedding on Saturday and everyone's going to be happy and have fun. It's costing me enough, that's the least they can do, right?"

"But Mrs. Uzzi, if your family needs to deal with your husband's issues, maybe . . ."

"Phst, don't worry about Drunder. You can't be convicted of something you didn't do, now can you?" Cassandra paused, apparently listening to another conversation. "You just have everything ready for the rehearsal on Friday. I'll make sure everyone's there. Including my husband."

Mia set down her phone after seeing that Cassandra had ended the call. She sipped her iced tea and didn't say anything until the buzzing in her head stopped ringing. "Well, they paid for a wedding. I guess I'm going to have it ready for them. I just hope we have a bride and groom that day."

"At least you have a limo to take them to the airport now." Trent sat and piled potato salad on his plate, handing the container to Mia. "This was made in-store. Mom's recipe."

"Actually, the potato salad is my Aunt Tilly's recipe. She was such a good cook. I'm sorry she's not around to meet you, Mia. I'm sure the two of you would have had a lot in common." Abigail held up the container of macaroni salad. "Now, *this* is my recipe. Aunt Tilly's macaroni salad had mustard in it. I'm not much of a mustard fan."

As they ate lunch, Mia's thoughts were on the wedding and why someone was trying to stop it. Had Drunder killed Chelsea? That didn't make any sense because he'd fired her a few days before. If she'd found out about Magic Springs's worst-kept secret—that witches and well, now, shifters, were real—he or one of his family could have done a memory wipe and kept the more-experienced wedding planner. Instead, he'd fired her. Mia knew he'd thought Chelsea had been dipping into the wedding fund for her own use. Had Baldwin really arrested Drunder or just taken him down to the station for questioning? Too many unanswered questions.

"Penny for your thoughts." Abigail broke into Mia's mind chaos.

She looked down at her plate and realized she hadn't touched any of her food. She picked up a fork and took a taste of Abigail's macaroni salad, which Mia didn't remember even putting on her plate. "Actually, I was thinking about the likelihood that Drunder killed Chelsea. It doesn't make any sense. In a normal town if Drunder had a secret that Chelsea found out, he might have killed her. But we all know Magic Springs isn't normal."

Abigail held up a finger. "Baldwin has a deep faith in his God and his religion. And most of all, in justice. He wants to do the right thing. All we have to do is either point out that Drunder has a rock-solid alibi or point him in another direction."

"I have more of a motive to kill Chelsea than Drunder. I was the one who got the job because she was fired." Mia dug into her sandwich. She set it down on the plate and took a drink of water. "Although I already had the job when she was killed, so I guess that waters down my motive. That and the fact that I didn't kill her."

Trent chuckled. "Yeah, there's that."

"I want to go down to see if I can talk to Drunder. Do you think Baldwin would let me?" Mia focused on finishing her meal. "Maybe I can say I need his permission to continue the wedding planning because he hired me?"

Trent nodded toward her plate. "Finish your lunch and then I'll drive you down to the station. Mom mentioned that I forgot to get the tower stands from the bakery for the cake anyway. I can run and get those while you're in with Baldwin and Drunder."

"They're called pillars. No wonder she didn't give you everything. You didn't ask for the right stuff." His mother closed the salad containers and stacked them before standing to go back into the kitchen. "I'll put these in the fridge. I need to check on my cakes."

After she left, Trent cleared the rest of the table but didn't move to take the plates and glasses inside. "I'm not sure I like the idea of you talking to Drunder. He has a reputation."

"You think he's going to flirt with me?" Mia paused the sandwich on its way up to her mouth. Trent's lips tightened. "You're kidding, right? I know he's married. Why would anyone take him seriously?"

"Not that kind of reputation, but now that I think about it, you are his type. He likes witches he can groom into their power. His wife, Cassandra, didn't even know she was a witch before she met Drunder." He stacked one last fork on the dirty plates. "No, he has a lot of power and he's not afraid to use it for his own benefit."

"But what about the rule you can't use magic for your own benefit? It was the first rule Grans taught me." She cleaned up the rest of the potato salad and popped the forkful into her mouth. Her plate was going to be completely empty by the time she finished eating.

"Well, it's more of a guideline than a rule." He glanced at the school and the kitchen. "Mom doesn't like me talking about it, but there are ways to get around it. Like if you think you're doing something for your family and you just happen to benefit too. Like wishing for a new house for your wife and children to be safe and secure.

You get to live there too. He's straddling a line on most of this, but then again, people know. And that's why he has a reputation."

"Okay, that's good to know. I'll keep that in mind as I question him." She finished her sandwich and pushed the empty plate toward Trent's stack. "Do you know anything about Cassandra's assistant, Selena Andrus?"

"Nothing factual. A lot of rumors. I do know that she doesn't like Drunder much. She's very devoted to her boss. And I've heard her state several times that Drunder doesn't deserve Cassandra." He studied her. "What are you looking for?"

"I don't know. Maybe nothing."

Trent put the last plate on the stack. "I'll run the dishwasher when we get back. Mom's been making a mess in your kitchen. I'm glad you don't have to be working in there until Monday."

"I'm just thankful for her help. Even if the wedding is canceled, at least we'll have cake to drown our sorrows." Mia arranged the glasses together.

"I have a feeling the wedding is going to go on as scheduled. You're too focused to let anything get in your way when you believe in something. And you like the idea of Tok and Amethyst." Trent headed to the kitchen door. "Besides, I like cake."

Mia gathered the glasses and the napkins, making sure they'd picked up everything before she followed Trent into the school. He was right. When she got something in her head she was determined. Now she just had to make it happen.

* * *

Drunder was sitting in the waiting room at the station when she arrived. Baldwin saw her come in and shook his head, but he didn't say anything as he went back to his office. She sat next to Drunder. "I take it you're not arrested?"

"Apparently, having an alibi is a good thing." Drunder glanced at his watch. "Cassandra is on her way down to pick me up. They only offer one-way rides around this taxi stand."

Mia bit back a smile. "Quick question for you. Why did you fire Chelsea?"

He laughed, but then looked closer at her. "You're serious."

"Actually, yes. I need to know where I stand as the next wedding planner. I've heard rumors, but I'd rather hear it from you." Mia paused, then asked the real question she'd come down to find the answer to. "And who would want to stop the wedding? Do you think Chelsea was killed because someone thought taking out the wedding planner would stop the wedding?"

He leaned back and closed his eyes. When he turned back to her sorrow showed on his face, along with age lines she hadn't seen before. "I didn't kill her. I fired her because she was skimming money off the top of all the vendor charges. I stopped by the florists to get Cassandra a bouquet of roses. She had a question because some of the flowers Amethyst ordered were pricy. She showed me the invoice and it was two thousand less than what Chelsea had claimed on the budget the day before, citing the same reason for the high cost. I don't work with someone I don't trust, and after checking the budget with a couple other vendors, I fired her."

"I don't understand why she would overcharge. You offered me a lot more than what I'd originally agreed to." Mia felt surprised at his answer. Money wasn't even first on her guesses about why Drunder had fired Chelsea.

"You're honest. I checked with several people, including James, after Cassandra called and asked you to take on the job. I reward good work from people I can trust." He patted her arm. "As for why anyone would want to stop the wedding, I'd talk to the McManns. Brody has been against these two getting together since we found out they were dating. He even came to my office and told me to keep my daughter away from his son. Like Amethyst was some sort of siren or something. They fell in love. Tok wasn't my first choice for a son-in-law, but you can't fight love."

As he said that, the door opened behind Mia and she saw his eyes light up.

"Drunder, are you all right?" Cassandra hurried over to him. Drunder stood and pulled her into an embrace.

Mia's eyes teared up as she watched the two. They'd been married for years and still they loved each other. That was obvious. *You can't fight love*, she thought.

"Okay, well, I need to check in with Baldwin about an issue at the house. I'm glad you're out of custody or whatever." Mia didn't think it was appropriate to say what she was thinking: *I'm glad you didn't kill Chelsea.*

"Mia, I didn't see you there." Cassandra took her arm. "I was serious when I told you to continue with the wedding planning. Besides this, are there any hiccups we need to talk about?"

Mia though about the limo and the canceled cake order. "Not that I can think of. Anything you need to tell me?"

"As soon as I get her father home, Amethyst will be right as rain. She was still clinging to Tok when I left. Those two are deeply in love and no one is going to stop this wedding. Not on my watch." Cassandra's eyes flashed, reminding Mia of a mama bear protecting her cub. "I'll see you tonight for our check-in?"

"Six p.m. at the Lodge. I'll be there." Mia moved toward Baldwin's office, but Cassandra stopped her.

"Bring Christina. I'd like to get to know her a little more before the wedding. She seems like such a sweet girl. I'm surprised she's friends with Bethanie."

"Now Cassie, you know Amethyst adores Bethanie," Drunder said as he pulled his wife closer into his arm, showing a united front. "Although, the girl can be a little selfish."

"Bethanie is all about herself. I don't know why anyone would be her friend," Cassandra said, then covered her mouth with her hand. "Sorry, I shouldn't let out our dirty laundry, but we've had concerns about Amethyst and Bethanie's friendship for years. However, the more we pointed out her faults, the more Amethyst pulled her closer. My daughter sees the best in people, even when it's not there to see."

"I think Amethyst and Christina have a lot in common." Mia said her goodbyes, then went up and knocked on Baldwin's door.

"Come in," the police chief called out absently.

She opened it and found his office just like she'd imagined it. Sarah had decorated it, that was clear. A framed picture of the snow-covered city hall sat on one wall, and on the other one several pictures of Baldwin at different stages of his life, including graduation from both Boise State and the police academy. His wedding, and a picture of him and Sarah with a sonogram of the baby that was soon to arrive. Professional, but with a touch of humanity. If Sarah had her way, Baldwin wouldn't end his career here in Magic Springs. He'd be in a much bigger role in a bigger town.

"Do you have a minute?" She stood in the doorway, waiting.

He waved her inside. "Come in and close the door. It won't do for my staff to know you're always out there investigating murders alongside them. They might feel like there's a competition. I just want the darn crime solved. Especially when our best suspect just walked out of here with his wife, who gave him an alibi."

"He was with her?" Mia sat in one of the visitor chairs.

"He was with a bunch of people at the party you attended, and then the two of them went for a drive to Twin Falls for a doughnut. They have the receipt that puts them an hour away at the estimated time of death. And a limo driver who took the pair down the mountain." He rolled his shoulders. "I'm about out of suspects. I considered you, but you already had the job before she was killed, so you have no motive."

"And I really didn't want the job in the first place," Mia added. "I thought we were getting a weekend off. But Drunder waved too big a check in front of me to turn down. I think the heater's going out at the school and I spent the money I had saved for that on a security system."

"Speaking of that, I double-checked with Trey. They

didn't pick up any disturbance on that gym door. So your intruder must have just tried it and then left. There was a slight blur from the kitchen back door camera at that time, but you don't have a dedicated camera on the gym door. Which is probably why the guy went there to try to get inside." He took a report out of the folder and handed it to him. "Here's the report from Trey's company for that entire forty-eight hours."

She picked up the printout and scanned it. Nothing jumped out at her. "Well, thanks anyway."

As she started to stand, he held out his hand. "Can I ask you one question?"

When she nodded and sat back down he swallowed and continued. "Do you have any suspects in Chelsea's murder? I've learned to trust your hunches."

"Actually, no." She rosed, then paused. "Except I've been finding that a lot of the wedding stuff has been canceled. I've had to renegotiate a lot of the vendor contracts. Now, I know some of that was Chelsea's doing right after she got fired. But several of the cancellations happened after her death. It looks like someone is trying to keep this wedding from happening. Is it a stretch to think they might have killed the wedding planner thinking that would stop the ceremony?"

"Which, if your theory is true, puts you in danger." He reopened the file he'd taken the printout out from. "Combined with the faxed threat, that makes this attempted break-in maybe more than that."

"Yeah, that's what I'm afraid of." She held on to the back of the chair. "Look, Trent and Levi are hanging out with Christina and me until this wedding is over, but if anything in the murder investigation looks odd to you, can you tell me? I promise, I'm not sticking my neck out to solve this murder. I don't want to be the guy or gal's next target."

"I'll keep you in the loop. But Mia, you need to be careful." He stood and walked her to the office door. "From what you just told me, you might already be on his hit list."

CHAPTER 14

Trent was waiting in the lobby for her and stood when she came out of Baldwin's office. The two men shook hands and exchanged greetings, but to Mia it felt like she'd just been handed over from one bodyguard to another. "Ready to go? I picked up one more thing my mom didn't even notice was missing."

"What was that?" Mia followed him out of the station and out into the bright light of the early afternoon. Soon the light would dim. It got dark early in this mountain town, even at the beginning of summer, but with the town lights you didn't notice it unless you were out by the school, where there were no streetlights except for those on the greenbelt by the river.

He opened his truck door and pointed inside. "The tiny bride and groom. Tess, the girl who's running the place while Nellie is on vacation, had it set aside for me with the pillars. I guess she knew we'd be back sooner or later."

Mia climbed into the truck and put on her seat belt. Then she picked up the box that held the dark-haired bride and her handsome groom in a standing spoon position, her head turned up toward his, waiting for a kiss. They were lovely, and the statues even looked like Amethyst and Tok. She set the box on her lap and looked up to see Christina crossing the street. Except it wasn't Christina, just someone who looked like her without the electric blue hair. A lot like her, especially with her hair down and colored strawberry blond, which was her born-with shade. She pointed the woman out to Trent. "Who does that look like?"

"That better not be Christina alone or Levi's going to get a stern talking to." He started back out of the truck, but Mia caught his arm.

"It's not her. I thought the same thing, but her face is different. I think it's the nose, or maybe the shape of the mouth. And she doesn't have a row of studs in her earlobe." Mia pointed out the differences. "And her hair isn't blue."

Trent leaned over the steering wheel, trying to get a better look at the woman, who appeared to be heading for a local bar on that side of the street. "If I'd met her on the street, I would have thought it was her, though. Her clothes are even the same style Christina wears. Kind of a shabby, rich-chic-trying-to-look-cool style."

"Goodness, don't let Christina hear you say that. She's been trying to look more normal than when she lived with her folks. Mother Adams has a certain idea of what's appropriate for a young girl to wear. Which, of course, was nothing Christina liked. It was a constant fight when she

stayed over at my house." Mia grinned at the memory of
the fights Christina and Isaac would have on the day
Christina was supposed to go home. "Christina started
leaving the clothes we'd buy together at my house. She
had her own room and closet. That way her mom wouldn't
be able to trash them when she went to school or out."

Trent started the truck. "Poor little rich girl. My heart
bleeds for her."

"Stop it. She's a good kid." Mia leaned back in her
seat and thought about her next step. She needed to get
back to the book to confirm the rest of the vendors before
six p.m. Then she needed a final guest list for the rehearsal
dinner, the wedding, and the reception afterward. That
would probably take most of the discussion time. Christina was going to get a quick course in wedding planning
whether or not she wanted one. She picked up her phone.
"Speaking of, I need to tell her she's coming to the Lodge
with me at six tonight. The mother of the bride wants to
get to know her better."

"I'll have Levi hang out with Mom and help with the
cakes. I'll wait for you in the bar." He winked. "Drinking
something unleaded."

"Sounds like a plan. Thank you again for stepping in. I
appreciate you being here. I know you have an actual
business to run, so hanging around acting like my bodyguard this week is appreciated." She called Christina and
chatted with her for a few minutes. When she ended the
call she turned toward Trent. "I think your brother is
going to be mad at me. I just broke their date tonight."

"He needs to get used to it. Dating someone in the
catering or hospitality field isn't just a nine-to-five job.
I'll chat with him when I tell him that he's babysitting

Mom tonight." Trent pulled the truck into the parking lot of the school. Then he leaned over and kissed her. "Thanks for putting up with me and my family this week."

"Believe me, I'm getting the better end of this deal." Mia climbed out of the seat and started toward the front door.

Trent shook his head and aimed her to the backyard. "Let's go in that way. It's more protected."

"As long as no one's on the community trail that runs behind the school. I need to get a quote for putting up a fence next week. Drunder's generosity on this job is buying me a fenced yard so I don't have to worry so much."

"If only that were true." Trent opened the back door and they stepped into the kitchen. The smells of vanilla and sugar greeted them. "Hey, Mom, we just found out that Mia and Christina have a planning meeting tonight, so I'm going to have Levi stay with you. He can cook dinner while you're baking."

"Your brother. Cook dinner?" Abigail laughed, the sound bright and airy.

Mia smiled as she entered the kitchen. It felt like a kitchen should. Happy, filled with people who loved one another. And she could feel the school was enjoying the new cook as well. "I'll leave out a few of our family meals and he can heat those up. There are instructions in the wrapping. Meat loaf or chicken marsala?"

"Chicken, please. I've heard talk that your food is amazing. Thank you for offering to feed me." Abigail glanced at Trent. "Your father is on a hunting trip, so I'd be home alone if I wasn't here helping."

"Then I guess it all worked out. Great timing." Mia glanced at her watch. "I've still got a few more calls to make, so I'll get the food out now and leave it in the fridge. Then, when Christina and Levi get back, I'll get ready and we can go."

"I'll be in here helping Mom." Trent moved toward the sink and washed up. He turned to his mother. "What can I do?"

Mia pulled out three packets of chicken marsala, just in case Grans didn't have dinner plans. Then she grabbed some water and headed back into her office to work on the wedding. About five, Christina came in and sat on one of the chairs.

"What do you think of my new old look? I thought Amethyst might appreciate me going with my natural hair color rather than the electric blue." Christina had an ice cream cone she was finishing in her hand. "After I got my hair done Levi and I went strolling around town to see if we could pick up any gossip."

"Sounds like the gossip chain was humming at the ice cream place." Mia nodded to the cone.

"Actually, it was. Bethanie was there and in a tizzy. I guess she'd thought she saw Amethyst's cousin in town, but when she tried to catch up with her, the woman was gone. I told her she was being silly. You just don't walk away from a medical degree graduation." Christina finished the cone in one large bite. After she waved away the brain freeze she stood. "I'll go get showered. I feel so bad for Amethyst. To have so many family members not happy with her choice of groom? And then her father was arrested?"

"He was questioned, not arrested. And he's out now anyway," Mia corrected her. She stood and tucked the book into her tote. "I've confirmed all the vendors and everyone should be there tomorrow to start the decorating. You and I will go over at eight and stay there until it's done. Then we should have tomorrow night off. Unless Abigail needs help with the cakes."

Christina held the door open for Mia. "She's really nice, isn't she?"

"Amethyst?"

Christina shook her head. "No, Abigail. She makes me wish she was my mother."

Mia nodded, and they headed upstairs to the apartment to get ready. She was in the living room waiting when Trent came upstairs.

"Fifteen-minute warning," he called toward Christina's room. Then he sat next to Mia. "How are you doing? You've been quiet today."

"Thoughtful. Your mom's really generous to do this."

He leaned back and twirled the keys to his truck. "She's loving helping out. I think she missed working in the bakery when she and Dad retired. Now she bakes all the time and sends stuff home with Levi and me."

"Well, I appreciate it. I'll pay her out of the wedding budget, but I think I'll do something special from my budget too. What would she like?" Mia considered the easy options: flowers, cakes, maybe a spa day?

"Honestly, I think she'd love a girl's day with you and Christina. Maybe your grandmother too. Mom doesn't hang with a lot of women. Mostly because she was either working or, well, the coven women can be a bit harsh at times." He squeezed her hand. "She's a loner, like you."

"I'm not a loner, I just don't have a lot of time to play, what with my business." Mia closed her eyes. She really hadn't had a friend outside of Christina for a long time. Probably before she'd started dating Isaac. "Okay, you're right. I don't make friends easily. One, I'm always working. And two, there's the witch thing. The same issues your mom runs into. I'll figure out something for us all to do. Maybe a weekend at the Lodge with a spa package."

He leaned over and kissed her on the forehead. "You're the best."

"Uh-oh, am I interrupting?" Christina stood in the doorway watching them.

"Actually, no, we're waiting on you." Mia stood and grabbed her tote. "Let's get this run-through done and over. If I've forgotten anything, I'd like to know tomorrow so maybe I can get it fixed."

Trent held open the door. "You worry too much."

"I think you just told me that a few hours ago." Mia walked past him and started down the stairs.

"And nothing's changed since I told you that." Trent closed the door and checked the lock. "Is Mr. Darcy inside?"

"He's sleeping on my bed. I left the door open, although I'm not sure it matters," Christina glanced down the hallway. "I shut the door before I left this morning, yet there he was when I came back."

"He like the sunshine your room gets in the afternoon." Mia stepped outside into the fading light. "A few more weeks and it will be nice in the evening. We'll have to start walking the trail."

"I'm not sure I like that idea," Trent grumbled as he unlocked his truck with the remote.

Mia climbed into the front passenger seat. "Now who's the worrier?"

Everyone was gathered when Mia and Christina stepped into the small conference room. Drunder stood and pulled out a chair for Mia. Christina sat next to Amethyst. "I'm sorry we're late."

"You're not late, dear, we were just catching up." Cassandra glanced around the table, a warning showing on her face. "Anyway, we just wanted you to walk us through the schedule for the next few days. And, of course, spend some time getting to know the two of you. Christina, tell us about how you arrived in Magic Springs. I understand you work with Mia?"

As Christina told the story of Mia's almost engagement to Isaac, Christina's brother, Mia took the time to get settled and pulled out the wedding book. She had several copies of the time line for the next few days and she set that on the table. Then she helped herself to a cup of tea and a cookie. When Christina finished the story with a throwback to Mia and the business, she held up the schedules. "So, now that you know our history, do you want to go over the schedules?"

"Yes," Drunder said as he picked up the papers and started to pass them around.

"As you can see, tomorrow you all are free to rest up or enjoy yourselves. The dresses and tuxes are all picked up, so now it's down to the rehearsal on Friday. We'll start at three, so please try to be on time. We need to be courteous to the minister's schedule. I understand he has some preparation to do on Friday night before the actual ceremony and wants to be done with the rehearsal no later than four thirty."

She continued to walk them through the specifics, noting when toasts would be made and letting them know that the dragon groom's cake would be ready for the rehearsal dinner.

"Dude, you so didn't order a dragon cake, did you?" Gary slapped Tok on the back. "You gave up playing with dragons years ago."

"Hulk, you know me. I never gave up dragons. Now I just collect them, and if you want to come over to my new dragon man cave when Amethyst and I get back from the honeymoon, you can play dragon war with me." He held up his hand into a high-five, which Gary slapped back.

"Boys, the adults are talking here." Marilyn McMann smiled at her sons and then met Mia's gaze. "Sorry, dear, go ahead."

"Well, that's about it. The guests have been confirmed and we're five people under the max for the ballroom. That number has been given to James for the catering. And the ceremony is set for one on Saturday. The limo will be here at six to take the happy couple to the airport, and the only other things you'll have to do is sorting through the photographer's pictures when you return and writing all the thank-you notes. But as of six p.m. Saturday, I'm done telling you all what to do and pushing you around." Mia widened her smile and saw the involuntary jerk of both Marilyn's and Cassandra's head. They hadn't expected her to say anything like that. Or take charge like she had. Yes, being a wedding planner was totally different from just catering an event. Here, she had to be in charge or the inmates would take over the asylum. That wasn't happening on her watch. "Any questions?"

They all looked at one another, then down at the schedule. Cassandra tried to grab back the reins with a question, but Mia could tell her heart wasn't in it.

"Great, so I'll see you all on Friday at three for the rehearsal. Of course, if you need me, I'll be here most of the day making sure the ballroom and the reception hall are decorated." Mia smiled at Tok and Amethyst. "I think you're going to love the aisle protectors. It took some doing, but I found twenty concrete dragons to place at the end of each set of chairs. The florist is putting flowers on them to match the rest of the room."

"Dragons eat flowers," Tok said, but Amethyst slapped his hand.

"You'd better hope these ones behave until after the ceremony." She kissed him. "I'd hate to have to use my magic on them while I walk down the aisle."

Mia shook her head. "You won't have to use your magic. I've got everything under control."

Mia had her own surprises for the ending of the ceremony. She hoped it would work out, but with so many magical people in one room, it might be a little dangerous. Of course, what hadn't been a problem since she took on the job?

Christina gave her a thumbs-up in approval of the way she'd taken over the meeting. Mia just hoped the rest of the days would be as clear-cut as the schedule seemed to imply it would be. The one thing Mia knew about plans was that they changed all the time.

She gathered up her paperwork and motioned to Christina that they would be leaving. The meeting had gone well, without any fights, and Mia wasn't going to take a chance of that changing.

Three more days to get through. Just three more days.

CHAPTER 15

Thursday morning Mia sat at the table drinking coffee when her phone rang. It was the Lodge. She met Trent's gaze and shook her head. "Crap."

"You might as well answer it. Bad news or good news, you need to know it." Trent nodded to the phone. "Do you want me to answer?"

"No, I'll do it." She set down her cup and put the call on Speaker. "Good morning."

"Good morning, Mia." James chuckled on the other end of the line. "Why do you sound like someone just stood you in front of a firing squad?"

"Are you?" Mia reached for a muffin and unwrapped it, putting a small bit into her mouth as she waited for the news.

"No, I'm not. Actually, I just wanted to call to see if you have final numbers for the rehearsal dinner on Friday. I hear one of our party had a chat with Baldwin yesterday."

Mia couldn't tell if he was fishing for information or just really needed the number. "I sent that over yesterday with the reception count. Didn't you get it?"

She heard the paper rustling. "No. I have a list of reception guests here. Seriously, is the former governor coming?"

"Yep. And apparently, so is his security staff. Although I hear they won't be eating or drinking, but they will be tasting the governor's food in the kitchen before his plate is brought out. He has some trust issues." Mia saw Trent's surprise and shrugged. "Okay, I'll send the rehearsal dinner list again as soon as I get downstairs. It's forty-five, if I remember right. Which is huge for what's supposed to be a family dinner."

"Some families are bigger than others. Especially when they have money. Excuse me a second." He paused and then answered someone in the kitchen. When he came back on the line he said, "I've got to go finish breakfast. The front desk asked me to tell you there's a package for you at the desk."

"A package? It's probably for the decorating today." She took another bite of the muffin. "I'll be in at about ten and I'll pick it up then."

"Sounds good. Three more days, girl. Three more days."

Mia ended the call and groaned. "That's what I said yesterday, but James must count today as not done yet."

"And you think as long as you've started the day, it's over." Trent took a muffin. "Levi's going to take you and Christina over to the Lodge. I'm picking up Mom at nine and taking her shopping. She says she needs stuff from the specialty supply store in Boise. I'll be out of town for most of the day. Unless you want me to stay and send Levi."

"I'm just decorating a couple of rooms. I'm sure your brother's protective eye will be enough. And I'd rather have you gone today than tomorrow." She finished her muffin. "I might need my own run to the supply store if Chelsea didn't order enough tulle."

"Are you sure you like this wedding planner career? It seems like a lot of details and a lot of fanfare for just one day." Trent didn't meet her gaze, but she knew he was watching her.

"I like doing the detail stuff. I think if this had been my wedding from the beginning, it would be a lot more fun. Maybe I should just do nonmagical weddings. I'm sure normal families might come with a little less baggage."

"Have you talked to a normal family? I'm pretty sure you wouldn't want to do Christina's wedding, especially with her mother." He stood and held out a hand. "Families are always a pain in the butt. Magical or not."

When they arrived at the Lodge Mia stopped at the front desk. She turned to Christina. "You go ahead and see who's shown up for decorating. I'd like to be out of here no later than five. Trent said he'd stop in Twin for some take-and-bake pizzas on his way back from Boise."

"Sound good. I'll go crack the whip." Christina made a whipping motion with her hand.

Maybe she actually could install fear in a vendor or two. First thing up had to be the arch, then setting up the holders for the flowers. She needed to see the magic come to life; drawings just didn't work for her.

"Can I help you?" A young man in a black suit came up to her.

Mia stopped daydreaming and smiled. "I'm Mia Malone. I've got a package?"

He frowned and glanced around. "Sorry, no package for a Ms. Malone."

"James said someone from the front desk called him about one this morning?" Mia tried to keep the exasperation out of her voice, but she knew it wasn't working.

"Oh, that was me. But the package says wedding planner for the Uzzi-McMann wedding, not Mia Malone. Sorry, that must be you?" When she nodded, he pulled out a box from underneath the counter. "Here you go."

She took the package over to a couch and ripped the tape off the top. The box felt off, like it didn't want her to open it. Why had someone sent a magical object to her? She pulled out a book and set it on the table. Then she sat on the couch and watched it. There was no question, she was looking at a grimoire.

She tucked the book back into the box. Then she picked up her cell. "Levi? Can you come back for a minute? I need you to take something back to the house."

"Sure, I'm just sitting in the parking lot." Levi's response came back quickly.

She met him at the front entrance of the Lodge. He frowned when he got out of the truck and approached her. "What in the heck is in that box? I can feel it from here."

"I'm not sure, but I can't deal with this now. Just take it to the school and put it in my office." After he took the box she wiped her hands together as if they were sticky or covered with mud. The book was tainted. Even with her limited magical knowledge, she knew that.

Throughout the morning Mia ignored the slight headache that was growing larger by the moment. When they broke for lunch she just wanted to sleep, not eat. Instead, she ordered soup and a sandwich and picked her way through lunch.

"Seriously, if you're sick, you should go home. I'll call Levi and have him come get you. I can deal with the rest of the day." Christina winced as Mia's phone rang. "Another issue?"

"Who knows? I can't believe there have been so many tiny problems that just keep adding up. The flowers were the wrong color. The dragons weren't decorated. The chairs were for some conference rather than a wedding." Mia let the call go to voice mail as she dug in her purse for one of her grandmother's headache blockers. Ten times better than any pain reliever she could buy off the shelf. She shook out two and took them with a swig of soda. "This is my second dose of these. If they don't do the trick, I must be dying."

"Don't joke about that." Christina crossed herself. "I need this job at least until I graduate. You know if I go home, my mom will have me married off to the first up-and-coming businessman she finds. Even if he does have a comb-over and a wandering eye."

"It's always all about you." Mia smiled, but even she felt the lack of emotion. "Let's just finish the ballroom as much as possible. We can do the rehearsal room tomorrow morning if you don't mind an early start."

"Works for me." Christina took a bite of her flatbread pizza and groaned. "This is so good."

Mia hoped the smell of the food wouldn't make her

throw up the little bit of food she'd managed to keep
down so far. But the food mixed with Grans's medicine
seemed to be helping cut the edge from the pain. She pulled
out her notebook. "Only three more things on the list.
Let's say you take one and me the other. First one to finish gets to start the third, but the other one has to work on
it too."

"Sounds great. As long as you think you can deal with
losing. I'm going to be the first one done. Always am, always will be." Christina glanced around the crowded dining room. "Don't you think it's odd we haven't seen
either family today?"

"Maybe they're off doing something fun. I told them
we didn't need anyone to show up until Friday afternoon." Mia pushed away the food. "I can't eat anymore
and I can't sit here. Tell James to charge the meal to my
account and I'll meet you back in the ballroom."

"You just want to get a head start." Christina's light
answer didn't match the concern Mia saw on her face.

"Just enjoy your lunch and don't hurry. I'm fine." Mia
tucked her notebook back into her tote and left the dining
room.

The white wooden chairs for the ceremony had arrived
while they were gone and the hotel staff was setting them
up. Mia grabbed the white tulle and wound it through the
first two rows of chairs. She was waiting for the third set
of chairs to be set up when Gary strode into the room. His
face lit up when he saw her, but then Mia saw it turn into
concern as he hurried toward her.

"Don't tell me I look that bad." Mia started wrapping
the chairs.

"No. I mean, yes, you look like death warmed over. Are you sick or have you just been pushing yourself too much?" Gary picked up the scissors to cut the tulle so she could cross the aisle and get to the other side.

"I have a headache, that's all," Mia explained, pausing as she caught her breath. She might just have to skip dinner and sleep this off. "Do you need something besides complimenting my beauty? Or lack thereof?"

"Actually, my mother wanted to make sure there wasn't anything you needed for the decorations." He took the tulle from her and wound it through the next set of chairs. "You shocked her a bit last night."

Mia had to admit he was a quick study. "I didn't mean to shock her. I was just tired of everyone poking their nose into what's supposed to be Amethyst's and Tok's wedding. They need to be the ones to make the decisions. Not your mother or Mrs. Uzzi."

"Well, she got the point." Gary pointed to a chair. "Sit down before you fall down. I'll finish this. Don't you have a helper?"

"Christina's finishing her lunch. I wasn't hungry." She watched as he finished all the chairs and then tucked the empty tulle roll into a box. "You didn't have to do that."

"I know. I'm finding it quite enjoyable. Please don't tell my brother. I'll never live this down." He sat in a chair a row away. "I think you should take a break and go home. This can be finished in the morning."

"After Christina gets back we'll finish up and be out of here." She rubbed her neck. "Hopefully, I'll feel better in the morning."

"This wedding is cursed. Nothing is going right. You

would think that Tok and Amethyst would get a clue and cancel it." He glanced at his phone, then tucked it into his pocket.

"You need to be somewhere else?" she guessed.

He shrugged. "In a minute. I can wait for Miss Christina."

"So, why do you think the wedding is cursed?"

He laughed, but the sound was harsh, not funny. "You don't? Chelsea gets killed. The vendors have been less than helpful. And now you're sick."

"What do you know about the vendors?" Now this was interesting, especially because she hadn't said anything to the family.

"I called the bakery this morning and she said they didn't have an order for a dragon cake." He stared at her. "Are you doing the cake?"

"Maybe. First tell me why you called the bakery."

He blushed. "I wanted them to make the frosting pink. Tok hates pink."

She couldn't help but laugh, but then the sound and motion made her head hurt.

Christina came running to her side. "Mia? Are you okay?"

"I'm just not feeling well." She tried to focus on Christina, but her face was fuzzy. "Maybe you should finish up the decorating."

"I'll take you home." Gary held out a hand.

Christina stepped in between Mia and Gary. "Thanks, but we have transportation coming. Mia, where's your tote?"

Mia pointed to the wall by the door, then let her hand drop. "Over there. My notebook is on the first row of chairs by the tulle. Call Levi and have him come get me and I'll send him back to help when I get into the house. I can't believe I'm this sick."

"Levi's on his way already. He called when I was finishing lunch." She pulled her phone out of her pocket. "He's at the entrance. Maybe it's food poisoning?"

"All I ate at the house was a muffin." Mia tried to stand but fell back down on the chair. The next thing she knew, Gary had picked her up and was carrying her out of the conference room. Mia saw Christina following along with her tote. When she got outside the fresh air woke her up a bit. "I'm sure I could have walked."

Gary tucked her into the truck after Christina opened the passenger door. "I'm not. She's all yours, dude."

As they started to drive off, Levi picked up her wrist. "Your pulse is strong. What's going on? Should I take you to the hospital?"

"No, take me home. I just need some sleep." Mia leaned her head back and looked straight ahead. Closing her eyes made her nauseous.

"Trent and Mom are already back at the house. They found a shop in Twin that carried what she needed, so they didn't have to go to Boise. He called you earlier but it went to voicemail. He was unloading the supplies or he would have come to get you." Levi dropped her wrist and, with both hands free, increased the truck's speed. "I don't like the way you look."

"I don't like the way you look in that blue shirt," Mia shot back. "So, are we done criticizing each other's appearance?"

"That's not what I meant and you know it. Man, you must keep my brother on his toes. Glad it's him and not me." Levi turned off the stereo.

Mia blessed him for the quiet as they drove the few minutes to the school. When he parked the door flew open and Trent gathered her up in his arms. "Doesn't anyone think I can walk? I've been doing it most of my life."

"What is she talking about, Levi?" Trent hurried into the lobby and set her on the couch.

Abigail leaned over her. She reached for her, then pulled her hands back. "Step back. She's been cursed."

"Mom? What are you talking about?" Trent took two steps away from the couch, but Mia could see the fear in his eyes.

"I'm just sick. I need to sleep this off," Mia mumbled.

"Levi, go make a pot of coffee and bring me a cup heavy with cream and sugar. Then you get back to be with Christina." Abigail took a quilt from a display rack and covered Mia with it. "Trent, call her grandmother. I'm going to need some help getting this off her."

"Gary McMann was with her when I got there. He carried her to the truck," Levi said as he headed to the kitchen. "Maybe he slipped her something."

"No, this is a curse, not a poisoning. It was something else she must have touched." Abigail glanced around the room. "Was she okay when she left here? No headache?"

Trent shook his head. "She was tired of the wedding issues, but she seemed fine."

"I'm sitting right here while you all talk about me. If you think I was cursed, it had to be from the grimoire. Ask Levi where he put it." Mia adjusted a pillow behind her back, trying not to give in to the strong need to sleep.

When Levi came back into the lobby he put a cup of coffee into her hands. "Drink this."

"Where is the box I sent you home with?" She sipped

the too-sweet drink. At least it was warm. She was freezing.

"It's over there by the stairs. I left it there when I came back from the Lodge." He pointed to an area by the door where a coat closet was tucked under the stairs. "I'm going back to help Christina. We'll see you in a few hours."

"Be careful, dear," his mother called after him. Then she nodded to Trent. "Bring that over to the table and let's see what we have to deal with here."

CHAPTER 16

When Grans arrived Abigail was examining the book, after putting on rubber gloves and using tongs to get it out of the box. Grans glanced at the grimoire on the table, then at Mia. "I can't believe you even picked up that thing. If you were a normal human, you would be dead by now."

"Well, it's a good thing I didn't let Christina pick up the package, then." Mia sat up on the couch after Abigail had performed several healing spells over her. At the last one Mia had heard the crack of the spell as it broke under Abigail's determination. Immediately, she'd started feeling better. Her headache was all but gone and her stomach had settled. She sipped a cup of hot chocolate now, rather than the overly sweetened coffee. Chilled, she kept the blanket over her, but she'd moved so Trent could sit beside her. "What's the spell? And who's grimoire is that?"

"Good question." Abigail stood and took off her gloves, stepping away from the book. "It won't let me open it. The book's witch is still alive or it would have disappeared by now. One more question: Who was the spell meant for? Mia? Or maybe Chelsea?"

"The box was addressed to the Uzzi and McMann wedding planner. It could have been either of us, but if I was guessing, I think it's been sitting for a while, so it was meant for Chelsea. Maybe this was the first attempt on her life, then when it didn't take, the witch came and finished the job." Mia rubbed her eyes. "Chelsea's room was a complete and utter mess when I found her."

"Wait, are we saying a witch killed Chelsea? But Drunder was cleared. He had an alibi." Grans took off her coat and sat next to Mia, patting her hand. She looked around at the group staring at her. "What? The Magic Springs rumor mill runs quite fast through these parts. I heard that this morning, first thing. I shouldn't have left last night to pick up my car. I'm staying here until this wedding is over."

"Well, if it is the same person, we have one clue that Baldwin's never going to have. This grimoire. If we can get it to tell us who its master is, we can send that person's name to the station and see what they do with that lead." Abigail focused her attention on Grans. "I need to do some baking, but you can give the book a go if you want."

"I trust your abilities. I think we should broadcast a lost grimoire through the coven and see if anyone comes looking for it." Grans pulled Mia closer. "And when they come for it I'll teach them a lesson for messing with my granddaughter."

"After the wedding. I need to get through this," Mia said. "But seriously, would someone actually come for it if they'd used it to deliver a killing curse?"

The front door opened and Christina and Levi came in from outside. Christina hurried to Mia's side and put a hand on her cheek. "I'm so glad you're feeling better."

"Me too." Levi shut the door. "Operation ballroom is complete. If you give Christina a list, we can finish up what we need to do for the rehearsal. Then you just have to show up after lunch and let us know what we did wrong."

"Whatever. I'm sure it's perfect." Mia pointed to the book. "I'm more worried about that."

"Well, let's get dinner in the oven and I'll lock this up in your office." Trent picked up the book. "We'll figure out who sent it after we get the wedding set up. Mia, do you have anything else on your to-do list for tonight?"

"Actually, no."

"Then Mom, you get what you need to get done today. Christina, can you help her? Mia, Mary Alice, and I will go upstairs and get dinner ready. Everyone cool with that?"

When they all nodded Trent smiled. "Good, then let's get things handled."

As they were slowly on their way upstairs, Mia looked over at Trent. "You're good with this delegation stuff."

He let out a chuckle. "Many years of practice and some watching my dad at the store. You'll get the hang of it as a business owner."

"Well, when I figure out who poisoned that book, I'm going to have a really strong talking to with them. I can't believe they left out something that dangerous that just anyone could pick up." Mia yawned. "I'm still dead tired. Any problem with me taking a shot nap while you all get dinner ready?"

"I don't think so." Grans waited at the top of the stairs for them to catch up. "I've scanned you for additional symptoms, but I didn't find anything. Abigail did a really nice job with her healing spell."

"Mom's pretty practiced on that healing spell. Between all three of us boys, I think she had to use it a lot. Besides, she didn't trust the local doctors, so we didn't go in for anything except our shots. I don't think she would have let them do those, except the schools demanded proof of immunizations." He put his arm around Mia. "You go rest. I can handle putting two pizzas in the oven and making a salad."

As he opened the door, Mr. Darcy came running up to see Mia. Then the cat led her to her bedroom and lay on her feet, purring until she gave up and fell asleep.

As she slept, she dreamed of the wedding. The flowers and the white tulle made the room look magical, ethereal. Mia sat in the back row, Trent in a suit by her side. The groom and his groomsmen were up front already, as were the bridesmaids and the maid of honor. Their shimmering silver dresses kept changing from pink to blue to red and back to silver. Then the dresses would repeat the color mix. It was all so beautiful. The wedding march started, and all of a sudden it was her walking up the aisle toward Trent. But instead of Christina being up at the front, another woman stood in her maid of honor spot. A woman Mia didn't know. She turned to Dorian, who was out of Mr. Darcy's body and alive again in the dream. He was also walking her down the aisle. "Where's Christina?"

"She's right up there. Waiting for you." He pointed to the woman Mia didn't know.

Mia stopped walking. "That's not her."

"Of course it is . . ." Dorian turned to her, but now Mr. Darcy's face was on Dorian's body.

"That's not Christina." She turned to look around the venue to see if she could see Christina in the crowd.

"Mia, Trent's waiting . . ."

She heard the knocking on the door.

Christina called through the closed door, "Mia? Pizza's ready. Trent said we had to wait for you to wake up before we could eat. Mia? Are you awake?"

Mr. Darcy sat at the end of the bed, watching her.

"Strange dream, don't you think?" She rubbed his head and sat up, slipping her feet into her shoes as she did. She pushed away the too-real dream and stood.

Mr. Darcy didn't move.

"It was a dream, right? Otherwise I'm not quite sure what it all means." She watched him.

Christina knocked on the door again. "Mia?"

Mr. Darcy let out a cry and ran to the door. As he pawed at it, the door opened and he took off down the hallway.

Christina stood in the hall, her mouth open and her hand held up to knock again. "I swear I didn't open the door."

"I know. Dorian was just showing off." Mia walked over to meet her. Stretching her arms as she went, she felt better. Not 100 percent yet, but the headache was almost totally gone. "Let's go eat."

They'd set up the food buffet style on the cabinets, but Abigail and Grans sat at the table in the middle of the kitchen, eating. Mia picked up a plate and filled it with salad and two slices of the veggie pizza she loved—everything but olives. She started to sit at the table, but Grans waved her away. "Go sit with the others in the living room. We're talking about the coven and I don't want you to misconstrue what we're saying."

"Which means you're gossiping, and you don't want me to hear," Mia translated her grandmother's words.

"Don't be smart." Grans's words didn't match her smile. "Abigail, I think you did a good job on her healing. She's bright and sassy again."

"I like her that way. Especially where Trent is involved. He needs a strong-minded woman in his life. If only to remind him of his sainted mother." Abigail smiled at Mia.

Trent snorted from the doorway. "If you're done listening to the stories this one makes up, we have a spot for you in the living room. We're planning for the Saturday night party after the wedding is over."

"All I'm doing Saturday night is sleeping," Mia grumbled, but she followed him into the living room and sat on the couch. She moved the coffee table closer and set down her plate. Waving Mr. Darcy away, she picked up a piece of pizza.

"What we were thinking is we'd rent two rooms at the Lodge, or maybe a suite if it's cheaper. Then we could crash for a couple of hours, hang out at the bar that night after dinner, and then do spa stuff all the next morning." Christina filled her in on what they'd been talking about.

"When I'll be sleeping in and ignoring the spa stuff," Trent added.

Levi shook his head. "Not me, dude. Have you ever

had a massage from Olga? She gets down in the muscle. I felt like I was going to sleep for weeks."

"If that's what you guys want, that's fine. I was going to suggest a weekend in Boise. We could go to the art museum, the zoo, hit a couple of restaurants, and then find a local theater show." Mia glanced around at the group. "And maybe some shopping before we come home?"

"Shoot me now," Trent muttered.

At the same time Levi said, "Art museum? Are you crazy?"

"Let's compromise. We'll do this now and in a few months you and I can take off and go to Boise." Christina patted Levi's arm. "You don't want to subject these boys to any culture. They might melt."

"I think the literary reference is water." Mia focused on her pizza. Now that the effects of the curse were off her, she was starving. "I feel like I haven't eaten all day."

"You didn't eat much." Christina picked a mushroom from the pizza and popped it in her mouth. "Any idea who that curse was for? You said the box was for the wedding planner. Who doesn't know that Chelsea's dead?"

"The thing is, we don't know when the box was sent or delivered." Mia frowned as she tried to remember. "I don't think I saw a shipping label."

"There wasn't one. It had to have been dropped off. If Baldwin accepted the coven as real, we could tell him about this and have him see if the front desk has cameras. Or if anyone knows when it was delivered. As it is, if we told him about it, he'd want to see the grimoire, and if he touched it, well, he isn't such a bad police chief. We don't want to have to replace him," Trent pointed out. "And he is going to be a father."

Christina shuddered. "I wouldn't want to be the one to tell Sarah. She'd have everyone who even thought about saying they were a witch rounded up and dunked in the lake."

"She can be a little over-the-top with all things otherworldly," Levi agreed. "No, we have to keep this curse under wraps. As far as anyone at the wedding or the Lodge goes, Mia was working too hard and didn't eat enough.

"Gary might know. I can't remember what I told him when he was carrying me out of the building." Mia tried to remember the conversation, but it was gone.

"Excuse me, why exactly was Gary carrying you out of the building?" Trent stared at her.

"My fault. I told him we didn't need a ride because Levi had just pulled up." Christina jumped into the conversation. "I asked him to help get her to the door. I didn't expect him to pick her up."

"Look, he was being helpful." Mia yawned, the food making her sleepy again. "I'm just not sure what I said to him. He did help decorate the ballroom. Anyway, as fun as this has been, I'm crashing again. I'll see you all first thing in the morning and we're all going over to make sure both rooms are beautiful before three p.m. Then you two are free until after the rehearsal dinner. Christina gets to stay because she's part of the wedding party."

"I'll stay too," Trent said, and then quickly added, "just in case you need a runner. With Christina busy, you may need to send me on errands."

"Nice save, bro." Levi tried to high-five his brother, but Trent ignored it.

"And Levi can come back and help Mom out with any last-minute cake issues," Trent added.

"We'll need to send him to get the groom's cake as soon as the rehearsal starts. Then he and Abigail can bring it over and set it up. We'll have a special table for the cake." Mia nodded. The plan was coming together. "Thanks, everyone, for your hard work this week. And for getting me back here so Abigail could cure me before the curse took too much from me."

"You are most welcome," Christina said. "Besides, my college fund thanks you. Mom's been delaying my living expenses checks later and later each month. If you didn't charge me peanuts for living here, I'd be in real trouble."

"Your mother is . . ." Levi started, then saw the look Christina was giving him, "calendar challenged. Maybe she doesn't realize a month has passed by when she needs to send the check?"

"Not even close to a save, bro." Trent laughed, then picked up Mia's empty plate. "Are you sure you don't want more pizza?"

"No, I'm full. I'm just worn out." Mia stood and gave him a quick kiss. "Thank you for worrying about me, though."

He chuckled. "You heard my mom. I need a strong woman in my life to keep me in line."

"Mom says that about all her sons. I heard her tell Jilly the same thing at Thanksgiving." Levi grabbed Christina's hand. "What about you? Has she given you the strong-woman speech?"

Christina blushed bright red.

"Well, that's a definite yes," Levi observed.

She slapped his arm. "Stop teasing me."

"I'll see you all tomorrow." Mia followed Trent into the hall. "Keep an eye on Christina, will you?"

"Why? Something going on?" He glanced back into

the living room, where Christina and Levi were scrolling through the television channels looking for something to watch. "Is it Levi?"

She shook her head. "Not Levi. Nothing I can put my finger on."

"Then why do you look like you expect her to disappear at a moment's notice?"

Trent's words made her shiver.

"Mia, what's wrong?" He set the plate in the kitchen on the counter and walked with her into the bedroom. He closed the door with his foot, then sat on the bed next to her. "Tell me why you're upset. Is it just a reaction from the curse?"

"Maybe. I'm not sure." When she saw Trent looked as confused as she felt, she held up her hand. "So don't laugh."

"Right now I'm ready to pop you into the truck and take you to the hospital or out of state or something. Laughing at you is not my first choice." He took her hand and held it with both of his. "Tell me what's wrong."

She told him about the dream. It was already feeling a bit fuzzy and she felt her face warm when she mentioned the fact that the wedding turned into one for her and Trent. "But as I was walking up the aisle, there was a strange woman at the altar with you guys. I didn't know her, but Dorian, who was walking me to you, said it was Christina."

"Dorian, the cat, was walking you?" Trent glanced over and saw Mr. Darcy sitting near the now-open door, watching them.

"No, it was Dorian, the man. Before he died I'd met him once, at the food bank." She shook her head. "I don't know why I'm concerned over a dream." Mia took her hand out from Trent's grip and pushed her hair away from her eyes.

"Just tell me the rest of it," Trent prodded. "Dorian was walking you to the aisle and a woman was there who wasn't Christina."

"Yeah, that was about it. Then Dorian said Trent was waiting for me and I heard Christina at the real door to my bedroom telling me dinner was ready." She smiled at Mr. Darcy, who had just jumped up on her lap. "I asked him if it was a dream, but he didn't answer."

"You asked the cat if it was a dream?"

"I told you not to laugh." Mia rolled her shoulders. "All I want to do is get through tomorrow and Saturday with no poisonous curses or disappearing vendors."

"It's funny how specific your ideas for a good day have become. And what a low bar you are setting." Trent stood and crossed the room, then stopped at the doorway. "I'll keep an eye on Christina until she goes to bed."

"Thanks. I appreciate it." Mia didn't respond to his statement about her wishes. She just wanted her first wedding planning event to go off without any more hitches. Oh, and having no more murders, that would be good too.

CHAPTER 17

Friday morning the sun was shining when they drove over to the Lodge. Mia saw the rain clouds coming in from the west. She checked the weather app on her phone. "It's supposed to rain this morning. Thank the Goddess we didn't plan an outdoor event."

"I'm sure it will stop by noon. That way the rehearsal should go fine without anyone getting drenched coming into the hotel." Trent pulled into the Lodge and stopped in front of the entry. He left the truck running and got out to help Mia with her tote. "Levi, park the truck. And park in the back, where you have some room. I don't want a dent in the door just because you parked too close to one of those Hummers."

"I think the back is just as filled with high-end trucks." Levi climbed out of the back, then held out a hand to help Christina and then her dressing bag out of the truck. "You should listen to Trent about the weather, though, Mia. He's got a talent for predictions."

"Is that so?" Mia handed Trent a box filled with more ribbon she'd found in her office. "I'll be sure to remember that. I like working with your family, Trent. I've learned so much about you this week."

"If they start telling you about my third-grade crush, that's when I'm drawing the line and banning you from talking with my mother. Levi I can threaten with violence to get him to shut up, but Mom's not scared of me one bit." He followed her into the lobby.

Mia laughed, but the sound caught as she saw the same guy at the front desk who had given her the box. "Hold up a second. I want to talk to him for a minute."

The front desk clerk saw her walking up and grinned. "Good morning, Miss Malone. Lovely to see you again."

"Thank you," she glanced down at his tag, "David. Can you answer a question for me?"

"I'd be glad to help in any way possible." He leaned against the counter.

"That box you called James to have me come get it. Why?"

He frowned and shrugged. "It had been here a while, and I knew because of the schedule they gave us that the wedding was tomorrow. I thought it might be important. Why do you ask?"

"Do you know how long it was sitting there?" Mia asked. "Think for a minute. It's important."

"Let me see. I work Wednesday through Sunday, and I'm pretty sure it was here last Sunday when I left. I saw it was for this week's wedding. I left a message for Monday's staff to figure out who was in charge of the wedding. There wasn't anyone listed on the schedule. When it was still here on Wednesday, I was going to figure it out myself and deliver it, but we were swamped. So that night, before I left, I called James because he was doing the food. I figured he'd know the wedding planner." He leaned closer. "I'm sorry, was that wrong?"

"No, it was fine. Thank you for the explanation. I was just wondering." Mia left the front desk and fell into step with Trent.

"He seemed genuine to me," Trent said after they were out of earshot.

Mia considered the information. "Yeah. I think that package was meant for Chelsea. Which means it wasn't one of the McManns unless it was Marilyn. She's the only one who would have the magic."

"Whoever sent it is missing their grimoire. Marilyn would have retrieved hers once Chelsea was dead." Trent opened the door to the ballroom. "Your grandmother is going over to the school this morning to stay with my mom. Maybe while she's waiting, she can whip up a rebound spell. I'd love to get this player caught before we fall into more of her booby traps."

Mia took a second to consider what Trent had just said. "You called the murderer a she. Any reason why?"

"The grimoire. They tend to take the gender personality of their owner. I'd bet money it belongs to a female." He sighed. "Which means Marilyn can't be totally crossed off the suspect list."

"Maybe. Drunder can, unless he was working with someone like Cassandra. But I don't think so. They seem like they're supporting the wedding now. Maybe Tok wasn't their first choice as a son-in-law, but they seem to see how in love the two of them are. I can't see either of the parents being part of this. They want what's best for the kids. Even if it's crossing their traditional dating lines."

He kissed her on the forehead. "Sometimes you talk like there's no difference between humans and the rest of us."

"There isn't. We all need water, food, and companionship." She squeezed his arm. "And meaningful work. So let's get busy. We've got a wedding here tomorrow."

Mia divided the group into two sets. Christina and Levi took the rehearsal dinner hall and she and Trent finished up the final touches on the wedding site. Tomorrow morning they'd have to reset the rehearsal hall for the reception, but this room needed to be finished today for tonight's run-through and tomorrow's big event.

The last things she set up were the dragon statues on every other line of chairs, staggering them so it started with one on the groom's side, then the second on the bride's side, second row. She grinned up at Trent as she adjusted the faces to aim toward the main aisle. "There's a spell I made especially for tomorrow. When they turn back around the dragons will spit out confetti and shower the couple as they walk through the community as man and wife."

"The cleaners are going to hate you." Trent watched as she went back to move a dragon just a little more to face the aisle.

"I know. It's going to be amazing. We'll all have confetti on us throughout the reception." She stood and scanned the room. "Besides, it could be worse."

"How, real fire?" Trent watched as she walked down the aisle toward him.

She laughed, feeling the joy of being part of making this beautiful for a special event. She took his arm and grabbed her tote, moving out of the room. "It could be glitter."

They went to get Levi and Christina for lunch. Sitting in the dining room, Mia felt a little light-headed, thinking about the spell that had almost taken her out yesterday.

"I'm glad to see you're better," Gary said from somewhere behind her.

She turned around and he stood there, watching the table. "I'm much better. Thank you for your assistance yesterday."

"From the look your man is giving me, I suppose I won't get the chance to carry you out of a building again." He held out a hand to Trent. "Gary McMann."

"Trent Majors. I think we met a few years ago out on a river float down Hells Canyon." Trent stood and shook Gary's hand.

"You're right. I'd forgotten about that. Tok and I hadn't ever been down that far through the canyon. It was breathtaking," Gary remarked.

Trent nodded. "The entire week was pretty amazing. Thanks for helping out Mia yesterday. She got hit by a pretty potent poison spell that someone aimed at the wedding planner."

Gary blanched. "I told you this was going to happen. Someone doesn't want this wedding to happen tomorrow. I'm glad you brought backup today. You need to be careful and not be alone."

"No one's going to hurt me again. I was careless. I felt the spell but didn't realize it was affecting me until it was almost too late." She focused her gaze on Gary's face. "Is there any chance your mother is involved?"

"I shouldn't be telling you this, but I'm going to anyway." Gary tucked his hands into his jeans as he glanced around the crowded dining room. He leaned forward to reduce his chances of being overheard. "It's not a secret that my mother isn't happy about the wedding. She thinks Tok is destined for tribe leadership. With a witch for a wife, that won't happen. He'll be sidelined, just like my father was from his right to leadership."

"I'm afraid stopping the wedding will only postpone the actual bonding. Those two are going to get married. Either tomorrow or they'll elope, and no one will be able to celebrate with them," Mia pointed out the flaw in the killer's plan.

"You and I know that. Heck, even my mom knows that. She likes Amethyst. She'd just like her more if she was of shifter blood. But it is what it is." Gary's phone beeped and he looked at the display. "Lunch is being served in our suite. I've got to go. Please be careful."

And with that last warning he was gone.

"Well, there goes our theory that the killer is Marilyn." Christina said, digging into her salad.

"Maybe. Or maybe if they say it's not her enough, they can convince themselves," Trent pointed out. "Gary's afraid of something, I just can't tell what."

"Amethyst's family seems to be on board with the wedding," Christina announced. "At least her mom and dad. She has three uncles who refused to come to the ceremony if the McManns were going to be there. Of course, they didn't totally diss her. They sent a large check for the happy couple. She told us during the mani-pedi party."

"Three uncles and a cousin who 'says' she's graduating this weekend. It's a little early for graduations, isn't it?" Mia pondered the idea.

"Depends. My college graduation was on May 7 because that was when they could get the auditorium," Trent said.

"The college in Twin does the weekend near the fifteenth," Christina announced. "Two more years and I'll be wearing that stupid hat."

"And I'll be looking for a new sous chef." Mia smiled at her assistant.

"Maybe."

"Believe me, you'll want to do something else. Besides, I won't be able to afford to pay you what you deserve by then." Mia shook her head, ending the conversation. "Anyway, we do have some narrow-minded parties on the Uzzi side of the aisle, unless they all decided not to attend."

Trent finished his burger and threw his napkin on the table. "I guess it's too late to even consider that Chelsea could have been killed by someone who just didn't like her. She wasn't the nicest person from what I've been told."

"Well, that's the angle that Baldwin is looking at now that Drunder was cleared." Mia shrugged. "He can work that side of the investigation and we'll work the magical side. We'll see who finds the real killer first."

"But will we be able to explain why we think someone's the killer if it's about the magic?" Trent asked before he stepped away from the table to answer his phone.

Christina leaned into the table. "Trent's right."

"Well, I guess we'll just have to make sure the wedding goes on and ruin their master plan. I'm not in law enforcement. Right now I'm a wedding planner, and I'd hate to have my first wedding go down the tubes because someone can't see past their own prejudices. So, tell me what's still left to do on the rehearsal dinner hall." Mia pushed away her plate and a server came up quickly to take it from the table. She didn't look up as the woman started to step away, but she held up a hand, then pointed to Trent's napkin-covered plate. "He's done as well."

The server paused, then picked up Trent's plate and left.

Mia pulled out her notebook and set it on the table where her plate had been. "Go ahead. I'll check things off the list."

For the next few minutes Christina, with Levi jumping in, walked Mia through all the things she'd completed that morning. And a list of what she thought still needed to be done. Then she asked, "What time should Levi go get the cake?"

"I'm thinking at two. That way, you and I can go get ready as soon as he gets back and we'll be done with the room before we have to be at the rehearsal. James got us the use of a hotel room to change in that we have access to from two to four. We shouldn't need it that long, but that gives the guys time to grab our bags and take them out to the truck." Mia wondered what was taking Trent so long on the call.

He was back in the dining room just as Christina was finishing her salad. "Sorry about that. Your grandmother wanted to run some things by me. I think her tracing spell is going to work."

"We'd better get back to work before we run out of time." Mia stood and left out her notebook. "We've got two hours before Levi has to get the cake. And there's a lot of table setup to get done."

"Yes, master." Trent grinned as he followed her out of the dining room. "I live to serve."

"Whatever." Mia giggled as she moved through the lobby area. A woman caught her eye and she grabbed Trent's sleeve and pointed toward her. "There's that woman who looks like Christina."

"Who?" Trent turned his head just as the look-alike went out the front doors. "I don't see anyone."

"You just missed her." Mia thought about going to see if she was still in the parking lot, but there was a lot to do. She didn't have time to chase down Christina's doppelgänger just for Trent's confirmation of what she'd been seeing. "Let's go. We've got things to do."

"Yes, ma'am, but for the record, we're waiting on you." He dodged the swat she aimed at him and then held the door open as they walked into a room that hadn't even been set up. Boxes, linens, tables, and chairs all lined the walls. But nothing was set up.

Mia stood staring at the room in shock.

Christina grabbed her arm. "It wasn't like this when we left for lunch. You know that. You peeked in when you came to get us for lunch. All the tables were up, the linens on, and we were ready for the catering staff to come in and set up the tables for dinner."

"I know. I saw it."

Levi came running back into the room. "This is the right room. The other one is half this size and set up for a conference lecture."

"What on earth happened here?" Mia glanced at Trent. She squeezed her eyes shut and quickly reopened them, but the result was the same. The room had been torn down while they were at lunch. "Crap. Trent, go check the wedding chapel."

He ran out of the room as Mia pulled out her diagram.

"Okay, people, let's do this again, but twice as fast as this morning."

She started hauling out chairs from the walls and rolling tables out in the approximate places on the floor. She set up a gift table as well as a head table. Christina came after her and put a fresh linen on the table. "Who does this kind of thing? It's mean and thoughtless."

"Someone who doesn't want the wedding to happen, I guess." Mia glanced up as Trent came into the room. "Well?"

"The wedding chapel is still intact and now, after I grabbed James, locked." Trent grabbed a table and set it up as he was talking. "He says it definitely wasn't one of his guys. And he can hold off staff coming in here until three, when the rehearsal starts. And as soon as we leave the chapel, he'll lock it back up."

"Someone really doesn't want this wedding to happen." She thought of Gary talking to them in the restaurant. Had he been making sure they didn't notice their work being torn down? Or was he truly worried about her getting through the wedding alive? At least this attack just set them back. It hadn't stopped the wedding. But it was meant as a warning. She was giving them an out. *Leave before someone gets hurt* had been the message.

Mia didn't negotiate with terrorists.

CHAPTER 18

Somehow they got the room back into shape for the rehearsal dinner even with sending Levi to get the cake at two. Mia sent Christina out to get changed at two thirty. After she'd left, Levi and Abigail hurried into the hall with the groom's cake. And, after helping Abigail set in place the fake fire spell, Trent pulled her aside.

"Go get ready. We can finish up." He held up her notebook. "I've got this."

"Are you sure? I mean, I could wear this." She looked down at the now-dirty jeans and less-than-clean T-shirt and shook her head. "No, you're right. I need to look like I'm not off the street and crashing the event."

"I usually am right." He started to turn, but she grabbed the notebook.

"Let me just glance through this before I go. We still

need to set up the centerpieces. Thank the Goddess we hadn't gotten them out of their boxes yet." Mia looked around the room.

Trent turned back and took the notebook out of her hands. "I can read. Besides, in a few minutes James and his crew are going to be in here setting up for the dinner. We're done except for the centerpieces."

"And the hearts on the floor. You'd better do it before James comes in because he doesn't like glitter." She leaned over and kissed him. "I've got to run."

Christina was already in the room, putting on makeup, when Mia came in using her key. She whistled. "You look amazing. Good thing Levi's here to keep all the McMann boys in line."

"As long as Levi stays away from grabby hands Bethanie, we'll be fine. I know how to politely turn down another's interest in me. I was taught that skill by my mother. She felt it was a needed talent because she thought she'd be the one to pick my future husband by the size of his wallet." Christina finished the look with a swipe of lipstick. "Go get changed. I'll fix your hair really quick."

Mia pulled out her pantsuit and silver tank from the garment bag. She clipped her hair into a bun and stripped. "I'm going to run through the shower to get this sweat off me. I'll be right out."

"That will make your hair even curlier. That's a great idea." Christina put on earrings to match her dress.

As Mia showered and changed, she ran through everything still on her to-do list. Like helping the couple run through the ceremony. And keeping an eye out for whoever was trying to cancel Amethyst and Tok's special day.

She adjusted her jacket and slipped on a silver pendant her grandmother had given her for good luck. Mia figured it probably had a protection spell on the stone, and right now she appreciated her grandmother's foresight. She leaned into the mirror and applied her makeup. "Maybe my hair is fine. It's away from my face and out of the way of any food service."

"Don't be silly, it's a wedding. You need to look romantic too. Just in case Trent gets any ideas tonight." Christina's eyes flashed. "Just sit down on the bed. It won't take long."

True to her word, a few minutes later Christina led Mia to a mirror after asking her to close her eyes. When she opened them her hair made her look like a Grecian goddess. It even had tendrils hanging down. She looked beautiful. A word she didn't use about herself often. She hugged Christina. "Thanks. This is perfect."

"It softens the look of the suit. So you can be professional and sexy at the same time." Christina grinned.

Mia had to admit it the girl had talents. "It's almost three and I have to stop at the dining hall to get the key from Trent. Are you coming with me?"

"Sure. I don't think I can glam up any more than what I've done." Christina fluffed her now strawberry-blond hair.

"You don't need to either." Mia grabbed her tote, which had all sorts of things to get her through the next two days. Like a pair of scissors. And a roll of breath mints. "Let's get going. Someone needs to practice their wedding march."

"Too soon. Don't even say things like that. You'll jinx it." Christina covered her eyes three times.

"Superstitious much?" Mia held the door open for her.

Christina headed out into the hallway. "You don't understand. I've had my safe, human world and ideas blown away and now I'm sharing my life with people I read about in fairy tales. No offense."

"None taken. Unless you're saying I'm the witch out of 'Hansel and Gretel.'" Mia pulled on the door to make sure it locked. No use giving someone easy access.

"You do cook a lot." Christina pondered, tapping a finger against her lips. "And I've gained five pounds since I moved in."

"After losing ten or more when you lived in Vegas." Mia hurried to catch up with her. Then she folded her arm inside Christina's and they walked side by side. "Besides, it's not me you need to worry about. I'm about as harmless as they come. Now Levi and Trent, they're scary."

They were laughing when they came into the dining room. The lights had been turned down and fairy lights twinkled around the room. Mia nodded as she took in the full effect. "This is perfect."

"Are you doing this for the reception too?" Christina stared up at the ceiling. "It looks like a starry night."

"Then my plan worked. Yes, the reception will also have this lighting treatment. But on a bigger scale." She glanced around the room, watching the serving staff setting up the tables with china and silver. "Where are the guys?"

Christina pointed over to the corner, where they were stacking tubs and boxes. "Over there. It looks like they're getting ready to load the truck with the extra stuff."

"Let's get the key and then you can go ahead and unlock the room." Mia strolled across the room to where the three Majors stood talking. She reached Trent first. "Hey, I need the key to the chapel. This looks amazing. You did awesome."

He took out a key and handed it to her. "*You* did awesome. Levi and I will get these boxes out of here, then Levi's taking Mom home. I'll be in the lobby, waiting."

"You can come to the dinner if you want." Mia smiled at him. "I know the hostess. We can fit you in."

"That's okay. I've got stew warming at the school. We can eat when we get done here. I'd rather eat with you than eat while I watch you take care of everything else."

Christina glanced at her watch. "Do I need to come back with you guys?"

"You can. Or I can send Levi back to the Lodge to wait for you in the lobby. Do you think they'll be some bridal party after-hours action?" Trent winked at Mia.

Christina nodded. "I'm afraid so. I don't feel like I'm part of the group, but I don't want to offend Amethyst, she's been so nice. And you know I can't trust Bethanie to get a ride."

"No problem, kitten. I'll bring a book back and sit in the lobby reading until you're tired of the party." Levi took her hands. "You know I'm here for you. And wow, do you look amazing. Did I already say that?"

"No, you didn't. And thanks." She kissed him on the cheek and took the key. "Thanks for the ride home too. I really need to get me a car."

"Even if you had a car, you couldn't drive after hanging out with the bridal party. Those girls like their shots." Levi made a shooting motion with his hand.

"Another difference. I'm having one beer. Even though I'm part of the bridal party, I'm still working to-morrow." She hurried out of the dining hall.

"She's a good kid," Trent murmured for Mia's ears only.

She nodded and stepped closer to Abigail. "Thank you so much for all your help. Is the wedding cake done?"

"Yes, and I'll come over in the morning to help you transport it over and set it up." Abigail put her arm around Trent. "Your grandmother is still working on the tracking spell, but she feels like it's close. We ran it once, but it didn't get out of Magic Springs. Which could be right, but she wants to double-check some calculations before she gives you a better answer."

"She thinks the owner is still in town?" Mia had won-dered if the book hadn't belonged to Silas Miller, but he'd left town days ago. After telling her it wasn't safe here in Magic Springs.

"Maybe. Like I said, it was a preliminary report. She'll know more tonight, when you get back to the house." Abigail checked her watch. "Boys, your dad is going to be home in three hours and I don't have anything cooking yet."

"Hold on, Mom. Let us get these boxes out." Levi took an armful and moved toward the doorway. Abigail fol-lowed with an armful of her own.

"See you later, then." Trent kissed her on the cheek and grinned. "You are a knockout tonight."

Mia left the dining hall and noticed a security guard standing near the entrance. He nodded at her as she left. James was taking this threat seriously, then. The guy had to be a bouncer somewhere. He was dressed in black with the Lodge logo on his chest. She paused, but he smiled.

"Now don't you worry, miss. No one's going to mess up your work here. Not while I'm watching out for it. I've been hired for the weekend. You can relax." He nodded again and crossed his arms.

"I'll have to thank James for the help." The guard didn't say anything. Apparently, the conversation was over, so Mia hurried to the chapel until she ran into a group of the McManns heading that way as well. She fell in step with the matriarch. "Mrs. McMann, you look lovely."

"Thank you, my dear. It's not often your son mates with the love of his life, now is it? I hope I only have to do this once per child." She took in Mia's pantsuit. "You look perfect. Professional yet approachable."

That hadn't been what Christina had said, but Mia smiled anyway. "Thanks. I guess we'd better get this party started."

When she walked into the chapel, she was immediately surrounded by Amethyst and her bridesmaids, including Christina.

"I told you she was right behind me." Christina took Mia's arm. "Amethyst wants to tell you something."

"Okay," Mia tried not to flinch. What did the bride want now, at the last minute? Were there even any all-night bridal stores where Mia could find a different color tulle or beaded flowers? This was something she needed to know as a wedding planner. A plan B outlet. "What can I do for you?"

"Nothing. Absolutely nothing. I know you had to step in when Daddy fired Chelsea, and even though you didn't have much time, you made this room look like the wedding of my dreams. Chelsea kept telling me why I couldn't do something. All you did was make it happen. Thank you. Thank you." Then Amethyst pulled Mia into a hug and started crying.

"Oh, my, you are so welcome. I'm glad you like it." She waved at Christina to get her some tissues. "But you don't want to cry. You're going to mess up your makeup. No one wants racoon eyes for the random pictures you know everyone is going to be taking of you and Tok."

Christina pressed tissues into Mia's hand and she gently patted the bride's face with them. "I just did what I was hired to do. And besides, the wedding isn't over. Let's not jinx it."

Amethyst's face went into shock. Then she swallowed and took a deep breath. "Oh, the Goddess, you're right. Practice gratitude without expectations. Love without exception. Generosity for all."

Christina glanced at Mia, who shrugged. She assumed it was a family mantra, but it wasn't anything Grans had taught her.

"I think it's time to get the wedding rehearsal started. You want everything to be perfect tomorrow, right?" Mia squeezed Amethyst's hand.

"Not perfect but special." She squeezed back.

Mia really needed to do more studying on the coven rules and regulations. Especially if she was going to continue planning special weddings.

Gary came up and put his arm around Amethyst. "My brother is wondering where his bride is."

"You tell Tok I'll be there when I get there. We need to

practice the wedding." Amethyst shook her head. "He's already trying to get me to be at his beck and call. There's no way I'm going to be a version of his mom. That woman gave up her life for her husband and kids. I'm still going to practice law, which means long nights at work and lots of takeout food."

Gary grinned at his soon-to-be sister-in-law. "Which only means Tok will be hanging out at Mom's and Pop's place more to eat. You might want to rethink your strategy."

"Don't you worry about your brother and me. We'll be just fine. Now go find out where the minister is." Amethyst pointed toward the front.

"Someone was supposed to pick him up at the airport thirty minutes ago." Gary glanced at his watch and hurried out the door to the front desk.

Mia groaned and grabbed for her phone. "Let me check to see if the limo has picked him up yet."

Amethyst put a hand on the phone, shaking her head. "He's already arrived and is upstairs in his room. He told Dad he needed ten minutes to center himself and get ready. I just wanted to get Gary out of here. I've noticed he's been a little close this last week. Trent's a patient man, but Gary can be a little forward."

"It's fine. Trent knows everything." Mia blushed as she put the phone back in her pocket. "I don't keep secrets from him."

"Gary can be pushy. And he thinks he's all that. He was sniffing after Chelsea all last week. Of course, when she turned him down, he pretended like he hadn't even been interested." Amethyst leaned forward. "Between you and me? Tok says Gary has impulse issues. Always has. He's always watching out for his baby brother when they go out drinking. If Gary sees a woman he likes, he thinks he's Cupid or some other god of love. I've seen the way he looks at you. Like you're dinner and he hasn't eaten for a week."

"Well, one more day and I'll be back in my school and he'll be back north, right?" Mia reached out and adjusted Amethyst's jacket. "You look lovely."

The speed at which Amethyst grabbed Mia's hand and squeezed surprised her. "Listen to me. I'm afraid if Gary was the one who killed Chelsea, he might kill again to get you. Please be careful."

And after dropping that bombshell, Amethyst went hurrying back to where her parents stood chatting with the McManns. Mia was left standing alone, watching. Christina came up and put a hand on her arm.

"Are you all right? You look like you've seen a ghost."

Mia took one last look at Amethyst, took out her clipboard, and tucked her tote under a table. "Let's run through our list while we're waiting on the minister." Mia talked through the ceremony and the things that wouldn't arrive until tomorrow. Like the bouquets and boutonnieres. She made a note to call and leave the florist a reminder message as soon as this was over.

"I'm glad you're the one checking off the last-minute issues." James came into the room and glanced around. "This is cray-cray. How did you get everything set after the disaster in the dining hall? Is everything okay?"

"Of course. And thank you for hiring security for the event. I can't believe it's necessary, but at least I can sleep tonight knowing this room won't be torn apart while my eyes are closed. Literally." She watched the minister walk into the room.

"Mia, I didn't hire security. What are you talking about?"

Mia's eyes widened and she took off for the other room. The man was still standing there, arms crossed, keeping bad guys out of the hall. Or at least that was what she thought he was doing. Maybe someone was in there right now, tearing up the room. "Who are you and who hired you?"

CHAPTER 19

The man in black didn't move, just stared down at her. "I told you, I'm here to protect the wedding. That's all you need to know."

"No, you said James hired you." She paused, thinking about the conversation. "Wait, I said James first."

He lifted an eyebrow and nodded.

"But you're not going to tell me who hired you." Mia looked at James, who had now caught up with her.

He shrugged. "Don't look at me. All I know is I didn't hire you security. Although after that incident in the dining hall, I don't think it's a bad idea."

Mia opened the door and peeked into the room. It was still set up and the food was starting to be set up for the dinner. Her heart rate slowed a few beats and she thanked the Goddess that nothing had gone wrong.

"When you are in this room I'll move to the wedding

chapel room. Then, tonight, there will be two of us to keep both rooms from being vandalized." The man smiled, and if that was supposed to make her feel better, it didn't work.

"Okay, thank you." She glanced at her watch. "I need to get back to the rehearsal. The minister should be there."

James walked with her to the other room. "Do you want me to find out who hired him? I have some contacts in the security world."

"No, it was probably one of the families. They both seem to be on board with the wedding, but maybe one of them is just acting. Which could put the other family on edge. Either way, he seems like a good deterrent." Mia paused at the door. "Thanks for your help on this. I didn't want to be such a pain my first wedding planner job."

"You aren't any trouble at all. Now your families? That's another story. That Gary is a piece of work. And I hear there's a cousin that's a little high maintenance too. Hopefully, she just won't show up." He squeezed her arm. "Now go get this done so you can get out of here. Are you staying for the dinner?"

"For the beginning, then Trent's taking me home as soon as Levi comes back to watch out for Christina. Probably overkill, but at least I'll feel comfortable." She paused at the door, looking back the way they'd come. "Which is probably why someone hired Bruiser back there."

Mia went into the room and, as she'd been told, the minister had arrived. But everyone was still in their cliques and the practice hadn't even started. *Of course not, I'm in charge here*, Mia reminded herself. Which was a scary thought because she didn't feel in control at all.

She went to the front of the room and stood by the minister. "Okay, people, we've got dinner waiting for us, so let's get this show on the road. Bride and party, to the back. Mom and Dad's to the back. Groom and groomsmen to the front over here. Everyone else, split up and pretend that the ushers have just set you on the appropriate side." She pointed to a teenage boy. "You, are you part of the wedding?"

His eyes widened and he squeaked out a sharp, "No."

"Great, because today you're an usher." She pointed to the back of the room. "Go stand by the parents."

"My parents? They're sitting over here." He pointed to the groom's side.

Mia smiled and gentled her tone. "Nope. The bride and groom's parents, not your parents. Remember, you're an usher today. And that's not just a singer."

He blushed and hurried back to stand by the McManns.

"Okay, then, Tok, you stand here, waiting for Amethyst. Who's your best man?"

He pulled Gary to his side. "This guy right here."

"Great." Mia tried to keep a straight face. "Gary, do you have the rings?"

He shook his head. "No, they're in my room. Should I go get them?"

"No, we'll play pretend tonight, but tomorrow you're in charge of the rings. And I'm going to check on you to make sure you have them long before the ceremony starts." She made a note on her list. "Then who's your favorite brother or friend after that?"

The crowd watching chuckled as Tok put the other two in order.

"Okay, all three of you, head to the back. You'll walk

up with the bridesmaids in reverse order. Gary and Bethanie will be last." She called back to Amethyst. "Who's
the first bridesmaid to come up? Christina?"

Amethyst gave her a thumbs-up. "We didn't bring the
flower girl tonight. She's with a babysitter in a room upstairs. Should we go get her?"

"Nope, let her be. Besides, they're fun when they just
wing it." Mia made a note to chat with the flower girl first
thing before the wedding and she could have her practice
then. "Usher? Bring up the McManns."

Mia waited as the teenager handed his arm to Marilyn
McMann and Brody followed. The teenager winked at
her as he moved them to their seats. "Now the bride's
mother."

As soon as Cassandra had been seated, Mia grabbed
her phone and hit a key. The couple had chosen an oldie
for the procession, "Cherish." She turned up the music.
"Okay, music on. First up is flower girl."

A girl sitting on the bride's side ran to the back and
pretended to be the flower girl. Another chuckle from the
audience as she threw imaginary petals with a bit of
magic sparkle as she strolled down the aisle. Mia nodded
to a place next to the pew on the bride's side.

"First couple, Christina and least favorite brother."
Mia smiled as Christina passed her and took her place by
the fake flower girl. "And next."

The next two couples made their way up, and then she
changed the music to the wedding march. "Everyone,
please stand. Dad, bring your daughter down the aisle."

As Drunder and Amethyst walked to the front, Mia
heard a small sob from her left. She reached into her tote
and handed one of the packets of tissues she'd packed
just for this moment. Cassandra took the packet and nod-

ded. When they got up to the front Mia stepped behind Drunder. Then she turned off the music. "Okay, now the minister takes over."

The large man smiled at her. "Thank you for your exceptionally well-run practice. Drunder, I will ask you the question and your response should be, 'Her mother and I.' Do you think you can remember that?"

"Yes, Horace. I'm not senile," Drunder grumbled.

"You are giving up your only daughter." He smiled at Tok. "That can make a man a little emotional. You'll find out when it's your turn. Anyway, I ask, Drunder answers, then you step down and take her hand from her father. Then all eyes are on me."

The minister went through the rest of the service, pretty standard fare, until they finished the vows. Then he looked out to the families. "'As Amethyst and Tok have pledged their lives together, so also are their families joined. You will share in not only their love, but in their successes and their failures. The fragile bond of marriage is made stronger when both families and the community around them pledge to support the union. I ask you, will you be faithful and kind in your dealings with this new life, their marriage, and support it fully? If so, please say yes.'"

The few family members and friends there joined in with the pledge.

Smiling, the minister nodded. "Then I pronounce you blah and blah and you don't get to kiss the bride until tomorrow when you seal your contract."

Mia stepped in. "Okay, after the kiss and the round of applause from the audience, you turn and walk down the aisle. Greeting others is fine, but save the chatting and kissing until you get to the reception. You're going to have people behind you that are waiting to leave."

As the bridal party made their way out, Mia nodded toward the rehearsal dinner hall. "Go ahead and go into the next room. We'll set up a reception line tomorrow, but for now you can just go find your table. I'm sure you're all starving."

She waited for the room to clear before she picked up her tote.

"You did a good job with this wedding. Especially with its challenges. Do you have cards? I am often asked if I know anyone who can deal with special circumstances." The minister, Horace, stood next to her, his book in his hand.

"I have my catering cards, but this is my first wedding planner gig. I was brought in unexpectedly." She dug in her tote and handed him three. "I'll send you new ones if you give me your card."

He tucked the cards in his notebook, then pulled out one of his own to trade. "I'm serious. With all the issues that surrounded this marriage, a lesser planner might not have been able to keep up with the, well, family differences."

She nodded to the door. "Are you eating with us?"

"Of course. I never turn down a free meal. Do you want to sit at my table?" He fell in step with her as they walked out of the room.

"Actually, I'm making sure everything's fine, then heading home. Tomorrow's going to be a long day. And this is a family party anyway." She leaned closer. "Be sure to try the groom's cake. It's amazing."

"I will do that. Again, thank you for your work here. Herding this group is above and beyond." He paused at the door. "I will see you tomorrow, Miss Malone."

Mia glanced around the room, making sure no one had

left any personal items behind. When she didn't see anything she pulled the door closed and locked it with the key James had provided.

The security guard now stood near the locked door. "Have a good evening."

"You too." She glanced back at the room where the dinner was happening. "Do you want something? I could make you a plate."

"I'm fine. Don't worry." He smiled again, and this time Mia saw the humor behind the eyes. "Go have fun."

"Actually, I'm seeing it off, then I'm out of here. I've got things to do and people to see." Mia tucked her tote under her arm and started walking.

"Probably for the best. Especially if you've never been to a coven wedding before. They can get a little wild. Then add in the McManns? It's going to be crazy here until they leave Sunday morning."

"I guess it's good you're around, then." The security guard was wise to the Magic Springs secrets. She waved and headed over to the rehearsal dinner and made sure everything was set up. She had a glass of wine in her hand as she watched from the doorway.

Christina saw her standing there and waved, then excused herself from the table and hurried over. "Are you ready to go? I should leave with you."

"No, you should finish your dinner and spend some time with your new friends. Levi will be waiting in the lobby for you. He and Trent aren't here yet anyway, so I'm just watching. I've already grabbed everything from the hotel room, so don't worry about that when you're ready to come home. I'll put your stuff on your bed." She glanced around the gathering. "Everyone seems to be having a good time."

"You were a hit with the group. Everyone is talking about how nice you are, and yet you got everything run through without a hitch. I think this wedding planner gig is going to work out for you."

"We'll see." She nodded to the table. "They're serving the main course. Go eat. I'm fine."

"Okay, but if you need me, you know I'm here for you." Christina squeezed her hand. "This wedding has me feeling all the feels, you know?"

Mia laughed. "Yes, I do. And now that it's probably going to happen, I'm starting to get into the fun too. First, I'm going to enjoy my bath tonight. My feet are killing me."

She didn't have to wait long before Trent found her at the door. "Everything okay? Are you ready?"

"You don't know how ready." She moved toward the coat closet and grabbed the garment bags, which Trent took from her. "Where's Levi?"

"Sitting in the lobby, reading. He brought his car so he doesn't have to leave Christina alone while he drops us off. He's a little nervous."

"Someone hired security for the event. And it wasn't James." She leaned on his shoulder as they walked. "I'm so tired of worrying about the next shoe to drop. Tomorrow I'm going to crash hard."

"Tomorrow you'll be enjoying yourself with a room service meal after having a massage and whatever spa stuff you girls pick out," Trent reminded her.

Mia groaned. "I forgot. I guess it will just have to do."

"You sound like I'm torturing you." He waved at Levi as they passed by. "Seriously? You don't see it as a treat?"

"I will tomorrow. Especially during the massage. Right

now, it's just one more thing on my list to do. Relaxing is hard work." Mia went through the front doors and didn't wait for Trent to open the truck door for her.

When he climbed in the other side and started the truck he glanced over at her. "If relaxing is hard work, you're doing it wrong."

After dinner she went downstairs to fill tomorrow's tote bag with the essentials she thought she'd need, including the wedding book. When she was happy with what she'd packed and couldn't think of anything else she might need, she left it on the desk and locked the office. Then she unlocked the kitchen and stepped in to check on the cake.

She turned the lights on and the cake twinkled into view. It was beautiful. Whatever Abigail invoiced her, she was going to add 10 percent just for the craftmanship. Hopefully, she'd continue to do wedding cakes for her if Mia continued to do wedding planning. She reached out to touch the bride's dress but pulled back just before reaching it. If she dented it or messed anything up, she'd never forgive herself.

"It's lovely, isn't it?" a woman's voice asked from behind her.

When Mia turned she saw Dorothy Purcell hovering by the laundry area. "Dorothy, I didn't think I'd see you again. Weren't you going to cross over to be with Harry?"

"Harry isn't there so I came back." She came closer to the cake. "We had a very small wedding at the courthouse. No reception, no cake. My mother didn't approve of our union. She knew Harry was a witch and thought I could do better. Of course she was right, but not because of his small talent as a witch. Harry just never was a good husband."

"Sorry about that. It's nice to see you, no matter what the reason." Mia meant what she said. She liked the elderly ghost, even if she had, in the past, pushed Mia to do something that was impossible. "I'm a wedding planner too, now. What do you think about that?"

"I think people put too much emphasis on the wedding. Why spend thousands of dollars on the first day of your marriage when that money could go to a house or your future? I guess I'm just too practical for these fancy things." She turned back to the cake. "But Abigail did a lovely job on the cake. That I approve of."

"Yes, she did." Mia saw the sadness in the ghost's face. "Dorothy? Are you all right?"

"Just thinking, dear. I spent so much time getting back at Mr. Simpson all those years, I wonder if I missed my chance at true love." She turned to Mia. "What about you? You're getting older. Are you thinking about marriage? Maybe with Abigail's son?"

"I'm not that old. And I'm not thinking of marriage. Not right now. I have a business to get going." Mia felt her cheeks heat up. Sometimes ghosts could ask the most intrusive questions. It was all about the time they spent watching, Mia thought. "Anyway, I hear my bathtub calling my name. Will I see you again?"

"Most likely. I enjoy coming to visit. Of course, the older residents of the nursing home are good company too because they can see me without much trouble." She started to fade. "Young children have the gift too, but who wants to spend time with a group of five-year-olds? Not me."

The door to the kitchen opened and Trent walked in. He stopped just inside the door when he saw Dorothy disappearing from the room. When she was gone he turned to Mia. "Sorry, did I interrupt something?"

"No. Dorothy and I were just admiring your mom's cake. She did an amazing job." Mia crossed the room and double-checked the lock on the outside door. Then she walked toward Trent and turned off the lights.

"I thought she was gone. That she'd dealt with her unfinished business." Trent followed her out to the lobby and watched her lock the kitchen again.

"I think she found the other side boring. She likes being here, chatting with whoever will talk to her."

"As long as it's not five-year-olds," he repeated.

Mia put her arm in his. "Yeah, so you heard that. I don't blame her. Being around a bunch of kids is chaotic. Maybe Dorothy wants a quiet, thoughtful conversation."

"You're telling me that to get rid of your resident ghost, you're going to have to marry me and have a passel of kids?" He put his hand on his chin, thinking it through. "I guess I can take one for the team in that case."

"I didn't say that." Mia slugged him playfully.

He put his arm around her waist and they walked upstairs. "Yeah, but you didn't say no either."

"I'll be glad when tomorrow's over." Mia leaned her head into his shoulder. "Everyone has wedding fever."

CHAPTER 20

Saturday morning as Mia sipped her coffee while checking out the window for rain clouds, the day looked perfect. Like someone had ordered a mild spring day with blue skies and fluffy white clouds and temps in the mid-seventies from Mother Nature. Of course, with the families who were putting on the wedding festivities, someone might have called in a few favors with the Goddess. She felt Trent's presence in the kitchen before she turned around. "Good morning. Did Christina and Levi get in at a reasonable time last night? Wow, I sound like her mother."

"No, you sound like a boss who has a big day today and wants everything, even the things she can't control, to go her way." He wrapped his arms around her and kissed her neck. "Good morning, sunshine. I won't say I hope you slept well because there's something baking in the oven. Did you get any sleep?"

She leaned into him. He knew her too well. "Yes. After soaking in that tub I went straight to sleep, and I think I soaked out the aches in my feet. I need to order good shoes again. I had them when I did a lot of catering at the Boise hotel. They make a huge difference when you're on your feet for hours. Anyway, I got up at five. Which is almost sleeping in for an event day."

"I'm impressed." He glanced at his watch. "What time do we have to be at the Lodge? I want to run home to grab clean clothes and check on things at the store."

"I'd like to be there by nine. If you're busy, I can ride with Christina and Levi or drive myself." She went to the oven and turned on the light. "This should be ready in about fifteen minutes if you want to eat first."

"I'll have some coffee and eat before I leave. I'll go home tomorrow after we have our evening at the Lodge. Unless you want me to stay until Baldwin finds out who killed Chelsea. I'll have to work Monday, but I can stay the night."

"I'm not sure I'm going to need a bodyguard after the wedding. If Chelsea was killed to keep the wedding from happening, once it's over, I should be safe." Mia shivered as she talked about this person who was going to extreme measures to keep the wedding from happening. "I can't believe I'm talking about this so calmly. It's messed up."

"Did your grandmother trace down the owner of the grimoire yet?" Trent poured a cup of coffee for himself and refilled Mia's cup.

"Not yet. She did say that the owner is actually here in Magic Springs, so that limits the suspect pool from the entire world to residents, visitors, wedding guests, and anyone from the coven." She sat down and sipped her coffee. "And that's another fact I can't tell Baldwin without him discounting the information."

"He's just not a believer. If it doesn't fit into his well-ordered knowledge about life, he can't see it for anything but fiction. But he means well. And he wants to find Chelsea's killer. He just thinks it's a regular human. And there's a chance it is."

"Not anymore. Before we found and I was poisoned by the grimoire? Yes, there was a chance. Now it's definitely someone attached to the coven or a renegade witch." She lowered her voice. "I'd like to believe it's Bethanie and hopefully get her out of Christina's life, but that's just wishful thinking. I don't think she has the evil inside to be able to actually kill someone. Take their boyfriend, spend their money, use their friendship, yes, she could do all that because it benefits her. Killing someone is just a step too far."

The buzzer went off and Christina came into the kitchen, with Levi following close behind. "What's up, my simpatico friends? Are we ready for a kick-butt wedding?"

Trent shook his head. "That's a stretch, isn't it?"

"What, kick butt or simpatico?" Christina filled a cup of coffee and handed it to Levi.

Levi laughed. "Probably both. My brother likes his mornings a little quieter. He's not a night owl; you'd think he'd be brighter in the morning."

"Maybe I'm a nooner." Trent blushed. "I mean, I'm sharper midday."

"You said it, dude, own it." Levi sat at the table. "Who's going to get Mom?"

"You are. Christina and Mia will be here, getting ready. I'm running to my place and then the store and I'll be back just before nine."

The buzzer went off on the oven. "But first we're eating. We may not have time to eat again until dinner, but I'll try to get the guys a plate at the reception dinner. Christina, you'll eat with the wedding party."

"Sounds good. Except Cliff, the guy I'm walking with, keeps talking to me about relationships. I guess he's having issues with this girlfriend and how to still have a life with his buddies." Christina glanced over at Levi. "I'm glad we're not a drama couple."

"Right now, you mean." Levi corrected her, and Christina blushed.

"That was totally not my fault." She turned to Mia and changed the subject. "So, what's on your schedule today? I'm going straight to Amethyst's suite so I can get all glammed up. Wait till you see what they're doing to the dresses as we come down the aisle. This is the one time I wish I could have a magic wedding."

"You can if you marry someone who is part of the coven. Let me see, maybe we know someone like that." Levi rolled his eyes.

"Dude, that's not even close to a proposal. Besides, I'm not getting married until my career is established. Which means two more years of school and then I have to find an actual job. One that doesn't involve me working for my brother. Sorry, Mia, I know you enjoyed being the head of catering at the Owyhee, but I just can't work for Isaac. It would destroy my spirit."

"There are lots of jobs out there for someone with your skills. You don't have to work for Isaac." Mia dished up the strata and handed out plates. Or me, she thought, as she gave Christina her breakfast. "Anyway, it's too early to be talking the future. Let's just get through today. My job today, to answer your question, is to make sure nothing gets dropped. So I'll be in the suite with you making sure everyone's happy. Then checking on the venue, and the catering, and, I guess now, the security guys. And marking stuff off on my list as it gets done. Like when Abigail delivers the cake and we get that set up. By the end of the day my list should be all marked off and I'll be done."

"I'll check us into our suite and take everyone's overnight case up with me before the reception is over. That way, if you want to change or just relax for a few minutes, you'll have a place." Trent held up a fork of the strata. "This is so good."

"Sausage, peppers, onions, and a few tomatoes I had in the fridge. Oh, and sourdough bread that had gone stale." Mia recited the ingredients, then saw Trent's frown. He'd been trying to get her to just say *thank you* when she got a compliment instead of excusing it away or giving out a list of ingredients if it was a dish. She smiled his way. "Thank you."

"Better." He focused on his plate. "Anything else we need to do to make today easier on you?"

"Not that I can think of, but stay close and keep your phones on. I don't expect to be sending you out to pick up anything, but you never know." Mia finally took a bite of her breakfast, then another. It was good. And she was hungry. Which was good for the morning of an event. Maybe because she wasn't cooking, this event would feel better. Typically, on catering days, she always felt sick to her stomach with worry. Here, she was worried, but it felt different. She wasn't sure why.

After everyone had left to get on with their day and she was cleaning up the kitchen, the doorbell rang. "What did Trent forget this time?" Mia wondered aloud to Mr. Darcy, who was sitting on the window seat, looking for birds in the trees. She didn't bother checking the monitor, just wiped her hands with a towel and hurried downstairs.

When she opened the door she was surprised to see Grans standing there, a black tote in her hand and her witching hat on her head. Muffy, her dog, was on a leash beside her. Her hat didn't look like a witch's hat. It reminded Mia of the hats Jackie Kennedy used to wear—pillbox or something like that? Anyway, Grans wore it every time she spelled. According to her, it made her spells focus better by keeping her thoughts in her mind. Mia just thought she liked the way it looked. "Grans, what are you doing here this morning. I've going to the Lodge in a couple of hours and won't be home until tomorrow."

"I know that, dear. I told you I was staying close until the wedding was over. I just needed last night to get everything packed." Grans dropped her keys in Mia's hand and pointed to the car. "Go get my overnight case. And Muffy's too. Then lock the car back up. I'd hate to have someone steal it."

"I don't think there are random car theft rings in Magic Springs, Grans." But Mia did what she was told. Grans was still waiting in the lobby when she came back in with the rest of the luggage. "Are you staying for a while? You've got enough stuff packed in your car for the next three months."

"I know, it was strange. Every time I thought I was packed, I remembered a few more things I felt compelled to bring with me. I'm probably going to need some stuff for the spell, but I think I overdid it with the books. I must have packed most of my library, and I even brought over the two boxes of Adele's stuff I still need to go through. Maybe you can bring those in too, and set them upstairs in the apartment. I'll work on that tonight while you're gone."

"Okay." Mia never argued with her grandmother, but this was troublesome. She wondered if something was going on. "I'll take the overnight bags upstairs and put them in your room. Trent's picking me up around nine."

"Good. That gives me enough time to finish your talisman. I don't want you going into the wedding unprotected. And if I cast this spell right, it should warn you when anyone with bad intentions toward you comes close. I wanted to match it up with the grimoire, but the book was being stubborn and wouldn't let me attach to it." She set down both bags in the work area Mia had set up in the back of the lobby. It was there to allow them to put together baskets and marketing packets, but the long, clear table was also a great place to work a spell. As her grandmother had found out a few months ago.

One of the bags shot to the end of the table and stopped, right by the edge. Mia ran over to catch it, but the bag stopped on its own. "What was that?"

"The grimoire you found. Now that it's not covered with a poison spell, it's been active and a little hard to deal with. I thought about leaving it at the house, but I'm afraid it might tear the place up. The book really wants to be returned to its owner." Grans started taking out items from her bag and setting them on the table, including her own book of spells.

"Well, I'd love to do that because it would also tell us who the murderer is, but the book won't give up its owner. It's like it knows why we want to return it." Mia studied the items on the desk. "You already made me a protection spell."

"All I need is your amulet. I just need to up the protection spell and add the alarm so you'll know when to be careful."

"I'll be in a room with five hundred people. How will it know when I'm close to the killer?"

"Good point. I need to put a closer range on the spell. I can't have it going off during the ceremony. That would be embarrassing." Grans waved Mia away. "Go bring in my luggage. And don't forget the boxes. I need to have something to do tonight while I'm hanging out here."

Mia eyed Muffy, who covered his face with his hands. The dog had already taken up his spot on the couch, where he could watch Grans but be far enough away from the spell casting to be safe. Mia guessed he'd learned that lesson from what happened to Mr. Darcy. If animals talked to one another, that is. "I'll be upstairs if you need me. You can call on the house phone."

"I know how to reach you," Grans muttered. "Goddess knows you're pushing my buttons today. What, do you think I'm senile?"

Why? Because it appeared you packed your entire house into your car and showed up here to stay the night?

Why would that be odd? Mia had so many answers to Grans's question, but she didn't want to get into an argument. "I'll talk to you later, then."

Mia got her grandmother's stuff settled, then pulled out her clipboard to make one final checklist for the wedding. She went through all her notebook pages and found all the reminders she needed to check on before the ceremony. If she continued this wedding planner gig, she needed to automate the process somehow. She'd write up an Excel spreadsheet on all the tasks and to-do lists to see if she could make up a project management system to make the event planning even smoother. She'd catered large events before, feeding over a thousand people in a few hours, and planning a wedding was like that, but with a longer lead time and a lot more people involved in the planning process.

She'd just finished the list for today when Trent came into the kitchen. He went to the fridge and grabbed a soda. "I didn't know your grandmother was coming over. She and Mom are talking while Mom gets the cake ready to transport. We'll need to use your van. Do you want to come over now, or should I come back for you?"

"I don't know. I'm waiting for Grans to finish casting a protection spell." Mia tucked everything into her tote and nodded to the overnight bag in the living room. "My bag's over there and Christina should have her bag ready now. She needs to get over to the Lodge soon."

"Levi's ready to take her if we need to make two runs." Trent pulled her close and kissed her. "Stop worrying. Everything is going to be perfect today. Tok and Amethyst are going to have a magical wedding, thanks to you."

"I just hope whoever the murderer is has abandoned their plan to stop the wedding. I can't take any more surprises." She picked up Mr. Darcy and gave him a kiss. "Be good for Grans tonight and I'll see you in the morning."

He struggled out of her grasp, jumping to the floor and running to the window seat, where he turned his back to ignore her.

"You too, Dorian," she added a greeting to the spirit that lived in her cat's body. As they walked out to the apartment door, she glanced over at Christina, who was standing in the living room with her overnight case. "Are you ready for the big day?"

"Not my big day, it's Amethyst's, but yeah, I'm ready to do my part to make it perfect. She's so nice. I can't believe she's friends with Bethanie." Christina adjusted her tote on her shoulder.

"You're friends with Bethanie. Maybe Amethyst is thinking the same thing about you," Mia gently reminded her.

"Yeah, you're right. Bethanie reminds me of my high school friends. We were the popular, rich clique. Not one of them had a goal in life except to marry well and run a foundation. And by run, I mean set up charity events and have their assistant do the work. Amethyst's parents have money, but she seems more grounded. Did you know she passed the bar last year? She's going to join a law firm once they decide where they're going to live. Tok wants to build houses. They're so cute together." Christina chatted on about the soon-to-be married couple as they went downstairs.

Grans and Abigail were in the lobby, sitting on the

couch with coffee. Grans looked up as they came down-stairs. "Good morning. Don't you both look lovely today."

"I'm hoping the video we get of the wedding next week shows how amazing the dresses are. You think I look good now, just wait until I'm walking down the aisle." Christina twirled like she had the bridesmaid dress already on. "Usually dresses for the wedding party are horrid. I guess they want the bride to look amazing so the other girls look awful. But not Amethyst. She picked out dresses that are going to shine on everyone."

"I'm glad you're happy with being part of the event." Abigail shared a look with Grans. "I'm sure the bride appreciates you stepping in last minute."

"Oh, it's no bother at all. I'm having fun and meeting some other women my age. Of course, Bethanie swears they're all snobs, but I think they just don't like her. Which I can understand." Christina laughed. "Next week I'll be back working and finishing up this semester, but I've already made plans with Kelsey—that's Amethyst's other cousin—to go to lunch next weekend. She's thinking about going back to school next year and wanted to talk about options."

"That's nice, dear." Grans waved Mia over. "Come here and get your necklace. I've updated the protection spell and reactivated the tracking spell as well, so I'll be able to see if you leave the Lodge."

"Why would I leave the Lodge? I've got a wedding to plan." Mia took the crystal and slipped it over her head.

"Exactly. So if you leave of your own volition, just text me so I don't send Trent out looking for you. There's still someone out there who wants to stop this wedding. So keep your eyes open. I'm sure Tok and Amethyst's parents have done the same thing for them," Grans warned.

The necklace warmed on her skin making Mia shiver. This would be over one way or the other today. If the killer was going to stop the wedding, they only had a few hours to do it. If Chelsea had been killed for another reason, nothing bad would happen today. Mia hoped the latter was the truth, but the charms on her necklace gave her little comfort as she moved away from the safety of her home at the school and toward the Lodge, where anything could happen.

CHAPTER 21

The Lodge lobby was busy when they arrived. Trent had their suitcases for the evening activities, and he stopped at the front desk to see if they could check into their suite now. Mia would be headed to the reception-room-turned-chapel after she and Christina paused at the elevator to take her up to Amethyst's suite.

"The next time you see me, I'll be beautiful. Do me a favor and snap a pic of me on the way up to the aisle. I'm going to want to remember this." Christina hugged her and then bounced into the elevator when the doors opened.

A shiver went through Mia as she remembered her dream. Christina not being up at the altar with the wedding party. Of course, in the dream she'd been the one getting married to Trent, so maybe it was just all her jumbled-up thoughts that had caused the crazy dream.

Or residuals from the poisoned grimoire. She stared at the elevator doors and wondered if she should go up and warn Christina to be careful. But careful of what? She reached for the Up button.

"You're going the wrong way." James stood behind her and waved a hand toward the reception rooms. "I'm glad you're early. I want you to check out the sample plate I made for the reception dinner. I think I've outdone myself with the plating if I do say so myself."

Mia turned away from the elevator. She was letting a dream affect her decisions. Christina would be fine. "I'm sure it's beautiful, but I'd love to see it. From what I'm learning about wedding planning, you need to eat when you're offered food because you'll be too busy later."

"Isn't that the truth? My first catering gig I almost passed out after I realized I hadn't eaten in over twenty-four hours." James chatted as they made their way to the kitchen. "I bet you're glad to get this job over with. I hear you and your crew are staying over and celebrating being done with us tonight. Make sure they give you the up-grade at the spa. I'll spring for the champagne and appetizers in the spa room. Heck, I might even join you."

"That's thoughtful of you." Mia took a deep breath and pushed away her concerns. All she had to do was get her checklist done and everything would be ready for a beautiful wedding.

The next hour was filled with catering decisions, checking on the florist, and helping get the chapel ready for the event. Then she moved to the reception hall. As the security guard had promised, there were men stationed discreetly by both rooms. She recognized the one she'd talked with the day before. "How's it going?"

"All quiet last night. Anything wrong with the wedding event room?" He nodded toward the room she'd just left.

"Not that I could see. I appreciate you doing this."

"Ma'am, it's a job. I'm being paid, but thank you for the acknowledgment. A lot of times we are just part of the furniture at events like this. No one sees us unless something goes wrong; then we're needed or it's our fault that someone snuck in." He actually smiled at her. "I appreciate you as well."

"I guess the wedding planner gig is a lot like yours. Today I should be invisible unless I'm needed or something goes wrong." Mia glanced into the room, which looked fine. The catering staff was still setting up the tables. So she decided to check in with the bridal party to see if everything was okay upstairs. "I'll be back in a few minutes. If someone's looking for me, they can reach me on my cell."

"Sounds good. I'll be here, waiting." He chuckled at his joke.

Mia made it to the elevator without being stopped, which she took as a sign she was heading the right way. When she reached the suite the door was open, and women were crowded into the large living room.

Cassandra saw her and grabbed a mimosa from a tray on the bar. "Come in. I was wondering when I'd see you this morning."

"I was downstairs making sure everything is ready. The food for the dinner is divine. The roast beef and lobster, perfectly matched." Mia took the mimosa and took a small sip. She didn't want to be rude, but, on the other hand, being a drunk wedding planner was probably a bad idea as well.

"We're having a beauty party up here. All the girls are

getting their makeup and hair done. Their nails just need a touch-up. I'm sure we can fit you in as well if you're not too busy." Cassandra pointed out the stations where Bethanie, Christina, and Amethyst were sitting. The other bridesmaid was talking to Marilyn on the couch. Everyone had a mimosa in their hand or nearby. The chatter was happy and excited. Just like a prewedding group should be. "Not that you need it, you're a natural beauty."

Mia shook her head and sipped her drink. "That's okay. I was just checking in with you all. Now I have to see that the guys are awake. They are so lucky. All they have to do is get dressed and come downstairs."

"It's probably a good thing for you to make sure Tok's here at least. The boys went out last night and did some hunting, from what I was told." She nodded over to Marilyn. "Even Brody went along. I guess it's a McMann tradition on the night before a wedding. When she told me that last night when I saw her drinking alone in the bar, I was furious. But what are you going to do? Families have their own ways of celebrating."

"Sounds like I *should* check in with Tok. I'm sorry Marilyn was alone last night. That must be hard." Mia glanced over at the mother of the groom, who seemed to be doing more listening than talking.

"Don't worry, I invited her to join Drunder and me at our table. We had a nice chat about what happens after the wedding and ways we could merge the families a bit more. I think this detente is long overdue and time for old wounds to heal. Now if we can just get the coven to get their broomsticks out of their butts." Cassandra chuckled at her joke.

Mia wondered just how many mimosas Cassandra had drunk, but before she could ask a woman came up.

"Mrs. Uzzi, you're up for the nail salon." The beautician glanced at Mia, reaching out to touch her hair. "Oh, I didn't realize we had another guest. Do you want me to put you in the rotation? I'm sure we can fit you in and do something with this."

Mia glanced in the mirror; her hair looked fine. Normal even. Self-consciously, she reached up but caught her hand before she touched her hair. "No, I'm fine. I was just checking in on how things were going in here."

"Mia!" Amethyst walked over holding her mimosa with two fingers and holding up her nails to keep them from smudging. She had on a white robe with the word "bride" embroidered on the lapel. "Come get pretty with us. This is half the fun of the wedding."

"No time, I'm afraid. I've got things to check on to make sure the wedding goes smoothly. Just wanted to see if everything was fine in here." Mia waved at Christina, who was getting her hair done in an upsweep.

"We're having a massage therapist come in to do chair massages. I should have had her come first so we could have full body massages and not mess up our hair." Amethyst hugged her. "Come back for that, okay? You need to relax too."

"I've got a massage booked as soon as you get into your limo to go to the airport." Mia hugged the happy bride back. Maybe she did love wedding planning. All the crap you had to do to get to this day may just be worth it. "Anyway, I'm heading over to the guys' room. Anything you want me to tell Tok?"

"I love him so much. We're going to be the happiest couple in Idaho. No, in the world. Tell him that." She waved toward the makeup specialist who was trying to get her attention. "And if I haven't said it before, thank you for everything. I'm going to remember this day for the rest of my life."

Mia left the bride's suite hoping that Amethyst's memories would be positive and that she hadn't just jinxed the day. When she knocked on the men's suite the door opened and Gary smiled out at her.

"Well, if it isn't our wedding planner. What can we help you with today?"

"Just checking in to see if everything's all right." Mia heard the television on in the room. "Are you all decent? Can I come in for a minute?"

"We're all dressed, if that's what you mean." Gary opened the door and she saw Tok and the other grooms-men, as well as Mr. Uzzi and Mr. McMann, standing around the television. "Come on in. We're watching last year's Fiesta Bowl, where BSU was cheated out of winning."

"They're showing football in May?" Mia shook her head. She didn't want to know. "Whatever. Gary, do you have the rings?"

He pulled out a ring box from his jeans pocket. "Right now, yes. Ask me again once I get into the monkey suit. I don't want to forget them up here in my pants."

"I trust you won't forget." Mia moved toward the group just as a play on the television caused an uproar on the couch. When the men had calmed down Tok finally saw her.

"Hey, Mia, what's happening? Did Amethyst send you to make sure I was still here?" Tok left the pack of men watching the game and Gary took his place.

"No, but she did say to tell you that she thinks you'll

be the happiest couple in the world." Mia looked around the room. Tuxedos were hanging on doors all through the room. "Are you going to be ready in time?"

"Of course. It's just about ten and we don't have to be down to the lobby for hours. I'm not sure why we're here so early, but I guess it gives us some time to talk. And watch the game." Tok glanced over at the television and Mia could see she was losing his attention.

"Okay, if you don't need anything." Mia moved toward the door, but Drunder Uzzi stopped her before she could leave.

"Mia, if I could have a minute in the hallway?" He held the door open and the two left the room, which smelled of nachos and beer. A far cry from the bridal suite, where mimosas were flowing and it smelled of jasmine and lilac. Of course, they had more flowers in the room due to the bouquets than the men's boutonnieres.

"What can I help you with?" Mia started to grab her clipboard, but he stilled her hand.

"Sorry, I heard the security I hired upset you yesterday. I should have let you know I was bringing in people. I didn't think, and for that I apologize." He took her hand in his. "After what happened to Chelsea, and then the reception hall, I thought it best that we add a few layers of protection for you and your staff, as well as the families and their guests."

"You don't have to apologize. I was surprised, that's all." Mia removed her hand from his. "If that's all, I've got things to check on."

"Of course, I don't want to keep you." He nodded toward the door. "Don't worry about them. I'll have all of them in the prep room before the ceremony so we can finally get this wedding done. I'll sleep like a baby to-night."

She moved toward the elevator, still feeling the tingle of the comfort spell he'd tried to douse her with as he held her hand. That was why she didn't plan on becoming part of the coven. Too many people—like Drunder—thought it fine to use magic without someone else's consent. In her world you asked before you spelled someone, even if it was going to make them feel better. Grans's amulet glowed green, showing Mia it was working to banish all traces of Drunder's spell. As she went back downstairs, she checked her hair in the elevator mirror. She might need a bit of a trim. She'd deal with it next week. She wasn't part of this wedding and she had work to get done.

Next on her list was to check in with James. At least she knew what she'd get when she entered the kitchen.

Except she was wrong. James wasn't in the kitchen. She stopped a waiter as he moved toward the dining room. "Do you know where James is?"

"He had to run to Majors for something. He said if anyone from the wedding came in to tell them that the food would be ready in time." The man moved toward the door, leaving her standing in the entryway. And in the way.

Mia hurried out of the kitchen and found a corner where she could check her list. She'd talked to Gary about the rings. James was MIA but had left a clear message. Nothing was wrong. She decided to go check the reception hall again to see if it was at least set up and how the cake looked.

Before she could make it to the room, Trent caught up with her. "You need to come with me, now."

"Trent, I'm a little busy." She turned and saw his face. Fear hit her as she took in his expression. "What's wrong?"

"I'll have you back here in less than thirty minutes. But you need to see this." He pulled her arm and they moved toward the entry. When they were in the truck and they were finally alone, she turned toward him.

"Okay, tell me now."

He didn't look over at her. "Someone broke into your grandmother's house and trashed the place."

"Oh, no. Grans was still at the school, though, right?"

He nodded. "She is. Mom's there, and Dad's going over as soon as some things are cleared up at the house. I don't want anyone alone right now."

"What were they looking for? Grans doesn't keep much money at the house. Thank the Goddess. Adele used to keep piles of cash around the house, but Grans has always felt more comfortable with using a card than cash." Mia stopped talking. She knew she was scared and chatting to cover her fear.

"Mia, they didn't just trash the place. They tried to set it on fire. Luckily, your grandmother had some strong protection spells in place, but she's still going to need some remodeling in the living room and the kitchen." He stopped the car at a stoplight and took the time to turn toward her. "I'm sorry. I know this isn't the best time to hear this news."

"It's the killer. He or she is still trying to stop the wedding."

"By setting your grandmother's house on fire?" Trent turned back to the road and shook his head. "I don't think so. I think they were trying to cover their tracks. And trying to get back their grimoire."

"You might be right." Mia closed her eyes and tried to calm down. Being upset wasn't going to get her list done. "Wait, James isn't at the Lodge."

"So?"

"Maybe he was the one who broke into Grans's?" Mia sat up straight in her bucket seat. "And he had access to the reception hall, well, until Drunder hired his security guards. Maybe James is a witch and has been hiding it all this time."

"Okay, I'll play your game. But why, then, would he want to stop the wedding? He's making a killing for the Lodge with this one event. If it's successful, he'll get more bookings because you know everyone wants to mirror Amethyst's actions." Trent listed off all the reasons it couldn't be the kitchen manager. "And he's not magical. Not at all. He'd have to be very powerful to pull off a job like that. Your grandmother said the grimoire was owned by a less-mature witch. And probably a female one."

"Sorry, I'm seeing zebras rather than horses." She rubbed her forehead, feeling the headache coming on. "Hey, does my hair look all right?"

"It's just like it normally is, maybe a little fancier. Why?" He pulled over the car behind a cop car where Baldwin stood, watching them.

"Nothing. I'm just feeling insecure about everything today." She sighed as she opened the truck door. "I have a feeling he's not going to have good news for us."

Trent got out on the other side of the truck and met her on the sidewalk. "Does he ever?"

CHAPTER 22

The conversation with Baldwin had been quick. He didn't know anything. "Seriously? Someone had to have seen something."

He squinted at her. "Where is your sidekick today?"

"Christina? She's at the Lodge, getting ready for the wedding. She's one of Amethyst's bridesmaids." Mia frowned as his implication hit her. "Now don't you be trying to pin this on her. There are a bunch of women back in the hotel who can prove where she's been for the last three hours."

"I'm not trying to pin anything on her. It's just a neighbor described seeing someone who looked like Miss Adams near your grandmother's house just before she noticed the fire." He rubbed a hand over his face. "It hasn't been a good week around Magic Springs. Let's hope your wedding goes off without a hitch. There's some bad Karma floating around town this week. Those kids deserve a better start to their lives than another tragedy."

He then repeated that they didn't know anything and she didn't need to be here. Mia got back into Trent's truck and closed her eyes. Maybe her grandmother might have a little more insight into why her house had been attacked or who could have done it. She called her while Trent drove them back to the Lodge. "Hey, Grans, are you all right?"

"I'm fine. I'm just glad I packed extra treats for Muffy. I think we're going to be here a bit longer than I expected." She sighed. "I needed to replace that wallpaper anyway."

"I can't believe you're being so calm about this. I'm freaking out right now," Mia admitted as she tried to relax her shoulders.

"Which is why I told Trent to leave you at the Lodge and not take you down there. I guess your amulet hasn't gone off yet today?"

Mia thought about her encounter with Drunder. "Once. Drunder tried to put a calming spell on me when I stopped in to see Tok. I don't understand. Why would he do that?"

"He's a control freak. If you're calm, the wedding should go off without a hitch." Grans paused. "I don't think you have to worry about him. Anyway, it probably surprised him when you caught the spell so fast. He's been known to set the entire city council into a spell by just shaking hands with the group."

"Well, your protection spell is pretty strong." Mia smiled at Trent as he pulled into the parking lot and turned off the truck. She held up a finger, indicating she wanted to finish this conversation before going inside.

"It wasn't my protection spell that stopped him. It was you. You've always been good at protecting yourself from random spells. My amulet is set for things that would actually harm you. Drunder's spell was more like someone giving you a glass of wine."

"I'm going to drink an entire bottle by myself as soon as this is over." Mia said goodbye and climbed out of the truck. "You could have just dropped me at the front door and gone to park. I'll be okay."

"You're not leaving my sight for the next twenty-four hours or so. Too many crazy things are happening. I take it your grandmother didn't know who would break into her house?" He reached over and took her tote from her and then put his arm around her shoulders as they walked into the building.

"Not a clue. At least that she'd tell me. Right now she thinks hiding things from me to keep me from getting upset is the way to go." Mia leaned into Trent's side. "It's like I'm a kid who she has to protect from the real world."

"You do have a lot on your plate."

Mia stopped walking and glared at him. "What did you just say?"

He took her arm and started her walking again. "You didn't let me finish. You do realize that I drove you to your grandmother's house even after she told me to keep this from you, right?"

"Yeah, I heard that part. Sorry. I'm tired and grumpy and ready to have all this lovey-dovey wedding stuff over and done with so I can go back to being a grump." She walked through the main entrance, where Levi was waiting for them.

"James is looking for you. Apparently, you need to approve the dinner setup?" Levi nodded at his brother. "He's been here three times already."

"Yet where was he when I went looking for him?" Mia sighed as she took her tote from Trent and pulled out her clipboard. "He's up next on the list anyway. If you're coming, let's go."

"Levi, why aren't you with Christina?" Trent narrowed his eyes as his brother fell into step with him.

"Because she's in a room where women are getting dressed? Dude, there's no place to sit on that floor. And the hotel staff keeps asking if I need anything." He held up his phone. "I'm texting her every twenty minutes. If she doesn't respond, I'll go all knight-on-a-white-horse on her."

"And you'll be twenty minutes too late." He tapped on the phone. "Make it every ten minutes, and you have to visually see her every half hour. I don't want anything to happen to her."

"You think I want something to happen? Dude." He checked the time on his phone and then sent a text. "Fine, I'm going up to see her now. You're right, but sometimes I wish you weren't."

"Go do what I say, little brother." Trent's mouth quirked with a smile.

Levi punched him on the arm. "Whatever."

Mia watched as Levi moved toward the elevator. "You know how to push buttons."

"More than you know." He nodded toward the dining hall. "Shall we see what James has been up to since you've been gone?"

The next few hours before the wedding flew by, and as

the last of the guests filed into the chapel, Mia stood nearby, her checklist done and her job nearly over. She stood near the wedding gift table and had to grab one of James's staff to set up a second table with just a white tablecloth, there were so many gifts. When the minister came up to the altar Mia stepped out to make sure everyone was in their place.

"Where are you going now?" Trent fell in step beside her.

"It's showtime." She pointed a lost elderly couple to the right room, then moved to the staging rooms. One for the guys, one for the girls. She knocked on the guy's door first. Again, Gary answered.

"Well, hello again." His vocal tone changed when he saw Trent standing behind her. "We're getting ready to move. Drunder is in with his daughter and Dad has gone to collect Mom so they can be seated."

"And you have the rings?" Mia glanced into the room, where Tok and the others sat in a circle of chairs, in tuxedos.

Gary patted his suit. "Right here. I'll have them ready for the ceremony."

She called out to Tok, "It's time for you to get set up at the altar. Take deep breaths, Tok, it's going to be amazing."

He smiled, but from where she stood, the man looked a little green.

Gary shooed her out. "Don't worry about it. I'll get him to the chapel."

Mia turned and moved toward the bride's room, but before she could get there, the bridesmaids hurried out to the hallway by the chapel entrance. Christina saw her and waved. Mia stuck her head into the room where Mr. and

Mrs. Uzzi were sitting with their daughter. "Time to go and sit, Cassandra. The music is starting now."

Cassandra stood and leaned over to kiss Amethyst on the check. Then she wiped off any trace of lipstick. "I am so proud of you for the girl you were. The woman you've become. And the woman you're going to be in the future. Many blessing on you as you take this next step in your life."

Mia handed Cassandra a tissue pack as she passed by her on the way out of the door. "Just in case."

Amethyst glanced at the doorway where her mother had just left. "What about me?"

"Hold off a bit. Let me get everyone else settled and then I'll send Trent to get you. You're so beautiful. Tok's a lucky man."

"We're both lucky." Amethyst swallowed. "Thank you for everything, Mia."

"Don't thank me yet. We don't have that ring on your finger." Mia absently touched her amulet, but it was still cool. "I'll see you in a few minutes."

As they walked back toward the chapel area, Mia saw a flash of color down a dark hallway. She paused, trying to see what she'd glimpsed. Her amulet started burning her chest. "Trent, something's wrong."

"What?" He followed her gaze, then pulled a flashlight out of his pocket.

"Are you kidding me?" Mia pointed to the flashlight.

He shrugged. "Always prepared. I told you I was a Scout, didn't I?"

They walked down the hallway, and when they turned a corner a woman in only her underwear lay on the floor. It was Christina, and it didn't look like she was breathing. Mia rushed toward her. "Oh, no."

Trent handed her his phone. "Call Levi."

Mia found his brother's number. When he answered Mia blurted out, "You need to come now."

"I'm a little busy. Christina isn't with the other girls. Isn't she supposed to be at the chapel now?" Levi sounded winded.

"Come one hall over and between the restrooms, where the bride's room was." Mia tried to give him directions, but then stood and ran to the edge. "Just come to your right and I'll meet you. Levi, Christina's here. She's been attacked."

Mia didn't hear an answer, but she heard running feet, and then Levi turned the corner. She pointed toward Christina, then turned and made her way back to Trent. Levi was right behind her.

He checked her pulse and then sat back on his heels. "Call 9-1-1. Tell them to meet me at the kitchen door. It will be faster. I need to get her to the hospital. And call Mom. If it's the same poison that was on the grimoire, I might need a counter potion."

Trent already had his phone out and was dialing.

Mia pulled off her suit jacket. "Here, cover her up. She'd never forgive you."

"You're right." He took the jacket and laid it over her body. He picked her up in his arms. "That will have to do. Trent, don't forget to call Mom."

"Almost done here." He disconnected the first call and then called his mother as Levi hurried Christina away to the kitchen door. When Trent finished he nodded to the wedding. "Whoever did this is going to try to stop the wedding. We need to get them out of the chapel."

Mia nodded. "We need to call Baldwin."

"He's on his way. I told dispatch to tell him we'd found the murderer." He put his phone in his pocket and took her arm in his. "Let's go save a wedding."

When they got to the staging area in the back they saw a woman who looked like Christina and Cliff getting ready to step into the chapel. Mia hurried over and took the woman's arm from Cliff's. "Wait, the order's mixed up. That's not who goes first."

"Yes, it is." Cliff reached for Fake Christina.

Mia could see why everyone thought it was Christina. The woman must have had on colored contacts or maybe it was just a glamour to make Willow's hard edges look more like Christina's soft lines.

"Sorry, we made a change." Mia grabbed the other bridesmaid and pushed her toward Cliff. "You two go now. The flower girl is already at the altar."

Trent had the woman's arm in a death grip as she tried to move toward the next groomsman and into the chapel.

"Nope, sorry, you're not next." Mia waved Bethanie up and put her hand in the other groomsman's. "You two go in."

"Ms. Malone, I'm the maid of honor. I go last." Bethanie looked back at Amethyst, who was staring at Mia like she'd grown a third head. "I'm with Gary."

"Not today." Mia got behind them and pushed them to the door.

With four of the people out of the way, she pointed to Gary. "You are going to have to walk by yourself. She's a little occupied."

"What on earth is going on, Mia?" Gary glanced at the woman he thought was Christina and then back at Mia. "Did you two have a fight? Were pillows involved?"

"You're a freaking pig, but you need to go now." Mia pushed him toward the door and, with a shrug, Gary followed her orders.

"Mia, if you didn't want Christina to be part of the wedding, I'm sorry. The magic spell on the dress won't affect her at all. I can wipe her mind if you want me to later." Amethyst didn't move from her father's arm.

Mia glanced at Fake Christina, who now had her lips clamped together. Trent was chanting something under his breath. "Sorry, Amethyst. I can explain later, but for right now, you're down a bridesmaid. Now go do the important part and get married. Tok's waiting for you."

A smile filled her face and she nodded. "It's my wedding day and I'm in love."

After they paused in the doorway and the music changed to the wedding march, Mia closed the doors. "Move her over to the hallway where she left Christina. Maybe that will remind her why she's been a bad witch."

Trent stopped chanting and the woman glared at Mia. "You don't understand. They're going to ruin everything. There's a reason witches and werewolves aren't allowed together. It's against the Goddess's ways."

"No, it's because you're too bigoted to see that they are in love. What they are doesn't matter. What matters is who they are together." Mia waved Baldwin over when she saw him enter the lobby area and walk toward them.

"You have no proof I did anything," the woman spat at Mia. "I'll be out of jail before this ceremony is over and I'll burn down the Lodge if I need to."

"That sounds like part of a confession to me." Baldwin nodded at Trent and pulled out his cuffs. "Let me take care of this. You two have a wedding to get to."

"Thanks, Mark." She leaned into Trent as they started to walk away. "I think she broke into Grans's too."

"Well, that would explain the Christina sighting. I can't believe how much she looks like Ms. Adams." Mark nodded to his deputies, who now moved to take the woman out to the police car. "I hope she's going to be all right."

"Willow? I didn't think you were coming to the wedding. Why are you out here? What's going on?" Silas Miller came up on the struggling girl and blocked their progress out. He stared at Chief Baldwin. "Tell me why you have this girl in handcuffs."

"You know this woman?" Mark pulled out his notebook.

"Yes, this is Willow Uzzi, Drunder's niece. She's a medical student in Florida. I didn't think she was coming back for the wedding." He pointed to Mia. "That woman's friend is standing in for her in Amethyst's court."

A cheer came from the chapel room and Silas smiled. "I'm just in time for the party. I never was one for the ceremonies. But I'm good at a party. I'm glad I decided to come back."

"Well, we need to get this one down to the station." Mark nodded to Mia and moved around Silas.

When the police officers were gone Silas pulled out a journal. "I found this at the house and thought I'd bring it to you. I'm sure I'll find out more about Willow at the party. I'll see you there."

Mia and Trent leaned back against the wall and sank to the floor in a seated position. "Okay, so I can't believe that just happened. Do you think we'll find out why Willow wanted to stop the wedding?"

"From what she said, I'm thinking it was the feud.

People get crazy things in their heads." Trent turned her face toward him. "Are you all right?"

"I'm fine. Tired. Confused." She patted the journal. "I'm excited to read this, though. Maybe we'll find out what's going on at the school."

"Can we just stay here for a while?" Trent closed his eyes as he talked.

Mia groaned and stood. "No, I have to go play party planner. I don't want Amethyst to be surprised at the events. I'm sure she has a lot of questions. Can you check in with Levi and keep me informed about Christina? I should call her mother, but I don't want to worry them unless there's a reason." Honestly, Mia didn't want to talk to Mother Adams, but she'd do it for Christina's sake if she needed to.

"Don't worry about it. I'll take care of everything and keep you in the loop. I'm going to ask the Uzzis' bodyguard to keep an eye out for you."

"I'm sure I'll be fine, but call me as soon as you find anything." Mia kissed him and headed to the reception to finish out the wedding. She felt relieved that the wedding had really happened. Willow had a lot to answer for. Including her grandmother's house.

CHAPTER 23

Tok and Amethyst were in the reception line when Mia eased into the room. Amethyst caught her gaze and tried to wave her over, but Mia shook her head. She'd tell them later. After they had their magic reception. Bethanie walked over and handed Mia a flute of champagne. "Thanks. You should go mingle."

"I am mingling. I'm talking to you." She turned her back on Amethyst and pinned Mia with a look. "So, do you want to tell me why you pulled Christina out of the lineup for the wedding? Where is she? Don't tell me her folks came to get her. I swear they are going to send her to a boarding school in the Alps or something."

"Her folks didn't come to get her. She had an accident." Mia saw James over by the kitchen door and he was waving at her. "Sorry, duty calls."

"Mia . . ." Bethanie called after her.

Mia hurried over to James, hoping that Bethanie wouldn't follow her. He ushered her into the cramped hallway behind the fake walls of the room. "So what happened? All of a sudden I see Levi carrying an almost-naked Christina out of my kitchen and into an ambulance. Is she okay?"

"I don't know yet. Trent's on his way over to the hospital. I'll keep you in the loop as soon as I hear something." Mia leaned against the wall and closed her eyes. "I'm hoping she's all right."

"Has this got something to do with the murder? David at the front desk said that Baldwin and his guys pulled a woman out of here who appeared to be one of the bridesmaids. I'd put money on Bethanie, but I just saw you talking with her, so I guess it was one of the other ones?"

"Long story, but kind of." Mia moved out of the way so a waiter could come through the hallway out to the reception with a tray of filled glasses. "Look, we're in the way here. I'll tell you more after this wedding's done."

"Are you still staying over? I could buy you dinner to bribe the secrets out of you." James raised his eyebrows.

"Probably not. I suppose it's too late to cancel and get my money back." She wasn't going to let anyone talk her into doing something the night after a major event again. Especially because it seemed like she was always solving a mystery or finding a killer recently. Maybe this part of her life would be over.

"Don't worry about it. I'll take care of canceling your

room. If there's any baggage in there, I'll have them leave it at the front desk. We can always sell a room on a weekend, especially a suite. I'll cancel your spa appointments too." He turned and headed to the kitchen. "I just hope Christina will be okay."

"Thanks, James. I'll let her know you were asking about her." Mia rolled her shoulders. Man, she was going to miss that massage tonight. But as soon as the newlyweds were in the limo and heading to the airport, she was going to be heading to the hospital, even if she had to walk the three blocks. She checked her phone. Nothing. She texted a quick message to Trent but got no answer. Either he had his phone off or he didn't have an update. Or at least not one he wanted to deliver over text.

She pushed the bad mojo away and followed the next waiter out into the reception. She stopped and chatted at a few tables and handed out her card to several people who mentioned their own celebration coming up. If half the cards she gave out turned into events, this was going to be one productive wedding.

She waved the bride and groom over to the head table when the line ended. She knew they probably wanted a minute to themselves, but this was a wedding. They'd have time for that later, on the honeymoon. She stepped over to the headwaiter, who seemed to be scanning the crowd. "Should we get dinner going?"

He nearly jumped out of his skin and then looked down at her like he didn't understand the language she was speaking. "What?"

"Dinner. Should we start getting out the plates?" She noticed he didn't have the same uniform as the other servers. As she studied his face, she realized she'd seen the guy at the one coven meeting she'd attended after moving to Magic Springs. What was his name? Harry? Hank? "Hank, are you working for the Lodge?"

"Of course. I mean, yes, I'm a waiter. And my name's not Hank." He turned and took a tray from a guy passing by. Then, quickly, he moved to the exit door, leaving the full tray of glasses on the table.

"Your name is Hank and you're a bad liar." Mia hurried out to where the security guards stood, arms crossed and watching. "Grab that guy. I want to ask him a few questions."

"On it." The guy from last night stuck out a foot and the fake waiter went sprawling. It was a good thing he'd set down the tray.

The guy sat on the escape artist and braced his arms behind his back. Mia moved closer. "Were you looking for Willow?"

Recognition and hope sprang into his eyes. And Mia had her answer. "You really shouldn't play poker. Tell me why you're here and how much of this was your fault."

"You can't make me talk." His eyes flashed. "Where's Willow? If you kicked her out, let me go. I'll find her and we'll be out of your hair."

"I don't think they just let you walk away from murder, attempted murder, and theft. I think they are going to have to find a spot for you in our local jail for the night." She pulled out the phone. When the call was answered she smiled. "Baldwin, I know you're busy, but can you come get the other half of our problems this week?"

"I didn't do any murder and if the witch tells you I did, she's a big fat liar," the man yelled at her.

"I'll send someone down. Tell Jeff to put him in the security cell and watch him."

Mia hung up. "Jeff?"

When the guy raised a hand, she pocketed her phone. "Baldwin says lock him up until he sends a ride for him. Can you do that?"

"My pleasure." He looked at the other guy. "Radio Landon to come out and take my place."

Mia headed back inside the reception. The front table had been served and it looked like Amethyst hadn't been fed for a week the way she was eating. Of course, she'd probably had to starve for days to get into that dress. She'd wait for a bit before sending her up to change into her travel outfit. They still had the first dance and cake cutting to get through. Hopefully the dress had a little bit of give to the fabric.

Cassandra paused by her. "It was a lovely wedding. Too bad you didn't get to see the ceremony. I hear there was a bit of a mix-up with Christina and Willow. I hope your friend is all right."

"I'm sure she'll be fine. Do you know what Willow tried to do?" Mia didn't look at Cassandra, just kept scanning the room.

"Poor girl. She was so upset about adding Tok to the family. She doesn't realize if we don't expand, grow as a race, we'll die. Marilyn was the first to sacrifice herself for the good of the coven. And it turned out well for her. Brody adores her and she has a strong bunch of boys. Now, Tok and Amethyst will continue the tradition. By the time our great-, great-grandchildren are born, no one will ever know there was a feud." Cassandra waved at a table. "Sorry, I need to go make my rounds. Thank you for such a lovely wedding. Asking you to step in was the best decision I've made in years."

As Cassandra walked away, Mia was struck with what she'd just learned. Cassandra had known Willow might try something. The fact that she killed someone to stop the wedding didn't seem to faze Cassandra. All she knew was that the wedding needed to happen for a reason much bigger than just Tok and Amethyst's love.

She glanced at Marilyn, who was watching the couple from her spot at the first table. Had the two of them always been fated or designed by these women to fall in love? Had they ever had another choice? "Oh, my, Goddess."

Gary stopped by her. "Uh-oh. Looks like someone just figured out the bigger plan. The moms think they've been so smooth about this. Who bragged? It had to be Cassandra. She thinks that getting Tok and Amethyst together will save the world, or something stupid like that. I'm just glad I wasn't the chosen one in this case."

She studied Gary, who had a beer in his hand instead of a wine flute. "Did you know?"

"I suspected. Mom used to take Tok and me to the park, where we'd just happen to run into Cassandra and Amethyst. Those two have been forced together since they were born." He shook his head. "I'm sorry Chelsea got in the way of Willow's plans. She didn't deserve to die. She wasn't a nice person, but she didn't deserve to die. The girl is messed up. She thinks she's fighting for a greater good. Of course, so does Mom. That is why I stay out of politics."

"I guess Baldwin won't believe this even if I tell him

about the plan to move the two groups together." Mia grabbed a wine flute from a passing tray and took a sip. This was getting weird.

"Does it really matter? No one expected Willow to go off the deep end and kill someone. Yeah, Mom and Cassandra probably thought there would be some fallout, but the girl went crazy. Arguing in the coven meetings about merging the bloodlines is one thing. Killing someone, or poisoning them like what happened to your friend, who does that?" Gary watched as Tok and Amethyst tipped their heads together to steal a kiss at the table. "Was it worth it? For those two? I'd have to say yes."

"The question is who else in the coven is as upset as Willow and Hank. What repercussions will happen from this?" Mia glanced around the room, trying to see if anyone looked upset or worried. But everyone seemed to be happy and having a good time.

"You worry too much." He winked at her. "If you're not busy later, save me a dance."

Mia went about her work, all the time watching for the other shoe to fall. But by the time Tok and Amethyst climbed into the limo to leave on their honeymoon, she'd been able to pull off the wedding of the year as well as avoid dancing with Gary again.

As she stood in the parking lot, watching the limo drive away, she realized she was too tired to go back inside to make sure everyone was out of the reception hall and nothing had been left behind. She pulled her phone from her pocket and sat down on a bench to call Trent and check on Christina. A man sat down beside her, but she didn't look up. When the phone was answered she leaned back into the bench. "How is she?"

"Christina? She's good." The man sitting next to her answered her question and hung up his phone. Trent smiled at her. "You, on the other hand, look wiped. Are you sure you don't want to stay here a night and take advantage of their hot springs pool?"

"I have my bathtub at home. Besides, I really want to get out of here. And I need to tell you and Grans what I found out." She leaned her head into his shoulder. "Just as soon as I sleep for two or three days."

"Christina is staying overnight at the hospital. Mom gave her the antidote when the nurse was out of the room and she perked right up. But now the doctors want to make sure she's not going to regress again." He took her hand in his. "Modern medicine just can't accept the appearance of a miracle healing like they used to."

"Make sure you thank your mom for me. If I'd lost Christina over this job, I would have been heartbroken. That Willow and her boyfriend, Hank, they didn't care who they hurt as long as they got what they wanted." She looked in the direction that the limo had disappeared. "It was a lovely reception. I'm sorry I didn't get to see the wedding. I really wanted to see the dragons shooting confetti at the bride and groom on their way out."

"According to Christina, the dresses were spelled to change colors on their walk down the aisle." He rubbed his thumb against her hand. "And besides, you weren't the one who put Christina in danger. It was Bethanie who volunteered Christina to take Willow's place."

"As usual, it's always Bethanie when you look for the source of trouble. That girl's a problem waiting to happen, even when she means well." She glanced at her watch. "Come inside with me. I'll close this up and you can help carry the luggage out to the truck."

"Here to serve." He stood and held out his hands to help pull her upright. "Your grandmother and my mom are at the apartment making dinner. Dad's hanging out with them. Levi's going to stay at the hospital, so Mom will take down a basket for him and Christina."

"Why does all that sound so normal and lovely?" She let him pull her up and they walked into the Lodge together.

"Maybe because the last couple of weeks have been stressful and crazy? Are you sure you want to do more wedding planning?" He nodded to the front desk clerk as they passed by on their way to the reception halls.

"I don't know. I guess I'm going to have to rethink expanding my business. Especially if the clientele is more than just human." She opened the door to the now-empty chapel. No one was in the room. And from the mess on the floor, the dragons must have done their jobs. "Walk around and see if anyone left anything. Other than that, I think we're done here. The hotel staff is contracted to do the cleanup. And the florist and rental place will come in later to pick up their stuff."

"In Magic Springs, everyone has a touch of magic, so I guess you'd just have to not do local weddings." He went over to the side of the room and checked each row.

Mia mirrored him on the other side of the chairs. "You're right about that. I don't know. I kept thinking if I'd planned it, I would have done this differently, or that. And I definitely wouldn't have had a dead body and a building break-in and fire in the middle."

"You just don't know how to expand your problem-solving skills." He stood at the arch and waited for her to finish with her side.

Laughing, she stepped up on the platform to meet him. "I guess that's true. Did you find anything?"

He gazed into her eyes for a long second, then leaned down to kiss her. "Yes, I think I found something very precious."

CHAPTER 24

The next Saturday, Mia was sitting in her kitchen on the window seat looking down at the garden that was just beginning to explode in color and produce. She'd already started using some of the garden's bounty in her dishes, but soon she'd either have to dry, freeze or can the overabundance of produce. It was a good problem to have.

Both Mr. Darcy and Muffy were on her lap as she drank coffee and thought about what she had in the garden and the recipes in her head. Maybe she'd try out a veggie stew with dumplings for tomorrow's dinner. She wouldn't have time today to get the vegetables out of the garden, then let the stew simmer and mix all the good flavors together.

Mr. Darcy pushed a book from the shelf and onto her lap, nearly hitting Muffy. She recognized it as the book

about Blaine County that had fallen when she was in the
library looking for wedding planning books. Taking the
hint, she opened the book and scanned through the pages
until she found the mention of the school. A grainy black-
and-white picture showed a young Silas Miller standing
in front of the just-completed school. And next to him
was a man who looked a lot like a young Brody Mc-
Mann. But it couldn't be him. Brody would have to be as
old as Silas now, and he had appeared to be in his late
fifties at the wedding. Except, for a shifter, maybe time
ran differently.

She scanned the book for more information, but besides that one picture, nothing stood out as important. At
least in the Magic Springs way. She set it aside and finished her coffee.

Today she was going to a teahouse with Abigail, Grans,
and a newly recovered Christina. She wanted to thank
Abigail for all the work she'd done on the wedding cakes
for last week's events. And she wanted to feel her out to
see if she was interested in doing some more work for
Mia's Morsels.

Trent came into the kitchen with grocery bags from
Majors. He set several bags on the table as she got up to
help him put the order away. "Mom's really looking forward to today's outing. I was over at their house last night
for dinner and all she could talk about was you and this
tea thing you're going to today."

"I'm glad she's excited. You didn't have to deliver our
groceries. I was going to head over as soon as they called
me to tell me the order was ready." She pulled cheese out
of one of the bags and put it into the fridge.

"I was coming by anyway to see if you wanted to take
a ride into Boise with me on Wednesday. If you're not

busy, we could spend the night and come back on Thursday. Maybe find something to do that night?" He set cans of tomatoes into the cabinet. After hanging around for so long Trent knew where everything in Mia's kitchen went. He also had the map to her heart if she was being honest with herself.

"I'll check the schedule, but I think I can do that. I've got a consultation for a possible wedding, but they are coming in on Friday to decide whether my company is a good fit for them or not." She put loaf of bread into the basket on the counter. "Christina wants to be part of a few wedding planning events to see if that's where she'll land when she graduates. I'm beginning to think I'm going to have a full-time employee when she graduates, unless she and Levi take off after they're married to live somewhere else."

"You really think they're heading down the path to marriage? They're both so young." He collected all the empty bags and put them in a drawer by the sink.

"Actually, most of their friends are already married." She poured them two glasses of tea and sat down at the table. "We're the hold outs for our age group. I think one of the girls I graduated with has had three husbands already. I can't even imagine that kind of change."

He sat and sipped his tea. "We haven't talked about where this is going. Do you want to?"

"Talk about us? Maybe. I'm fine where we are right now. You're happy, right?" She tried to read his face, but his expression was blank. "Or are you telling me you want more?"

He met her gaze. "I always want more, but I'm happy where we are if you are."

"How did we get on this conversation anyway?" She ran a hand through her hair. "I'm going to have to get ready soon. Our reservations are at eleven."

"Another reason why I delivered the groceries." He grabbed a notebook from the backpack he'd slung over the chair rail. "I found this in Silas Miller's plans for the school."

Mia waited for him to find the right page, then she stood and stepped behind him to see the notebook. "That's the school, right?"

Trent nodded. He pointed to the area on the other side of the building from the garden. "Mia, I think this is an old cemetery. I think you might have some unmarked graves on the property."

"Are you kidding me? I've walked the entire five acres that came with the building. Do you think the cemetery was here before the school was built? How come they didn't just move the bodies, then?"

"Probably costs. Miller's group did a protection spell out by the back door of the kitchen. The one that leads out to the driveway. Have you ever had issues back there?" He was watching Mia as she processed the information.

"Yes, but I didn't want to sound like I was crazy. And we'd been having some issues around the school, so I thought it was someone trying to get it. Or John Louis, trying to scare me off." She went back over and sat across from him. "Do you really think there might still be bodies out there?"

"I've asked Elizabeth to pull the records for the land to see if anyone moved them prior to the building, but you know the way buildings were built back then. I'll do some more research, but I wonder if that's part of the reason he told us to leave the protection spells in place. He didn't want us to deal with a bunch of angry ghosts in the building." Trent closed the notebook and leaned back. "It's still not too late to build your own building. I'm sure someone would buy this one."

"And tear the school down to build something new. I like repurposing the old school into to something the whole town can use." Mia shook her head. "If we have to move the graves into the current cemetery, what do you think that would cost?"

"Probably a lot. We'd have to talk to the historical society to see if they have insurance that might cover at least some of the costs." He stood and leaned over to kiss her. "But we're getting ahead of ourselves. You need to go play tea party with my mom and I'm heading over to the library to work with Elizabeth. See you Wednesday. Are we staying overnight?"

"I'll run down and check the calendar just to make sure, but as of right now, heck yes." She handed him the book on Blaine County. "You might want to check this out too. I found something interesting. Do you know how long shifters live?"

He frowned as he took the book. "I'm sure there's a logical reason you're asking this. But anyway, you plan Wednesday night's festivities. I'll even go to dinner theater if you find one open." He held up the book as he walked toward the door. "I'm sure we'll have a lot to talk about."

"I'm sure you timed our trip so there won't be any dinner theaters open." She followed him to the apartment door and then watched him leave before heading to her room to get ready.

* * *

Time for a Cuppa was the new shop in Magic Springs. The owner was a local coven member who had settled in Oregon after leaving home to attend college. When her mother died at the beginning of the year, Mahogany Medford returned to Magic Springs to close the estate. Instead, Mahogany opened a tea shop and now not only served high tea on the weekends, but had a cute little retail shop that she kept open during the week as well.

Abigail had volunteered to drive because she had an oversize SUV that not only looked better than Mia's van, but had back seats. Mia and Christina sat in the back while Abigail and Grans chatted in the front.

Mia liked seeing Grans hanging out again with a friend. Since her best friend, Adele, died a few years ago, Grans had kept to herself. She'd even stopped playing tennis at the local club after losing her doubles partner. Abigail was Mia's mom's age, but the two women seemed to have a lot in common.

Christina nudged her arm and pointed to the women in front of them. "That's good, right?"

Mia nodded and smiled. "That's awesome."

"I wondered how you'd feel, well, with dating Trent and all. If my mom started to be friends with Abigail, I'd know something was up." Christina turned and stared out of the car window. "I'm supposed to go home and clean out my room next week. Mom says if I'm not going to live under her roof, she's not keeping a shrine to my absence."

"Do you want me to go with you?" Mia knew how biting Mother Adams could be. She'd been the focus of that anger for years, when she'd lived with Isaac. Now that they'd broken it off, Christina's mother had found more time to torture her youngest child. "Don't worry about getting a storage place. We'll set your extra stuff in one of the second-floor classrooms. It's going to be a while before I do any remodeling there."

"Can I? I didn't want to ask. You're already giving me room and board with my job." Christina's face lit up for the first time that day.

"You earn that. I don't know what I'd do at Mia's Morsels without you. I thought we'd chat a bit about expanding our services today at tea. I want to see what Abigail thinks about being part of the team."

Abigail met her gaze in the rear-view mirror, but Mia didn't know what the look meant. Before she could ask, the car slowed and they pulled into a lot.

"We're here," Abigail announced as she parked and turned off the car. She climbed out of the car.

Mia did the same, hurrying to make sure Grans didn't need any help. She got a glare from her grandmother for her trouble.

"I don't need help getting out of a car, Mia." She slid down to the ground from the higher seat.

"It's set a little higher than your car." Mia closed her door and smoothed her skirt. She was in a fun sundress that made her feel young and free. She did a twirl as she stepped away from the car. "I love getting dressed up for a girls' day."

"We should always wear what makes us happy." Abigail waited for Grans, then took her arm as they walked toward the teahouse's front door. Mia and Christina followed behind.

"Are you feeling like a kid?" Christina pointed to the two in front of them.

Mia tucked her sparkle clutch under her arm. "A little.

And why is it okay for Abigail to walk with my grand-mother, but if I offer to help her out of the car, I'm being overprotective?"

"I heard that," Grans called back. "Just be quiet like good children."

Christina and Mia laughed as they made their way to the door. The hostess inside looked up as they came in.

"May I help you?"

Mia stepped around the others. "Mia Malone. We have a reservation for four?"

"Yes, miss. Come this way." She grabbed some menus as she came around. "And I'll let Ms. Medford know you're here."

"That's nice. Does she greet all her guests?" Mia followed the young woman to a table near a window that looked out onto a garden behind the house.

After the hostess got them seated she answered Mia's question. "It's not standard, no. But I was told to let her know as soon as you arrived. She said she needed to talk to you about something important."

As they settled in, Christina turned toward Mia. "Do you know the owner? Maybe she needs us to cater an event. Or maybe plan her wedding?"

"Are you still doing wedding planning? I thought maybe this last wedding would have scared you away from that line of work." Abigail seemed to be focused on admiring the garden, but Mia felt her intensity despite the lack of eye contact.

"Actually, I wanted to talk to you about that." Mia set her clutch on her lap and took a sip of water. "Would you be interested at all in doing cakes if Mia's Morsels were to expand their line of services? You're an excellent cake decorator and I don't know what I would have done without your help this time."

"If the original order hadn't been canceled, you would have been fine with the bakery cake. However, I did have a lot of fun working with you too. If I said yes, could I limit my involvement? I really don't want to work full-time again." Now Abigail was meeting her gaze. "Also I'd like to pick my projects. If your couple just wants a simple cake, I'm probably not going to accept that assignment."

"I think we could work around that. I'm not sure how many slots I'm going to open up for the service. Just a few for now to get our feet wet in the industry." Mia reached out to shake hands with Abigail. "You're hired. Well, probably as an independent consultant, but I'm so glad you agreed to continue working with us. Now, I can say I feel comfortable trying to plan another wedding event."

Christina clapped her hands. "This is going to be so much fun. I'm thinking about opening my own wedding planning business when I graduate. This will be like an internship."

Mia felt a bit of the light drain from her joy. She was going to miss the girl when she left for a real job. But that was tomorrow's worry, not today's. She focused on the discussion at hand. "And with Christina going back to school in the fall, I may have to keep the numbers low. Or hire someone to help."

"Bethanie's looking for another job. The real estate office she was working at had to close when John Louis went to jail again." Christina glanced back and forth from Mia to the others. "What? Bethanie is . . ."

"Well? Can you finish that sentence? I mean, you can't say a hard worker. Or trustworthy." Mia pointed out.

"I have to agree with Mia on that." Abigail patted Christina's hand. "I know the two of you are friends, but working with someone takes more than just being friends. You have to be able to trust that person."

The waitress dropped off the tea kettle and a basket of tea selections. "I'll be right back to get your order."

After she left Christina brightened. "I know what I can say about Bethanie. She knows her jewelry. She's got a good relationship with the local jeweler."

"True. But maybe that's where she should look for a job. Where she could talk gems and metals and shiny things." Grans put down her menu. "I think we should go all out and have the finger sandwich tray and the dessert tray."

"Maybe the fruit one too," Mia added, seeing the chocolate-covered items listed on the menu. "We're celebrating. Let's get all three."

But instead of the waitress approaching their table, a woman dressed in a black, flowy dress with long, black hair came up and set a stacked tray of chocolate-covered fruits on the table. "I'm so happy to meet you all. I'm the owner, Mahogany Medford."

"I'm Mia Malone." Mia introduced the others. "And we're so happy to be here today. You have a lovely shop."

"Thank you. I was wondering if I could speak with you alone for a minute, Mia? Maybe I could show you my garden? I have a lovely assortment of herbs you might be interested in." She stood back and held a hand toward the door that led to a patio area.

Mia met Grans's gaze and, when she nodded, stood.

She still wore the protection stone that Grans had supplemented with power last week, so at worst, they'd be able to find her if this was a residual attack from the coven and shifter tribe union last week. She picked up a chocolate-covered strawberry and set it on her plate. "Of course. I'll be right back, so go ahead and order while I'm gone."

They strolled over the deck to the stairs that led down into the garden. Then they walked a bit through the trees and vines before Mahogany spoke.

"I hope you don't think me forward, but I need your help." She pointed to a white iron bench near a pond. "Do you mind if we sit?"

"Not at all." Mia sat and took in the floral scent that filled her senses. The pond had goldfish floating around and she found them enchanting. But Mahogany's statement hung in the air. "What's going on?"

"I came back in January to bury my mother. Everyone said it was old age. The doctor. That Baldwin man from the police. Even the funeral home told me how lucky I was to have her for so long. But Mia, Mom wasn't that old. Fifty, maybe. I was born when she was a teenager and I'm only in my mid-thirties. I moved into her house, but no one questioned Mom's death besides me." She shook her head. "I'm not crazy, but I feel that way."

"Why are you telling me this?" Mia figured she knew she wasn't being asked to cater a celebration of life for Mrs. Medford. "I'm just a caterer."

"Oh, Mia, you are so much more than that and you know it." Mahogany went on to tell her what she needed.

By the time they got back to the table the food had arrived. Mia slipped into her chair and Mahogany left them alone after wishing them a lovely afternoon.

Grans poured Mia a cup of tea. "Do you want to talk, dear?"

Mia looked at the three women at the table and grinned. They were the perfect group to solve this mystery. If they wanted to try. Mia sipped her tea, and when she set down the cup she said, "Let me tell you a story . . ."

RECIPE

Magically Easy Peach Crisp

I grabbed a bag of fresh peaches from a local store this last week and remembered why I love them so much. Here's a recipe to use up a few of the fresh ones before they go bad, especially if you buy too many. This can also be made with canned peaches, but where's the fun in that?

Pre-heat oven to 400 degrees F.

Arrange 4 cups sliced fresh peaches (You can leave the skin on or peel these) evenly in an 8 x 8 inch baking dish. I always spray the dish with spray oil, just to keep it from sticking. Mix together 2 tbsp of brown sugar and a tsp of cinnamon and sprinkle over the top, mixing in with a spoon.

Mix the following into a bowl using a pastry cutter (or a fork) until evenly crumbled:

½ cup flour
½ cup brown sugar
½ cup cold butter
1 tsp ground cinnamon
½ tsp salt

Fold 1 cup rolled oats into the mixture, then press on top of the peaches.

Bake until lightly brown or 30 minutes. Serve warm with vanilla ice cream.

Visit us online at
KensingtonBooks.com
to read more from your favorite authors,
see books by series, view reading
group guides, and more!

Visit us online for sneak peeks, exclusive
giveaways, special discounts, author content,
and engaging discussions with your fellow readers.

Betweenthechapters.net

Sign up for our newsletters and be the first
to get exciting news and announcements about
your favorite authors!
Kensingtonbooks.com/newsletter